The Blind Owl
and Other Stories

Sadeq Hedayat

Translated by D.P. Costello
and Deborah Miller Mostaghel

CALDER

CALDER PUBLICATIONS
an imprint of

ALMA BOOKS LTD
3 Castle Yard
Richmond
Surrey TW10 6TF
United Kingdom
www.almaclassics.com

The Blind Owl first published as *Buf-e Kur* in 1937
Translated by D.P. Costello
First published by John Calder (Publishers) Limited in 1957
Translation © John Calder (Publishers) Limited, 1957
First published by Alma Classics in 2008. Repr. 2010, 2012

The other stories in this volume first published in *Buried Alive* (1930); *Three Drops of Blood* (1932); *The Stray Dog* (1942)
Translated by Deborah Miller Mostaghel, and edited by Nushin Arbabzadah
A translation of these stories first published by Alma Classics in the volume *Three Drops of Blood* in 2008. Reprinted 2010, 2012, 2017

This new edition of *The Blind Owl and Other Stories* first published by Calder Publications in 2017

Printed in Great Britain by CPI Group (UK) Ltd, Croydon CR0 4YY

ISBN: 978-0-7145-4458-8

Contents

Sadeq Hedayat: His Life and Works

S ADEQ HEDAYAT WAS BORN on 17th February 1903 and died on 9th April 1951. He was descended from Rezaqoli Khan Hedayat, a notable nineteenth-century poet, historian of Persian literature and author of *Majma' al-Fosaha*, *Riyaz al-'Arefin* and *Rawza al-Safa-ye Naseri*. Many members of his extended family were important state officials, political leaders and army generals, both in the nineteenth and twentieth centuries.

Hedayat is the author of *The Blind Owl*, the most famous Persian novel both in Iran and in Europe and America. Many of his short stories are in a critical realist style and are regarded as some of the best written in twentieth-century Iran. But his most original contribution was the use of modernist, more often surrealist, techniques in Persian fiction. Thus, he was not only a great writer, but also the founder of modernism in Persian literature.

Having studied at the exclusive St Louis French missionary school in Tehran, Hedayat went to Europe, supported by a state grant, spending a year in Belgium in 1926–27, a year and a half in Paris in 1928–29, two terms in Reims in 1929 and a year in Besançon in 1929–30. Having still not finished his studies, he surrendered his scholarship and returned home in the summer of 1930. This provides a clue to his personality in general, and his perfectionist outlook in particular, which sometimes resulted in nervous paralysis.

Back in Tehran, Hedayat became the central figure among the *Rab'eh*, or Group of Four, which included Mojtaba Minovi, Bozorg Alavi and Mas'ud Farzad, but had an outer belt including Mohammad Moqaddam, Zabih Behruz and Shin Partaw. They were all modern-minded and critical of the literary establishment, both for its social traditionalism and intellectual classicism. They were also resentful of the literary establishment's contemptuous attitude towards themselves, and its exclusive hold over academic posts and publications.

In the early 1930s, Hedayat drifted between clerical jobs. In 1936 he went to Bombay at the invitation of Sheen Partaw, who was then an Iranian diplomat in that city. Predictably, he had run afoul of the official censors, and in 1935 was made to give a pledge not to publish again. That was why, when he later issued the first, limited edition of *The Blind Owl* in Bombay, he wrote on the title page that it was not for publication in Iran, predicting the possibility of a copy finding its way to Iran and falling into the hands of the censors.

During the year in Bombay, he learnt the ancient Iranian language Pahlavi among the Parsee Zoroastrian community, wrote a number of short stories and published *The Blind Owl* in fifty duplicated copies, most of which he distributed among friends outside Iran.

He was back in Tehran in September 1937, although he had returned with great reluctance and simply because he did not feel justified in continuing to depend on his friend's hospitality in Bombay. In 1939, he joined the newly founded Office of Music as an editor of its journal, *Majelleh-ye Musiqi* (*The Music Magazine*). It was literary work among a small group of relatively young and modern intellectuals, including Nima

Yushij, the founder of modernist Persian poetry. He might well have regarded that as the most satisfactory post he ever had.

It did not last long. After the Allied invasion of Iran and abdication of Reza Shah in 1941, the Office of Music and its journal were closed down, and Hedayat ended up as a translator at the College of Fine Arts, where he was to remain until the end of his life. He also became a member of the editorial board of Parviz Khanlari's modern literary journal *Sokhan*, an unpaid but prestigious position. Even though the country had been occupied by foreign powers, there were high hopes and great optimism for democracy and freedom upon the collapse of the absolute and arbitrary government. The new freedom – indeed, licence – resulting from the Reza Shah's abdication led to intense political, social and literary activities. The modern educated elite were centred on the newly organized Tudeh Party, which was then a broad democratic front led by Marxist intellectuals, although by the end of the '40s it had turned into an orthodox communist party. Hedayat did not join the party even in the beginning, but had sympathy for it and had many friends among Tudeh intellectuals.

But the party's support for the Soviet-inspired Azerbaijan revolt in 1946, which led to intense conflicts within its ranks, and the sudden collapse of the revolt a year later, deeply upset and alienated Hedayat from the movement. He had always been a severe and open critic of established Iranian politics and cultural traditions, and his break with radical intellectuals made him a virtual émigré in his own land. This was a significant contribution to the depression he suffered in the late 1940s, which eventually led to his suicide in Paris in 1951.

For some time his close friend Hasan Shahid-Nura'i, who was serving as a diplomat in France, had been encouraging him to go to Paris. There were signs that his depression was deepening day by day. He was extremely unhappy with his life in Tehran, not least among intellectuals, many of whom were regularly describing him as a "petty-bourgeois demoralizer", and his work as "black literature".

Through his letters to friends one may observe, not far beneath the surface, his anger and despair, his acute sensitivity, his immeasurable suffering, his continuously darkening view of his own country and its people, and his condemnation of life. Through them, perhaps more than his fiction, one may see the three aspects of his predicament: personal tragedy, social isolation and universal alienation.

In a letter which he wrote in French to a friend in Paris four years before his last visit, he had said:

> The point is not for me to rebuild my life. When one has lived the life of animals which are constantly being chased, what is there to rebuild? I have taken my decision. One must struggle in this cataract of shit until disgust with living suffocates us. In *Paradise Lost*, Reverend Father Gabriel tells Adam "Despair and die", or words to that effect. I am too disgusted with everything to make any effort; one must remain in the shit until the end.

Ultimately, what he called "the cataract of shit" proved too unbearable for him to remain in it.

Hedayat's fiction, including novels, short stories, drama and satire, written between 1930 and 1946, comprises *Parvin*

Dokhtar-e Sasan (Parvin the Sasanian Girl), Afsaneh-ye Afarinesh (The Legend of Creation), Al-bi'tha(t) al-Islamiya ila'l-Bilad al-Afranjiya (Islamic Mission to European Cities), Zendeh beh Gur, (Buried Alive), Aniran (Non-Iranian), Maziyar, Seh Qatreh Khun (Three Drops of Blood), Alaviyeh Khanom (Mistress Alaviyeh), Sayeh Roshan (Chiaroscuro), Vagh-vagh Sahab (Mr Bow-Vow), Buf-e Kur (The Blind Owl), 'Sampingé' and 'Lunatique' (both in French), *Sag-e Velgard (The Stray Dog), Hajji Aqa, Velengari (Mucking About)* and *Tup-e Morvari (The Morvari Cannon).*

I have classified Hedayat's fiction into four analytically distinct categories, although there is some inevitable overlap between them: romantic nationalist fiction, critical realist stories, satire and psycho-fiction.

First, the romantic nationalist fiction. The historical dramas – *Parvin* and *Maziyar*, and the short stories 'The Shadow of the Mongol' ('Sayeh-ye Moghol'), and 'The Last Smile' ('Akharin Labkhand') – are on the whole simple in sentiment and raw in technique. They reflect sentiments arising from the Pan-Persianist ideology and cult which swept over the Iranian modernist elite after the First World War. 'The Last Smile' is the most mature work of this kind. Hedayat's explicit drama is not highly developed, and he quickly abandoned the genre along with nationalist fiction. But many of his critical realist short stories could easily be adapted for the stage with good effect.

The works in the second category of Hedayat's fiction, his critical realist works, are numerous and often excellent, the best examples being 'Alaviyeh Khanom' ('Mistress Alaviyeh') which is a comedy in the classical sense of the term, 'Talab-e Amorzesh' ('Seeking Absolution'), 'Mohallel' ('The Legalizer'), and 'Mordeh-khor-ha' ('The Ghouls'). To varying degrees, both satire and irony are used in these stories, though few of them could be accurately described as satirical fiction.

They tend to reflect aspects of the lives and traditional beliefs of the contemporary urban lower-middle classes with ease and accuracy. But contrary to long-held views, they are neither "about the poor or downtrodden", nor do they display sympathy for their types and characters. Wretchedness and superstition are combined with sadness, joy, hypocrisy and occasionally criminal behaviour. This was in the tradition set by Jamalzadeh (though he had more sympathy for his characters), enhanced by Hedayat and passed on to Chubak and Al-e Ahmad in their earlier works.

Coming to the third category, Hedayat's satirical fiction is rich and often highly effective. He was a master of wit, and wrote both verbal and dramatic satire. It takes the form of short stories and novels, as well as short and long anecdotes. They hit hard at their subjects, usually with effective subtlety, though sometimes outright lampooning, denunciation and invective reveal the depth of the author's personal involvement in his fictional satire.

Hajji Aqa is the longest and most explicit of Hedayat's satires on the political establishment. Superficial appearances and critical propaganda notwithstanding, it is much less a satire on the ways of the people of the bazaar and much more of a merciless attack on leading conservative politicians. Indeed, the real-life models for the Hajji of the title were supplied by two important old-school (and, as it happens, by no means the worst) politicians.

Hedayat would already have held a lasting and prominent position in the annals of Persian literature on account of what

I have mentioned so far. What has given him his unique place, however, is his psycho-fiction, of which *The Blind Owl* is the best and purest example. This work and the short story 'Three Drops of Blood' are modernist in style, using techniques from French symbolism and surrealism in literature, of surrealism in modern European art and of expressionism in the contemporary European films, including the deliberate confusion of time and space. But most of the other psycho-fictional stories – e.g. 'Zendeh beh Gur' ('Buried Alive'), 'Arusak-e Posht-e Pardeh' ('Puppet behind the Curtain'), 'Bon-bast' ('Dead End'), 'Tarik-khaneh' ('Dark Room'), 'Davud-e Guzhposht' ('Davoud the Hunchback') and 'Sag-e Velgard' ('The Stray Dog') – use realistic techniques in presenting psycho-fictional stories.

The appellation "psycho-fictional", coined by me in the mid-1970s to describe this particular genre in Hedayat's literature, does not render the same sense as is usually conveyed by the well-worn concept and category of "the psychological novel". Rather, it reflects the essentially subjective nature of the stories, which brings together the psychological, the ontological and the metaphysical in an indivisible whole.

Hedayat's psycho-fictional stories, such as 'Three Drops of Blood' and 'Buried Alive', are macabre and, at their conclusions, feature the deaths of both humans and animals. Most human beings are no better than *rajjaleh* (rabble), and the very few who are better fail miserably to rise up to reach perfection or redemption. Even the man who tries to "kill" his *nafs* – to mortify his flesh, or destroy his ego – in the short story 'The Man Who Killed His Ego', ends up by killing himself; that is, not by liberating but by annihilating his soul. Women are either *lakkateh* (harlots), or they are *Fereshteh*, that is, angelic apparitions who wilt and disintegrate upon appearance, though this is only true of women in the psycho-fictions, women of similar cultural background to the author, not those of lower classes in his critical realist stories.

As a man born into an extended family of social and intellectual distinction, a modern as well as modernist intellectual, a gifted writer steeped in the most advanced Persian as well as European culture, and with a psyche which demanded the highest standards of moral and intellectual excellence, Hedayat was bound to carry, an enormous burden, which very few individuals could suffer with equanimity, especially as he bore the effects of the clash of the old and the new, and the Persian and the European, such as few Iranians have experienced. He lived an unhappy life, and died an unhappy death. It was perhaps the inevitable cost of the literature which he bequeathed to humanity.

Homa Katouzian
St Antony's College and the Oriental Institute
University of Oxford

Bibliography

Michael Beard, *The Blind Owl as a Western Novel* (Princeton, NJ: Princeton University Press, 1990)

Nasser Pakdaman, ed., *Sadeq Hedayat, Hashtad-o-daw Nameh beh Hasan Shahid-Nura'i (Sadeq Hedayat, Eighty-two Letters to Hasan Shahid-Nura'i)* (Paris: Cheshmandaz, 2000)

Ehsan Yarshater, ed., *Sadeq Hedayat: An Anthology* (Boulder, CO: Westview, 1979)

By Homa Katouzian:

Sadeq Hedayat, His Work and His Wondrous World, ed., (London and New York: Routledge, 2008)

Sadeq Hedayat: The Life and Legend of an Iranian Writer, paperback edition, (London and New York: I.B. Tauris, 2002)

Darbareh-ye Buf-e Kur-e Hedayat (Hedayat's The Blind Owl, a Critical Monograph) (Tehran: Nashr-e Markaz, 5th impression, 2008)

Sadeq Hedayat va Marg-e Nevisandeh (Sadeq Hedayat and the Death of the Author) (Tehran: Nashr-e Markaz, 4th impression, 2005)

Tanz va Tanzineh-ye Hedayat, (Satire and Irony in Hedayat) (Stockholm: Arash, 2003)

The Blind Owl

(translated by D.P. Costello)

1

THERE ARE SORES which slowly erode the mind in solitude like a kind of canker.

It is impossible to convey a just idea of the agony which this disease can inflict. In general, people are apt to relegate such inconceivable sufferings to the category of the incredible. Any mention of them in conversation or in writing is considered in the light of current beliefs, the individual's personal beliefs in particular, and tends to provoke a smile of incredulity and derision. The reason for this incomprehension is that mankind has not yet discovered a cure for this disease. Relief from it is to be found only in the oblivion brought about by wine and in the artificial sleep induced by opium and similar narcotics. Alas, the effects of such medicines are only temporary. After a certain point, instead of alleviating the pain, they only intensify it.

Will anyone ever penetrate the secret of this disease which transcends ordinary experience, this reverberation of the shadow of the mind, which manifests itself in a state of coma like that between death and resurrection, when one is neither asleep nor awake?

I propose to deal with only one case of this disease. It concerned me personally and it so shattered my entire being that I shall never be able to drive the thought of it out of my mind. The evil impression which it left has, to a degree that surpasses human understanding, poisoned my life for all time to come.

I said "poisoned": I should have said that I have ever since borne, and will bear for ever, the brand mark of that cautery.

I shall try to set down what I can remember, what has remained in my mind of the sequence of events. I may perhaps be able to draw a general conclusion from it all – but no, that is too much to expect. I may hope to be believed by others or at least to convince myself; for, after all, it does not matter to me whether others believe me or not. My one fear is that tomorrow I may die without having come to know myself. In the course of my life I have discovered that a fearful abyss lies between me and other people and have realized that my best course is to remain silent and keep my thoughts to myself for as long as I can. If I have now made up my mind to write it is only in order to reveal myself to my shadow, that shadow which at this moment is stretched across the wall in the attitude of one devouring with insatiable appetite each word I write. It is for his sake that I wish to make the attempt. Who knows? We may perhaps come to know each other better. Ever since I broke the last ties which held me to the rest of mankind, my one desire has been to attain a better knowledge of myself.

Idle thoughts! Perhaps. Yet they torment me more savagely than any reality could do. Do not the rest of mankind who look like me, who appear to have the same needs and the same passion as I, exist only in order to cheat me? Are they not a mere handful of shadows which have come into existence only that they may mock and cheat me? Is not everything that I feel, see and think something entirely imaginary, something utterly different from reality?

I am writing only for my shadow, which is now stretched across the wall in the light of the lamp. I must make myself known to him.

2

IN THIS MEAN WORLD of wretchedness and misery I thought that for once a ray of sunlight had broken upon my life. Alas, it was not sunlight but a passing gleam, a falling star, which flashed upon me, in the form of a woman – or of an angel. In its light, in the course of a second, of a single moment, I beheld all the wretchedness of my existence and apprehended the glory and splendour of the star. After, that brightness disappeared again in the whirlpool of darkness in which it was bound inevitably to disappear. I was unable to retain that passing gleam.

It is three months – no, it is two months and four days – since I lost her from sight but the memory of those magic eyes, of the fatal radiance of those eyes, has remained with me at all times. How can I forget her, who is so intimately bound up with my own existence?

No, I shall never utter her name. For now, with her slender, ethereal, misty form, her great, shining, wondering eyes, in the depths of which my life has slowly and painfully burned and melted away, she no longer belongs to this mean, cruel world. No, I must not defile her name by contact with earthly things.

After she had gone I withdrew from the company of man, from the company of the stupid and the successful and, in order to forget, took refuge in wine and opium. My life passed, and still passes, within the four walls of my room. All my life has passed within four walls.

I used to work through the day, decorating the covers of pen cases. Or, rather, I spent on my trade of pen-case decorator the time that I did not devote to wine and opium. I had chosen this ludicrous trade of pen-case decorator only in order to stupefy myself, in order somehow or other to kill time.

I am fortunate in that the house where I live is situated beyond the edge of the city in a quiet district far from the noise and bustle of life. It is completely isolated and around it lie ruins. Only on the far side of the gully one can see a number of squat mud-brick houses which mark the extreme limit of the city. They must have been built by some fool or madman heaven knows how long ago. When I shut my eyes not only can I see every detail of their structure but I seem to feel the weight of them pressing on my shoulders. They are the sort of houses which one finds depicted only on the covers of ancient pen cases.

I am obliged to set all this down on paper in order to disentangle the various threads of my story. I am obliged to explain it all for the benefit of my shadow on the wall.

Yes, in the past only one consolation, and that a poor one, remained to me. Within the four walls of my room I painted my pictures on the pen cases and thereby, thanks to this ludicrous occupation of mine, managed to get through the day. But when once I had seen those two eyes, once I had seen her, activity of any sort lost all meaning, all content, all value for me.

I would mention a strange, an incredible thing. For some reason unknown to me the subject of all my painting was from the very beginning one and the same. It consisted always of a cypress tree at the foot of which was squatting a bent old man like an Indian fakir. He had a long cloak wrapped about him and wore a turban on his head. The index finger of his left hand

6

was pressed to his lips in a gesture of surprise. Before him stood a girl in a long black dress, leaning towards him and offering him a flower of morning glory. Between them ran a little stream. Had I seen the subject of this picture at some time in the past or had it been revealed to me in a dream? I do not know. What I do know is that whenever I sat down to paint I reproduced the same design, the same subject. My hand independently of my will always depicted the same scene. Strangest of all, I found customers for these paintings of mine. I even dispatched some of my pen-case covers to India through the intermediary of my paternal uncle, who used to sell them and remit the money to me.

Somehow I always felt this subject to be remote and, at the same time, curiously familiar to me. I don't remember very well... It occurs to me that I once said to myself that I must write down what I remember of all this – but that happened much later and has nothing to do with the subject of my painting. Moreover, one consequence of this experience was that I gave up painting altogether. That was two months, or, rather exactly, two months and four days ago.

It was the thirteenth day of Nouruz.* Everyone had gone out to the country. I had shut the window of my room in order to be able to concentrate on my painting. It was not long before sunset and I was working away when suddenly the door opened and my uncle came into the room. That is, he said he was my uncle. I had never seen my uncle in my life, for he had been abroad ever since his early youth. I seem to remember that he was a sea captain. I imagined he might have some business matter to discuss with me, since I understood that he was interested in commerce as well. At all events my uncle was a bent old man with an Indian turban on his head and a ragged yellow cloak on his back; his face was partly concealed by a scarf wrapped around his neck; his shirt was open and revealed a hairy chest. It would have been possible to count the hairs of the sparse beard protruding from under the scarf which muffled his neck. His eyelids were red and sore and he had a harelip. He resembled me in a remote, comical way like a reflection in a distorting mirror. I had always pictured my father something like this. On entering the room he walked straight across to the opposite wall and squatted on the floor. It occurred to me that I ought to offer him some refreshment in honour of his arrival. I lit the lamp and went into the little dark closet which opens off my room. I searched every corner in the hope of finding something suitable to offer him, although I knew there was nothing of the sort in the house – I had no opium or drink left. Suddenly my eye lighted on the topmost of the shelves on the wall. It was as though I had had a flash of inspiration. On the shelf stood a bottle of old wine which had been left me by my parents. I seem to remember hearing that it had been laid down on the occasion of my birth. There it was on the top shelf. I had never so much as given it a thought and had quite forgotten there was such a thing in the house. To reach the shelf I got up onto a stool which happened to be there. As I reached towards the bottle, I chanced to look out through the ventilation hole above the shelf. On the open ground outside my room I saw a bent old man sitting at the foot of a cypress tree with a young girl – no, an angel from heaven – standing before him. She was leaning forwards and with her right hand was offering him a blue flower of morning glory. The old man was biting the nail of the index finger on his left hand.

The girl was directly opposite me but she appeared to be quite unaware of her surroundings. She was gazing straight ahead without looking at anything in particular. She wore on her lips a vague, involuntary smile as though she was thinking of someone who was absent. It was then that I first beheld those frightening, magic eyes, those eyes which seemed to express a bitter reproach to mankind, with their look of anxiety and wonder, of menace and promise – and the current of my existence was drawn towards those shining eyes charged with manifold significance and sank into their depths. That magnetic mirror drew my entire being towards it with inconceivable force. They were slanting, Turkoman eyes of supernatural, intoxicating radiance which at once frightened and attracted, as though they had looked upon terrible, transcendental things which it was given to no one but her to see. Her cheekbones were prominent and her forehead high. Her eyebrows were slender and met in the middle. Her lips were full and half-open as though they had broken away only a moment before from a long, passionate kiss and were not yet sated. Her face, pale as the moon, was framed in the mass of her black, dishevelled hair and one strand clung to her temple. The fineness of her limbs and the ethereal unconstraint of her movements marked her as one who was not fated to live long in this world. No one but a Hindu temple dancer could have possessed her harmonious grace of movement.

Her air of mingled gaiety and sadness set her apart from ordinary mankind. Her beauty was extraordinary. She reminded me of a vision seen in an opium sleep. She aroused in me a heat of passion like that which is kindled by the mandrake root. It seemed to me that as I gazed at her long slender form, with its harmonious lines of shoulder, arm, breasts, waist, buttocks and legs, that she had been torn from her husband's embrace, that she was like the female mandrake which has been plucked from the arms of its mate.

She was wearing a black pleated dress which clung tightly to her body. Gazing at her, I was certain that she wished to leap across the stream which separated her from the old man but that she was unable to do so. All at once the old man burst into laughter. It was a hollow, grating laugh, of a quality to make the hairs of one's body stand on end; a harsh, sinister, mocking laugh. And yet the expression of his face did not change. It was as though the laughter was echoing from somewhere deep within his body.

In terror I sprang down from the stool with the bottle in my hand. I was trembling, in a state of mingled horror and delight such as might have been produced by some delicious, fearful dream. I set the bottle of wine down on the floor and held my head in my hands. How many minutes, how many hours I remained thus, I do not know. When I came to myself I picked up the bottle and went back into my room. My uncle had gone and had left the room door agape like the mouth of a dead man. The sound of the old man's hollow laughter was still echoing in my ears.

It was growing dark. The lamp was burning smokily. I could still feel the aftermath of the delicious, horrible fit of trembling which I had experienced. From that moment the course of my life had changed. With one glance, that angel of heaven, that ethereal girl, had left on me the imprint of her being, more deeply marked than the mind of man can conceive.

At that moment I was in a state of trance. It seemed to me that I had long known her name. The radiance of her eyes, her complexion, her perfume, her movements, all appeared familiar to me, as though, in some previous existence in a world of dreams, my soul had lived side by side with hers, had sprung from the same root and the same stock and it was inevitable that we should be brought together again. It was inevitable that I should be close to her in this life. At no time did I desire to touch her. The invisible rays which emanated from our bodies and mingled together were sufficient contact. As for the strange fact that she appeared familiar to me from the first glance, do not lovers always experience the feeling that they have seen each other before and that a mysterious bond has long existed between them? The only thing in this mean world which I desired was her love; if that were denied me I wanted the love of nobody. Was it possible that anyone other than she should make any impression upon my heart? But the hollow grating laughter, the sinister laughter of the old man had broken the bond which united us.

All that night I thought about these things. Again and again I was on the point of going to look through the aperture in the wall, but fear of the old man's laughter held me back. The next day also I could think of nothing else. Would I be able to refrain altogether from going to look at her? Finally, on the third day I decided, despite the dread which possessed me, to put the bottle of wine back in its place. But when I drew the curtain aside and looked into the closet I saw in front of me a wall as blank and dark as the darkness which has enshrouded my life. There was no trace of aperture or window. The rectangular opening had been filled in, had merged with the wall, as though it had never existed. I stood upon the stool but, although I hammered on the wall with my fists, listening intently, although I held the lamp to it and examined it with care, there was not the slightest trace of any aperture. My blows had no more effect upon the solid, massive fabric of the wall than if it had been a single slab of lead.

Could I abandon the hope of ever seeing her again? It was not within my power to do so. Henceforth I lived like a soul in torment. All my waiting, watching and seeking were in vain. I trod every hand's-breadth of ground in the neighbourhood of my house. I was like the murderer who returns to the scene of his crime. Not one day, not two days, but every day for two months and four days I circled around our house in the late afternoon like a decapitated fowl. I came to know every stone and every pebble in the neighbourhood but I found no trace of the cypress tree, of the little stream or of the two people whom I had seen there. The same number of nights I knelt upon the ground in the moonlight, I begged and entreated the trees, the stones and the moon – for she might have been gazing at that moment at the moon – I sought aid from every created thing, but I found no trace of her. In the end I understood that all my efforts were useless, because it was not possible that she should be connected in any way with the things of this world: the water with which she washed her hair came from some unique, unknown spring; her dress was not woven of ordinary stuff and had not been fashioned by material, human hands. She was a creature apart. I realized that those flowers of morning glory were no ordinary flowers. I was certain that if her face were to come into contact with ordinary water it would fade; and that if she were to pluck an ordinary flower of morning glory with her long fine fingers they would wither like the petals of a flower.

I understood all this. This girl, this angel, was for me a source of wonder and ineffable revelation. Her being was subtle and intangible. She aroused in me a feeling of adoration. I felt sure that beneath the glance of a stranger, of an ordinary man, she would have withered and crumpled.

Ever since I had lost her, ever since the aperture had been blocked and I had been separated from her by a heavy wall, a dank barrier as massive as a wall of lead, I felt that my existence had become pointless, that I had lost my way for all time to come. Even though the caress of her gaze and the profound delight I had experienced in seeing her had been only momentary and devoid of reciprocity – for she had not seen me – yet I felt the need of those eyes. One glance from her would have been sufficient to make plain all the problems of philosophy and the riddles of theology. One glance from her and mysteries and secrets would no longer have existed for me.

From this time on I increased my doses of wine and opium, but alas, those remedies of despair failed to numb and paralyse my mind. I was unable to forget. On the contrary, day by day, hour by hour, minute by minute, the memory of her, of her body, of her face, took shape in my mind more clearly than before.

How could I have forgotten her? Whether my eyes were open or closed, whether I slept or woke, she was always before me. Through the opening in the closet wall, like the dark night which enshrouds the mind and reason of man, through the rectangular aperture which looked onto the outside world, she was ever before my eyes.

Repose was utterly denied me. How could I have found repose?

It had become a habit with me to go out for a walk every day just before sunset. For some obscure reason I wanted desperately to find the little stream, the cypress tree and the vine of morning glory. I had become addicted to these walks in the same way as I had become addicted to opium. It was as though I was compelled by some outside force to undertake them. Throughout my walk I would be immersed in the thought of her, in the memory of my first glimpse of her, and I desired to find the place where I had seen her on that thirteenth day of Nouruz: if I should find that place, if it should be granted to me to sit beneath that cypress tree, then for sure I should attain peace. But alas, there was nothing but sweepings, burning sand, horse bones and refuse heaps around which dogs were sniffing. Had I ever really encountered her? Never. All that had happened was that I had looked furtively, covertly at her through a hole, a cursed aperture in my closet wall. I was like a hungry dog sniffing and rooting in a refuse heap: when people come to dump garbage on the pile he runs away and hides, only to return later to renew his search for tasty morsels. This was the state that I was in. But the aperture in the wall was blocked. For me the girl was like a bunch of fresh flowers which has been tossed onto a refuse heap.

On the last evening when I went out for my usual walk, the sky was overcast and a drizzling rain was falling. A dense mist had fallen over the surrounding country. In the fine rain which softened the intensity of the colours and the clarity of the outlines, I had experienced a sense of liberation and tranquillity. It was as though the rain was washing away my black thoughts. That night what ought not to have happened did happen.

I wandered, unconscious of my surroundings. During those hours of solitude, during those minutes which lasted I know not how long, her awe-inspiring face, indistinct as though seen through cloud or mist, void of motion or expression like the paintings one sees upon the covers of pen cases, took shape before my eyes far more clearly than ever before.

By the time I returned home I should think that a great part of the night was spent. The mist had grown denser, so much so that I could not see the ground immediately in front of my foot. Nevertheless, by force of habit and some special sense which I had developed, I found my way back to the house. As I came up to the entrance I observed a female form clad in black sitting on the stone bench outside the door.

I struck a match to find the keyhole and for some reason glanced involuntarily at the figure in black. I recognized two slanting eyes, two great black eyes set in a thin face of moonlit paleness, two eyes which gazed unseeing at my face. If I had never seen her before I should still have known her. No, it was not an illusion. This black-robed form was she. I stood bemused, like a man dreaming, who knows that he is dreaming and wishes to awake but cannot. I was unable to move. The match burned down and scorched my fingers. I abruptly came to myself and turned the key in the lock. The door opened and I stood aside. She rose from the bench and passed along the dark corridor like one who knew the way. She opened my door and I followed her into the room. I hurriedly lit the lamp and saw that she had gone across and lain down upon my bed. Her face was in shadow. I did not know whether or not she could see me, whether or not she could hear my voice. She seemed neither to be afraid nor to be inclined to resist. It was as though she had come to my room independently of any will of her own.

Was she ill? Had she lost her way? She had come like a sleepwalker, independently of any will of her own. No one can possibly imagine the sensations I experienced at that moment. I felt a kind of delicious, ineffable pain. No, it was not an illusion. This being who without surprise and without a word had come into my room was that woman, that girl. I had always imagined that our first meeting would be like this. My state of mind was that of a man in an infinitely deep sleep. One must be plunged in profound sleep in order to behold such a dream as this. The silence had for me the force of eternal life; for on the plane of eternity without beginning and without end there is no such thing as speech.

To me she was a woman and at the same time had within her something that transcended humanity. When I looked at her face I experienced a kind of vertigo which made me forget the faces of all other people. Gazing at her, I began to tremble all over and my knees felt weak. In the depths of her immense eyes I beheld in one moment all the wretchedness of my life. Her eyes were wet and shining like two huge black diamonds suffused with tears. In her eyes, her black eyes, I found the everlasting night of impenetrable darkness for which I had been seeking and I sank into the awful, enchanted blackness of that abyss. It was as though she was drawing some faculty out of my being. The ground rocked beneath my feet and if I had fallen I should have experienced an ineffable delight.

My heart stood still. I held my breath. I was afraid that if I breathed she might disappear like cloud or smoke. Her silence seemed something supernatural. It was as though a wall of crystal had risen between her and me, and that second, that hour or that eternity was suffocating me. Her eyes, weary perhaps with looking upon some supernatural sight which it is not given to other people to see, perhaps upon death itself, slowly closed. Her eyelids closed and I, feeling like a drowning man who after frantic struggle and effort has reached the surface of the water, realized that I was feverish and trembling and with the edge of my sleeve wiped away the sweat that was streaming from my forehead.

Her face preserved the same stillness, the same tranquil expression, but seemed to have grown thinner and frailer. As she lay there on my bed she was biting the nail of the index finger of her left hand. Her complexion was pale as the moon and her thin, clinging black dress revealed the lines of her legs, her arms, her breasts – of her whole body.

I leant over her in order to see her more plainly. Her eyes were closed. However much I might gaze at her face, she still seemed infinitely remote from me. All at once I felt that I had no knowledge of the secrets of her heart and that no bond existed between us.

I wished to say something but I feared that my voice would offend her ears, her sensitive ears which were accustomed, surely, to distant, heavenly, gentle music.

It occurred to me that she might be hungry or thirsty. I went into the closet to look for something to give her, although I knew there was nothing in the house. Then it was as though I had had a flash of inspiration. I remembered that on the top shelf was a bottle of old wine which had been left to me by my father. I got up onto a stool and took it down. I walked across on tiptoe to the bed. She was sleeping like a weary child. She was sound asleep and her long, velvety eyelashes were closed. I opened the bottle and slowly and carefully poured a glassful of the wine into her mouth between the two locked rows of teeth.

Quite suddenly, for the first time in my life, a sensation of peace took possession of me. As I looked upon those closed eyes it was as though the demon which had been torturing me, the incubus which had been oppressing my heart with its iron paw, had fallen asleep for a while. I brought my chair to the side of the bed and gazed fixedly at her face. What a childlike face it was! What an unworldly expression it wore! Was it possible that this woman, this girl or this angel of hell (for I did not know by what name to call her), was it possible that she should possess this double nature? She was so peaceful, so unconstrained!

I could now feel the warmth of her body and smell the odour of dampness that rose from her black, heavy tresses. For some reason unknown to me I raised my trembling hand – my hand was not under my control – and laid it upon a strand of her hair, that lock which always clung to her temple. Then I thrust my fingers into her hair. It was cold and damp. Cold, utterly cold. It was as though she had been dead for several days. I was not mistaken. She *was* dead. I inserted my hand into the front of her dress and laid it upon her breast above the heart. There was not the faintest beat. I took a mirror and held it before her nostrils, but no trace of life remained in her.

I thought that I might be able to warm her with the heat of my own body, to give my warmth to her and to receive in exchange the coldness of death; perhaps in this way I could infuse my spirit into her dead body. I undressed and lay down beside her on the bed. We were locked together like the male and female of the mandrake. Her body was like that of a female mandrake which had been torn apart from its mate and she aroused the same burning passion as the mandrake. Her mouth was acrid and bitter and tasted like the stub end of a cucumber. Her whole body was as cold as hail. I felt that the blood had frozen in my veins and that this cold penetrated to the depths of my heart. All my efforts were useless. I got off the bed and put on my clothes. No, it was not an illusion. She had come here, into my room, into my bed and had surrendered her body to me. She had given me her body and her soul.

So long as she lived, so long as her eyes overflowed with life, I had been tortured by the mere memory of her eyes. Now, inanimate and still, cold, with her eyes closed, she had surrendered herself to me – with her eyes closed.

This was she who had poisoned my whole life from the moment that I first saw her – unless my nature was such that from the beginning it was destined to be poisoned and any other mode of existence was impossible for me. Now, here, in my room, she had yielded to me her body and her shadow. Her fragile, short-lived spirit, which had no affinity with the world of earthly creatures, had silently departed from under the black, pleated dress, from the body which had tormented it, and had gone wandering in the world of shadows and I felt as though it had taken my spirit with it. But her body was lying there, inanimate and still. Her soft, relaxed muscles, her veins and sinews and bones were awaiting burial, a dainty meal for the worms and rats of the grave. In this threadbare, wretched, cheerless room which itself was like a tomb, in the darkness of the everlasting night which had enveloped me and which had penetrated the very fabric of the walls, I had before me a long, dark, cold, endless night in the company of a corpse, of her corpse. I felt that ever since the world had been the world, so long as I had lived, a corpse, cold, inanimate and still, had been with me in a dark room.

At that moment my thoughts were numbed. Within me I felt a new and singular form of life. My being was somehow connected with that of all the creatures that existed about me, with all the shadows that quivered around me. I was in intimate, inviolable communion with the outside world and with all created things, and a complex system of invisible conductors transmitted a restless flow of impulses between me and all the elements of nature. There was no conception, no notion which I felt to be foreign to me. I was capable of penetrating with ease the secrets of the painters of the past, the mysteries of abstruse philosophies, the ancient folly of ideas and species. At that moment I participated in the revolutions of earth and heaven, in the germination of plants and in the instinctive movements of animals. Past and future, far and near had joined together and fused in the life of my mind. At such times as this every man takes refuge in some firmly established habit, in his own particular passion. The drunkard stupefies himself with drink, the writer writes, the sculptor attacks the stone. Each relieves his mind of the burden by recourse to his own stimulant and it is at such times as this that the real artist is capable of producing a masterpiece. But I, listless and helpless as I was, I, the decorator of pen-case covers, what could I do? What means had I of creating a masterpiece when all that I could make were my lifeless, shiny little pictures, each of them identical with all the rest? And yet in my whole being I felt an overflowing enthusiasm, and indescribable warmth of inspiration. I desired to record on paper those eyes which had closed forever; I would keep the picture by me always. The force of this desire compelled me to translate it into action. I could not resist the impulsion. How could I have resisted it, I, an artist shut up in a room with a dead body? The thought aroused in me a peculiar sensation of delight.

I extinguished the smoky lamp, brought a pair of candles, lit them and set them above her head. In the flickering candlelight her face was still more tranquil than before; in the half-dark of the room it wore an expression of mystery and immateriality. I fetched paper and the other things necessary for my task and took up my position beside her bed – for henceforth the bed was hers. My intention was to portray at my leisure this form which was doomed slowly and gradually to suffer decomposition and disintegration and which now lay still, a fixed expression upon its face. I felt that I must record on paper its essential lines. I would select those lines of which I had myself experienced the power. A painting, even though it be summary and unpretentious, must nevertheless produce an emotional effect and possess a kind of life. I, however, was accustomed only to executing a stereotyped pattern on the covers of pen cases. I had now to bring my own mind into play, to give concrete form to an image which existed in my mind, that image which, emanating from her face, had so impressed itself upon all my thoughts. I would glance once at her face and shut my eyes. Then I would set down on paper the lines which I had selected for my purpose. Thereby I hoped to create from the resources of my mind a drug which would soothe my tortured spirit. I was taking refuge in the end in the motionless life of lines and forms.

The subject I had chosen, a dead woman, had a curious affinity to my dead manner of painting. I had never been anything else than a painter of dead bodies. And now I was faced with the question: was it necessary for me to see her eyes again, those eyes which were now closed? Or were they already imprinted upon my memory with sufficient clarity?

I do not know how many times I drew and redrew her portrait in the course of that night, but none of my pictures satisfied me and I tore them up as fast as I painted them. The work did not tire me and I did not notice the passage of time.

The darkness was growing thin and the windowpanes admitted a grey light into my room. I was busy with a picture which seemed to me to be better than any of the others. But the eyes? Those eyes, with their expression of reproach as though they had seen me commit some unpardonable sin – I was incapable of depicting them on paper. The image of those eyes seemed suddenly to have been effaced from my memory. All my efforts were useless. However much I might study her face, I was unable to bring their expression to mind.

All at once as I looked at her a flush began to appear upon her cheeks. They gradually were suffused with a crimson colour like that of the meat that hangs in front of butchers' shops. She returned to life. Her feverish, reproachful eyes, shining with a hectic brilliance, slowly opened and gazed fixedly at my face. It was the first time she had been conscious of my presence, the first time she had looked at me. Then the eyes closed again.

The thing probably lasted no more than a moment but this was enough for me to remember the expression of her eyes and to set it down on paper. With the tip of my paintbrush I recorded that expression and this time I did not tear up my picture.

Then I stood up and went softly to the bedside. I supposed that she was alive, that she had come back to life, that my love had infused life into her dead body. But at close quarters I detected the corpse smell, the smell of a corpse in the process of decomposition. Tiny maggots were wriggling on her body and a pair of blister flies were circling in the light of the candles. She was quite dead. But why, how, had her eyes opened? Had it been a hallucination or had it really happened?

I prefer not to be asked this question. But the essential was her face, or, rather, her eyes – and now they were in my possession.

I had fixed on paper the spirit which had inhabited those eyes and I had no further need of the body, that body which was doomed to disappear, to become the prey of the worms and rats of the grave. Henceforth she was in my power and I had ceased to be her creature. I could see her eyes whenever I felt inclined to do so. I took up my picture as carefully as I could, laid it in a tin box which served me as a safe and put the box away in the closet behind my room.

The night was departing on tiptoe. One felt that it had shed sufficient of its weariness to enable it to go its way. The ear detected faint, far-off sounds such as the sprouting grass might have made, or some migratory bird as it dreamt upon the wing. The pale stars were disappearing behind banks of cloud. I felt the gentle breath of the morning on my face and at the same moment a cock crowed somewhere in the distance.

What was I to do with the body, a body which had already begun to decompose? At first I thought of burying it in my room, then of taking it away and throwing it down some well surrounded by flowers of blue morning glory. But how much thought, how much effort and dexterity would be necessary in order to do these things without attracting attention! And then, I did not want the eye of any stranger to fall upon her. I had to do everything alone and unaided. Not that I mattered. What point was there to my existence now that she had gone? But she – never, never must any ordinary person, anyone but me, look upon her dead body. She had come to my room and had surrendered her cold body and her shadow to me in order that no one else should see her, in order that she should not be defiled by a stranger's glance. Finally an idea came to me. I would cut up her body, pack it in a suitcase, my old suitcase, take it away with me to some place far, very far from people's eyes, and bury it there.

This time I did not hesitate. I took a bone-handled knife that I kept in the closet beside my room and began by cutting open with great care the dress of fine black material which swathed her like a spider's web. It was the only covering she wore on her body. She seemed to have grown a little: her body appeared to be longer than it had been in life. Then I severed the head. Drops of cold clotted blood trickled from her neck. Next, I amputated the arms and legs. I neatly fitted the trunk along with the head and limbs into the suitcase and covered the whole with her dress, the same black dress. I locked the case and put the key into my pocket. When I had finished, I drew a deep breath of relief and tried the weight of the suitcase. It was heavy. Never before had I experienced such overwhelming weariness. No, I should never be able to remove the suitcase on my own.

The weather had again set to mist and fine rain. I went outside in the hope of finding someone who might help me with the case. There was not a soul to be seen. I walked a little way, peering into the mist. Suddenly I caught sight of a bent old man sitting at the foot of a cypress tree. His face could not be seen for a wide scarf which he wore wrapped around his neck. I walked slowly up to him. I had still not uttered a word when the old man burst into a hollow, grating, sinister laugh which made the hairs on my body stand on end and said:

"If you want a porter, I'm at your service. Yes. I've got a hearse as well. I take dead bodies every day to Shah Abdolazim* and bury them there. Yes. I make coffins, too. Got coffins of every size, the perfect fit for everybody. At your service. Right away."

He roared with laughter, so that his shoulders shook. I pointed in the direction of my house but he said, before I had a chance to utter a word:

"That's all right. I know where you live. I'll be there right away."

He stood up and I walked back to my house. I went into my room and with difficulty got the suitcase with the dead body across to the door. I observed, standing in the street outside the door, a dilapidated old hearse to which were harnessed two black, skeleton-thin horses. The bent old man was sitting on the driver's seat at the front of the hearse, holding a long whip. He did not turn to look in my direction. With a great effort I heaved the suitcase into the hearse, where there was a sunken space designed to hold the coffins, after which I climbed on board myself and lay down in the coffin space, resting my head against the ledge so as to be able to see out as we drove along. I slid the suitcase onto my chest and held it firmly with both hands.

The whip whistled through the air; the horses set off, breathing hard. The vapour could be seen through the drizzling rain, rising from their nostrils like a stream of smoke. They moved with high, smooth paces. Their thin legs, which made me think of the arms of a thief whose fingers have been cut off in accordance with the law and the stumps plunged into boiling oil, rose and fell slowly and made no sound as they touched the ground. The bells around their necks played a strange tune in the damp air. A profound sensation of comfort to which I can assign no cause penetrated me from head to foot and the movement of the hearse did not impart itself in any degree to my body. All that I could feel was the weight of the suitcase upon my chest. I felt as if the weight of her dead body and the coffin in which it lay had for all time been pressing upon my chest.

The country on each side of the road was enveloped in dense mist. With extraordinary speed and smoothness the hearse passed by hills, level ground and streams, and a new and singular landscape unfolded before me, one such as I had never seen, sleeping or waking. On each side of the road was a line of hills standing quite clear of one another. At the foot of the hills there were numbers of weird, crouching, accursed trees, between which one caught sight of ash-grey houses shaped like pyramids, cubes and prisms, with low, dark windows without panes. The windows were like the wild eyes of a man in a state of delirium. The walls of the houses appeared to possess the property of instilling intense cold into the heart of the passer-by. One felt that no living creature could ever have dwelt in those houses. Perhaps they had been built to house the ghosts of ethereal beings.

Apparently the driver of the hearse was taking me by a by-road or by some special route of his own. In some places all that was to be seen on either side of the road were stumps and wry, twisted trees, beyond which were houses, some squat, some tall, of geometrical shapes – perfect cones, truncated cones – with narrow, crooked windows from which blue flowers of morning glory protruded and twined over the doors and walls. Then this landscape disappeared abruptly in the dense mist.

The heavy, pregnant clouds which covered the tops of the hills sagged oppressively. The wind was blowing up a fine rain like aimless, drifting dust. We had been travelling for a considerable time when the hearse stopped at the foot of a stony, arid hill on which there was no trace of greenery. I slid the suitcase off my chest and got out.

On the other side of the hill was an isolated enclosure, peaceful and green. It was a place which I had never seen before and yet it looked familiar to me, as though it had always been present in some recess of my mind. The ground was covered with vines of blue, scentless morning glory. I felt that no one until that moment had ever set foot in the place. I pulled the suitcase out and set it down on the ground. The old driver turned round and said:

"We're not far from Shah Abdolazim. You won't find a better place than this for what you want. There's never a bird flies by here. No."

I put my hand into my pocket, intending to pay the driver his fare. All that I had with me were two *krans* and one *abbasi.** The driver burst into a hollow, grating laugh, and said:

"That's all right. Don't bother. I'll get it from you later. I know where you live. You haven't got any other jobs for me, no? I know something about grave digging, I can tell you. Yes. Nothing to be ashamed of. Shall we go? There's a stream near here by a cypress tree. I'll dig you a hole just the right size for the suitcase and then we'll go."

The old man sprang down from his seat with a nimbleness of which I could not have imagined him to be capable. I took up the case and we walked side by side until we reached a dead tree which stood beside a dry riverbed. My companion said:

"This is a good place."

Without waiting for an answer, he began at once to dig with a small spade and a pick which he had brought with him. I set the suitcase down and stood beside it in a kind of torpor. The old man, bent double, was working away with the deftness of one who was used to the job. In the course of his digging he came across an object which looked like a glazed jar. He wrapped it up in a dirty handkerchief, stood up and said:

"There's your hole. Yes. Just the right size for the suitcase. The perfect fit. Yes."

I put my hand into my pocket to pay him for his work. All that I had with me were two *krans* and one *abbasi*. The old man burst into a hollow laugh which brought out gooseflesh all over my body and said:

"Don't worry about that. That's all right. I know where you live. Yes. In any case, I found a jar that'll do me instead of pay. It's a flower vase from Rhages, comes from the ancient city of Rey. Yes."

Then, as he stood there, bent and stooping, he began to laugh again so that his shoulders shook. He tucked the jar, wrapped in the dirty handkerchief, under his arm and walked off to the hearse. With surprising nimbleness he sprang up and took his place on the driver's seat. The whip whistled through the air, the horses set off, breathing hard. The bells around their necks played a strange tune in the damp air. Gradually they disappeared into the dense mist.

As soon as I was alone I breathed a deep breath of relief. I felt as though a heavy weight had been lifted from my chest, and a wonderful sensation of peace permeated my whole being. I looked around me. The place where I stood was a small enclosure surrounded on every side by blue hills and mounds. Along one ridge extended the ruins of ancient buildings constructed of massive bricks. Nearby was a dry riverbed. It was a quiet, remote spot far from the noise and tumult of men. I felt profoundly happy and reflected that those great eyes, when they awoke from the sleep of earth, would behold a place which was in harmony with their own nature and aspect. And at the same time it was fitting that, just as she had been far removed from the life of

28

other people while she was alive, so she should remain far from the rest of mankind, far from the other dead. I lifted the suitcase with great care and lowered it into the trench, which proved to be of exactly the right dimensions, a perfect fit. However, I felt that I must look into the case once more. I looked around. Not a soul was to be seen. I took the key from my pocket and opened the lid. I drew aside a corner of her black dress and saw, amid a mass of coagulated blood and swarming maggots, two great black eyes gazing fixedly at me with no trace of expression in them. I felt that my entire being was submerged in the depths of those eyes. Hastily I shut the lid of the case and pushed the loose earth in on top of it. When the trench was filled in I trampled the earth firm, brought a number of vines of blue, scentless morning glory and set them in the ground above her grave. Then I collected sand and pebbles and scattered them around in order to obliterate the traces of the burial so completely that nobody should be able to tell that it had ever taken place. I performed this task so well that I myself was unable to distinguish her grave from the surrounding ground.

When I had finished I looked down at myself and saw that my clothes were torn and smeared with clay and black, clotted blood. Two blister flies were circling around me and a number of tiny maggots were wriggling, stuck to my clothes. In an attempt to remove the bloodstains from the skirts of my coat I moistened the edge of my sleeve with saliva and rubbed at the patches; but the bloodstains only soaked into the material, so that they penetrated through to my body and I felt the clamminess of blood upon my skin.

It was not long before sunset and a fine rain was falling. I began to walk and involuntarily followed the wheel tracks of the hearse. When night came on I lost the tracks but continued to walk on in the profound darkness, slowly and aimlessly, with no conscious thought in my mind, like a man in a dream. I had no idea in what direction I was going. Since she had gone, since I had seen those great eyes amid a mass of coagulated blood, I felt that I was walking in a profound darkness which had completely enshrouded my life. Those eyes which had been a lantern lighting my way had been extinguished forever and now I did not care whether or not I ever arrived at any place.

There was complete silence everywhere. I felt that all mankind had rejected me and I took refuge with inanimate things. I was conscious of a relationship between me and the pulsation of nature, between me and the profound night which had descended upon my spirit. This silence is a language which we do not understand. My head began to swim, in a kind of intoxication. A sensation of nausea came over me and my legs felt weak. I experienced a sense of infinite weariness. I went into a cemetery beside the road and sat down upon a gravestone. I held my head between my hands and tried to think steadily of the situation I was in.

Suddenly I was brought to myself by the sound of a hollow, grating laugh. I turned and saw a figure with its face concealed by a scarf muffled around its neck. It was seated beside me and held under its arm something wrapped in a handkerchief. It turned to me and said:

"I suppose you want to get into town? Lost your way, eh? Suppose you're wondering what I'm doing in a graveyard at this time of night? No need to be afraid. Dead bodies are my regular business. Grave-digging's my trade. Not a bad trade, eh? I know every nook and cranny of this place. Take a case in point – today

I went out on a grave-digging job. Found this jar in the ground. Know what it is? It's a flower vase from Rhages, comes from the ancient city of Rey. Yes. That's all right, you can have the jar. Keep it to remember me by."

I put my hand into my pocket and took out two *krans* and one *abbasi*. The old man, with a hollow laugh which brought out gooseflesh all over my body, said:

"No, no. That's all right. I know you. Know where you live, too. I've got a hearse standing just near here. Come and I'll drive you home. Yes. It's only two steps away."

He put the jar into my lap and stood up. He was laughing so violently that his shoulders shook. I picked up the jar and set off in the wake of the stooping figure. By a bend in the road was standing a ramshackle hearse with two gaunt black horses harnessed to it. The old man sprang up with surprising nimbleness and took his place on the driver's seat. I climbed onto the vehicle and stretched myself out in the sunken space where they put the coffins, resting my head against the high ledge so that I should be able to look out as we drove along. I laid the jar on my chest and held it in place with my hand.

The whip whistled through the air; the horses set off, breathing hard. They moved with high, smooth paces. Their hoofs touched the ground gently and silently. The bells around their necks played a strange tune in the damp air. In the gaps between the clouds, the stars gazed down at the earth like gleaming eyes emerging from a mass of coagulated blood. A wonderful sense of tranquillity pervaded my whole being. All that I could feel was the jar pressing against my chest with the weight of a dead body. The interlocking trees with their wry, twisted branches seemed in the darkness to be gripping one another by the hand for fear they should slip and crash to the ground. The sides of the road were lined with weird houses of individual geometrical shapes, with forlorn, black windows. The walls of the houses, like glow worms, gave forth a dim, sickly radiance. The trees passed by alarmingly in clumps and in rows and fled away from us. But it appeared to me that their feet became entangled in vines of morning glory which brought them to the ground. The smell of death, the smell of decomposing flesh, pervaded me, body and soul. It seemed to me that I had always been saturated with the smell of death and had slept all my life in a black coffin while a bent old man whose face I could not see transported me through the mist and the passing shadows.

The hearse stopped. I picked up the jar and sprang to the ground. I was outside the door of my own house. I hurriedly went in and entered my room. I put the jar down on the table, went straight into the closet and brought out from its hiding place the tin box which served me as a safe. I went to the door, intending to give it to the old hearse-driver in lieu of payment, but he had disappeared; there was no sign of him or of his hearse. Frustrated, I went back to my room. I lit the lamp, took the jar out of the handkerchief in which it was wrapped and with my sleeve rubbed away the earth which coated it. It was an ancient vase with a transparent violet glaze which had turned to the colour of a crushed blister fly. On one side of the belly of the vase was an almond-shaped panel framed in blue flowers of morning glory, and in the panel…

In the almond-shaped panel was *her* portrait… the face of a woman with great black eyes, eyes that were bigger than other people's. They wore a look of reproach, as though they had seen me commit some inexpiable sin of which I had no knowledge.

They were frightening, magic eyes with an expression of anxiety and wonder, of menace and promise. They terrified me and attracted me and an intoxicating, supernatural radiance shone from their depths. Her cheekbones were prominent and her forehead high. Her eyebrows were slender and met in the middle. Her lips were full and half open. Her hair was dishevelled, and one strand of it clung to her temple.

I took out from the tin box the portrait I had painted of her the night before and compared the two. There was not an atom of difference between my picture and that on the jar. The one might have been the reflection of the other in a mirror. The two were identical and were, it seemed obvious, the work of one man, one ill-fated decorator of pen cases. Perhaps the soul of the vase-painter had taken possession of me when I made my portrait and my hand had followed his guidance. It was impossible to tell the two apart, except that my picture was on paper while the painting on the vase was covered with an ancient transparent glaze which gave it a mysterious air, a strange, supernatural air. In the depths of the eyes burned a spark of the spirit of evil. No, the thing was past belief: both pictures depicted the same great eyes, void of thought, the same reserved yet unconstrained expression of face. It is impossible to imagine the sensations that arose in me. I wished that I could run away from myself. Was such a coincidence conceivable? All that wretchedness of my life rose again before my eyes. Was it not enough that in the course of my life I should encounter one person with such eyes as these? And now two people were gazing at me from the same eyes, *her* eyes. The thing was beyond endurance. Those eyes to which I had given burial there, by the hill, at the foot of the dead cypress tree, beside the dry river bed, under the blue flowers of morning glory, amid thick blood, amid maggots and foul creatures which were holding festival around her, while the plant roots were already reaching down to force their way into the pupils and suck forth their juices – those same eyes, brimful of vigorous life, were at that moment gazing at me.

I had not known that I was ill-starred and accursed to such a degree as this. And yet at the same time the sense of guilt that lurked in my mind gave rise to a strange, inexplicable feeling of comfort. I realized that I had an ancient partner in sorrow. Was not that ancient painter who, hundreds, perhaps thousands, of years ago, had decorated the surface of this jar my partner in sorrow? Had he not undergone the same spiritual experiences as I? Until now I had regarded myself as the most ill-starred of created beings. Now I understood for a space that on those hills, in the houses of that ruined city of massive brick, had once lived men whose bones had long since rotted away and the atoms of whose bodies might now perhaps be living another life in the blue flowers of morning glory; and that among those men there had been one, an unlucky painter, an accursed painter, perhaps an unsuccessful decorator of pen-case covers, who had been a man like me, exactly like me. And now I understood (it was all that I was capable of understanding) that his life also had burned and melted away in the depths of two great, black eyes, just as mine had done. The thought gave me consolation.

I set my painting beside that upon the jar and went and kindled the charcoal in my opium brazier. When it was burning well I set the brazier down in front of the two paintings. I drew a few whiffs of the opium pipe and, as the drug began to take effect, gazed steadily at the pictures. I felt that I had to concentrate my thoughts, and the only thing that enabled me to do so and to achieve tranquillity of mind were the ethereal fumes of opium.

I smoked my whole stock of opium, in the hope that the wonder-working drug would resolve the problems that vexed me, draw aside the curtain that hung before the eye of my mind and dispel my accumulation of distant, ashy memories. I attained the spiritual state for which I was waiting and that to a higher degree than I had anticipated. My thoughts acquired the subtlety and grandeur which only opium can confer and I sank into a condition between sleep and coma.

Then I felt as though a heavy weight had been removed from my chest, as though the law of gravity had ceased to exist for me and I soared freely in pursuit of my thoughts, which had grown ample, ingenious and infinitely precise. A profound and ineffable delight took possession of me. I had been released from the burden of my body. My whole being was sinking into the torpor of vegetable existence. The world in which I found myself was a tranquil world but one filled with enchanted, exquisite forms and colours. Then the thread of my thoughts snapped asunder and dissolved amid the colours and the shapes. I was immersed in a sea the waves of which bestowed ethereal caresses upon me. I could hear my heart beating, could feel the throbbing of my arteries. It was a state of existence charged with significance and delight.

From the bottom of my heart I desired to surrender myself to the sleep of oblivion. If only oblivion were attainable, if it could last forever, if my eyes as they closed could gently transcend sleep and dissolve into non-being and I should lose consciousness of my existence for all time to come, if it were possible for my being to dissolve in one drop of ink, in one bar of music, in one ray of coloured light, and then these waves and forms were to grow and grow to such infinite size that in the end they faded and disappeared – then I should have attained my desire.

Gradually a sensation of numbness took hold of me. It resembled a kind of agreeable weariness. I had the impression that a continuous succession of subtle waves were emanating from my body. Then I felt as though the course of my life had been reversed. One by one, past experiences, past states of mind and obliterated, lost memories of childhood recurred to me. Not only did I see these things but I took part in the bustle of bygone activity, was wholly immersed in it. With each moment that passed I grew smaller and more like a child. Then suddenly my mind became blank and dark and it seemed to me that I was suspended from a slender hook in the shaft of a dark well. Then I broke free of the hook and dropped through space. No obstacle interrupted my fall. I was falling into an infinite abyss in an everlasting night. After that a long series of forgotten scenes flashed one after another before my eyes. I experienced a moment of utter oblivion. When I came to myself, I found myself in a small room and in a peculiar posture which struck me as strange and at the same time natural to me.

3

W HEN I AWOKE in a new world everything that I found there was perfectly familiar and near to me, so much so that I felt more at home in it than in my previous surroundings and manner of life, which, so it seemed to me, had been only the reflection of my real life. It was a different world but one in such perfect harmony with me that I felt as though I had returned to my natural surroundings. I had been born again in a world which was ancient but which at the same time was closer and more natural to me than the other.

It was still twilight. An oil lamp was burning on a shelf. There was a bed unrolled* in the corner of the room, but I was awake. My body felt burning hot. There were bloodstains on my cloak and scarf and my hands were covered with blood. But in spite of fever and giddiness I experienced a peculiar animation and restlessness which were stronger than any thought I might have had of removing the traces of blood, more powerful than the thought that the police would come and arrest me. In any case I had been expecting for some time to be arrested and had made up my mind, should they come, to gulp down a glass of the poisoned wine which I kept on the top shelf. The source of my excitement was the need to write, which I felt as a kind of obligation imposed on me. I hoped by this means to expel the demon which had long been lacerating my vitals, to vent onto paper the horrors of my mind. Finally, after some hesitation, I drew the oil lamp towards me and began as follows:

4

I T WAS ALWAYS MY OPINION that the best course a man could take in life was to remain silent; that one could not do better than withdraw into solitude like the bittern which spreads its wings beside some lonely lake. But now, since that which should not have happened has happened, I cannot help myself. Who knows? Perhaps in the course of the next few moments, perhaps in an hour's time, a band of drunken policemen will come to arrest me. I have not the least desire to save my carcass, and in any case it would be quite impossible for me to deny the crime, even supposing that I could remove the bloodstains. But before I fall into their hands I shall swallow a glass from the bottle of wine, my heirloom, which I keep on the top shelf.

I wish now to squeeze out every drop of juice from my life as from a cluster of grapes and to pour the juice – the wine, rather – drop by drop, like water of Karbala,* down the parched throat of my shadow. All that I hope to do is record on paper before I go the torments which have slowly wasted me away like gangrene or cancer here in my little room. This is the best means I have of bringing order and regularity into my thoughts. Is it my intention to draw up a last will and testament? By no means. I have no property for the State to devour, I have no faith for the Devil to take. Moreover, what is there on the face of the earth that could have the slightest value for me? What life I had I have allowed to slip away – I permitted it, I even wanted it, to go – and after I have gone what do I care what happens? It is all the same to me whether anyone reads the scraps of paper I leave behind or whether they remain unread for ever and a day. The only thing that makes me write is the need, the overmastering need, at this moment more urgent than ever it was in the past, to create a channel between my thoughts and my unsubstantial self, my shadow, that sinister shadow which at this moment is stretched across the wall in the light of the oil lamp in the attitude of one studying attentively and devouring each word I write. This shadow surely understands better than I do. It is only to him that I can talk properly. It is he who compels me to talk. Only he is capable of knowing me. He surely understands… It is my wish, when I have poured the juice – rather, the bitter wine – of my life down the parched throat of my shadow, to say to him, "This is my life."

Whoever saw me yesterday saw a wasted, sickly young man. Today he would see a bent old man with white hair, burnt-out eyes and a harelip. I am afraid to look out of the window of my room or to look at myself in the mirror, for everywhere I see my own shadow multiplied indefinitely.

However, in order to explain my life to my stooping shadow, I am obliged to tell a story. Ugh! How many stories about love, copulation, marriage and death already exist, not one of which tells the truth! How sick I am of well-constructed plots and brilliant writing!

I shall try to squeeze out the juice from this cluster of grapes, but whether or not the result will contain the slightest particle of truth I do not yet know. I do not know where I am at this moment, whether the patch of sky above my head and these few spans of ground on which I am sitting belong to Nishapur or to Balkh* or to Benares. I feel sure of nothing in the world.

I have seen so many contradictory things and have heard so many words of different sorts, my eyes have seen so much of the worn-out surface of various objects – the thin, tough rind behind which the spirit is hidden – that now I believe nothing. At this very moment I doubt the existence of tangible, solid things, I doubt clear, manifest truths. If I were to strike my hand against the stone mortar that stands in the corner of our courtyard and were to ask it, "Are you real and solid?" and the mortar were to reply, "Yes," I do not know whether I should take its word or not.

Am I a being separate and apart from the rest of creation? I do not know. But when I looked into the mirror a moment ago I did not recognize myself. No, the old 'I' has died and rotted away, but no barrier, no gulf, exists between it and the new one.

I must tell my story, but I am not sure at what point to start. Life is nothing but a fiction, a mere story. I must squeeze out the juice from the cluster of grapes and pour it spoonful by spoonful down the parched throat of this aged shadow. At what point should I start? All the thoughts which are bubbling in my brain at this moment belong to this passing instant and know nothing of hours, minutes and dates. An incident of yesterday may for me be less significant, less recent, than something that happened a thousand years ago.

Perhaps for the very reason that all the bonds which held me to the world of living people have been broken, the memories of the past take shape before my eyes. Past, future, hour, day, month, year – these things are all the same to me. The various phases of childhood and maturity are to me nothing but futile words. They mean something only to ordinary people, to the rabble – yes, that is the word I was looking for – the rabble, whose lives, like the year, have their definite periods and seasons and are cast in the temperate zone of existence. But my life has always known only one season and one state of being. It is as though it had been spent in some frigid zone and in eternal darkness while all the time within me burned a flame which consumed me as the flame consumes the candle.

Within the four walls that form my room, this fortress which I have erected around my life and thoughts, my life has been slowly wasting away like a candle. No, I am wrong. It is like a green log which has rolled to one side of the fireplace and which has been scorched and charred by the flames from the other logs; it has neither burnt away nor remained fresh and green; it has been choked by the smoke and steam from the others.

My room, like all rooms, is built of baked and sun-dried bricks and stands upon the ruins of thousands of ancient houses. Its walls are whitewashed and it has a frieze around it. It is exactly like a tomb. I am capable of occupying my thoughts for hours at a stretch with the slightest details of the life of the room – for example, with a little spider in a crevice of the wall. Ever since I have been confined to my bed people have paid little attention to me.

In the wall there is a horseshoe nail which at one time supported the swinging cradle where my wife and I used to sleep and which since then may have supported the weight of other children. Just below the nail there is a patch where the plaster has swelled and fallen away, and from that patch one can detect the odours from the things and the people which have been in the room in the past. No draught or breeze has ever been able to dispel these dense, clinging, stagnant odours: the smell of sweat, the smell of bygone illnesses, the smell of people's mouths, the smell of feet, the acrid smell of urine, the smell of rancid oil, the smell of decayed straw matting, the smell of burnt omelettes, the smell of fried onions, the smell of medicines, the smell of mallow, the smell of dirty napkins, the smell which you find in the rooms of boys lately arrived at puberty, the vapours which have seeped in from the street and the smells of the dead and dying. All of these odours are still alive and have kept their individuality. There are, besides, many other smells of unknown origins which have left their traces there.

Opening off my room is a dark closet. The room itself has two windows facing out onto the world of the rabble. One of them looks onto our own courtyard, the other onto the street, forming thereby a link between me and the city of Rey, the city which they call the "Bride of the World", with its thousandfold web of winding streets, its host of squat houses, its schools and its caravanserais. The city which is accounted the greatest city in the world is breathing and living its life there beyond my room. When I close my eyes here in my little room the vague, blurred shadows of the city (of which my mind is at all times aware, whether consciously or not) all take substantial form and rise before me in the shape of pavilions, mosques and gardens.

These two windows are my links with the outside world, the world of the rabble. But on the wall inside my room hangs a mirror in which I look at my face, and in my circumscribed existence that mirror is a more important thing than the world of the rabble men which has nothing to do with me.

The central feature of the city landscape as seen from my window is a wretched little butcher's shop directly opposite our house. It gets through a total of two sheep per day. I can see the butcher every time I look out of the window. Early each morning a pair of gaunt, consumptive-looking horses are led up to the shop. They have a deep, hollow cough and their emaciated legs terminated by blunt hoofs give one the feeling that their fingers have been cut off in accordance with some barbarous law and the stumps plunged into boiling oil. Each of them has a pair of sheep carcasses slung across its back. The butcher raises his greasy hand to his henna-dyed beard and begins by appraising the carcasses with a buyer's eye. He selects two of them and feels the weight of their tails with his hand. Finally he lugs them across and hangs them from a hook at the entrance to the shop. The horses set off, breathing hard. The butcher stands by the two bloodstained corpses with their gashed throats and their staring bloody-lidded eyes bulging from the bluish skulls. He pats them and feels the flesh with his fingers. Then he takes a long bone-handled knife and cuts up their bodies with great care, after which he smilingly dispenses the meat to his customers. How much pleasure he derives from all these operations! I am convinced that they give him the most exquisite pleasure, even delight. Every morning at this time the thick-necked yellow dog which has made our district his preserve is there outside the butcher's shop. His head on one side, he gazes regretfully with his innocent eyes at the butcher's hand. That dog also understands. He also knows that the butcher enjoys his work.

A little further away under an archway a strange old man is sitting with an assortment of wares spread out in front of him on a canvas sheet. They include a sickle, two horseshoes, assorted coloured beads, a long-bladed knife, a rat trap, a rusty pair of tongs, part of a writing set, a gap-toothed comb, a spade, and a glazed jar over which he has thrown a dirty handkerchief.

I have watched him from behind my window for days, hours and months. He always wears a dirty scarf, a Shuster cloak and an open shirt from which protrude the white hairs on his chest. He has inflamed eyelids which are apparently being eaten away by some stubborn, obtrusive disease. He wears a talisman tied to his arm and he always sits in the same posture. On Thursday evenings he reads aloud from the Koran, revealing his yellow, gappy teeth as he does so. One might suppose that he earned his living by this Koran-reading, for I have never seen anyone buy anything from him. It seems to me that this man's face has figured in most of my nightmares. What crass, obstinate ideas have grown up, weed-like, inside that shaven greenish skull under its embroidered turban, behind that low forehead? One feels that the canvas sheet in front of the old man, with its assortment of odds and ends, has some curious affinity to the life of the old man himself. More than once I have made up my mind to go up and exchange a word with him or buy something from his collection, but I have not found the courage to do so.

According to my nurse, the old man was a potter in his younger days. After giving up that trade he kept only this one jar for himself and now he earned his living by peddling.

These were my links with the outside world. Of my private world all that was left to me were my nurse and my bitch of a wife. But nanny was her nurse too; she was nurse to both of us. My wife and I were not only closely related but were suckled together by Nanny. Her mother was to all intents and purposes mine too because I never saw my parents but was brought up by her mother, a tall, grey-haired woman. I loved her as much as if she had been my real mother, and that was the reason why I married her daughter.

I have heard several different accounts of my father and mother. Only one of them, the one Nanny gave me, can, I imagine, be true. This is what Nanny told me:

My father and my uncle were twins. They resembled each other exactly in figure, face and disposition, and even their voices were identical. So it was no easy matter to tell them apart. Moreover, there existed between them a mental bond or sympathy as a result of which, to take an example, if one of them fell ill the other would fall ill also. In the common phrase, they were like two halves of the one apple.

In due course the both decided to go into commerce and, when they reached the age of twenty, they went off to India, where they opened up a business in Rey wares, including textiles of various kinds – shot silk, flowered stuffs, cotton piece goods, jubbahs, shawls, needles, earthenware, fuller's earth, and pencase covers. My father settled in Benares and used to send my uncle on business trips to the other cities of India. After some time, my father fell in love with a girl called Bugam Dasi, a dancer in a lingam temple. Besides performing ritual dances before the great lingam idol she served as a temple attendant. She was a hot-blooded, olive-skinned girl, with lemon-shaped breasts, great, slanting eyes and slender eyebrows which met in the middle. On her forehead she wore a streak of red paint.

At this moment I can picture Bugam Dasi, my mother, wearing a gold-embroidered sari of coloured silk and around her head a fillet of brocade, her bosom bare, her heavy tresses, black as the dark night of eternity, gathered in a knot behind her head, bracelets on her wrists and ankles and a gold ring in her nostril, with great, dark, languid, slanting eyes and brilliantly white teeth, dancing with slow, measured movements to the music of the sitar, the drum, the lute, the cymbal and the horn, a soft, monotonous music played by bare-bodied men in turbans, a music of mysterious significance, concentrating in itself all the secrets of wizardry, the legends, the passion and the sorrow of the men of India; and, as she performs her rhythmic evolutions, her voluptuous gestures, the consecrated movements of the temple dance, Bugam Dasi unfolds like the petals of a flower. A tremor passes across her shoulders and arms, she bends forwards and again shrinks back. Each movement has its own precise meaning and speaks a language that is not of words. What an effect must all this have had upon my father! Above all, the voluptuous significance of the spectacle was intensified by the acrid, peppery smell of her sweat mingling with the perfume of champac and sandalwood oil, perfumes redolent of the essences of exotic trees and arousing sensations that slumbered hitherto in the depths of the consciousness. I imagine these perfumes as resembling the smell of the drug box, of the drugs which used to be kept in the nursery and which, we are told, came from India – unknown oils from a land of mystery, of ancient civilization. I feel sure that the medicines I used to take had that smell.

All these things revived distant, dead memories in my father's mind. He fell in love with Bugam Dasi, so deeply in love that he embraced the dancing girl's religion, the lingam cult.

After some time the girl became pregnant and was discharged from the service of the temple. Shortly after I was born my uncle returned to Benares from one of his trips. Apparently, in the matter of women as in all others, his reactions were identical to my father's. He fell passionately in love with my mother and in the end he satisfied his desire, which, because of his physical and mental resemblance to my father, was not difficult for him to do.

As soon as she learnt the truth, my mother said that she would never again have anything to do with either of them unless they agreed to undergo "trial by cobra". In that case she would belong to whichever of the two came through alive.

The "trial" consisted of the following. My father and my uncle would be enclosed together in a dark room like a dungeon in which a cobra had been let loose. The first of them to be bitten by the serpent would, naturally, cry out. Immediately a snake-charmer would open the door of the room and bring the other out into safety. Bugam Dasi would belong to the survivor.

Before the two were shut up in the dark room my father asked Bugam Dasi if she would perform the sacred temple dance before him once more. She agreed to do so and, by torchlight, to the music of the snake-charmer's pipe, she danced, with her significant, measured, gliding movements, bending and twisting like a cobra. Then my father and uncle were shut up in the room with the serpent. Instead of a shriek of horror, what the listeners heard was a groan blended with a wild, gooseflesh-raising peal of laughter. When the door was opened my uncle walked out of the dark room. His face was ravaged and old, and his hair – the terror aroused by the sound of the cobra's body as it slid across the floor, by its furious hissing, by its glittering eyes, by the thought of its poisonous fangs and of its loathsome body shaped like a long neck terminating in a spoon-shaped protuberance and a tiny head, the horror of all this had changed my uncle, by the time he walked out of the room, into a white-haired old man.

In accordance with the terms of the contract Bugam Dasi belonged henceforth to my uncle. The frightful thing was that it was not certain that the survivor actually was my uncle. The "trial" had deranged his mind and he had completely lost his memory. He did not recognize the infant and it was this that made them decide he must be my uncle. May it not be that this story has some strange bearing upon my personal history and that that gooseflesh-raising peal of laughter and the horror of the "trial by cobra" have left their imprint upon me and are somehow pertinent to my destiny?

From this time on I was nothing more than an intruder, an extra mouth to feed. In the end my uncle (or my father, whichever it was), accompanied by Bugam Dasi, returned to the city of Rey on business. They brought me with them and left me with his sister, my aunt.

My nurse told me that my mother, when saying goodbye, handed my aunt a bottle of wine to keep for me. It was a deep red wine, and it contained a portion of the venom of the cobra, the Indian serpent. What more suitable keepsake could such a woman as Bugam Dasi have found to leave to her child? Deep red wine, an elixir of death which would bestow everlasting peace. Perhaps she also had pressed out her life like a cluster of grapes and was now giving me the wine which it had yielded, that same venom which had killed my father. I understand now how precious was the gift she gave me.

Is my mother still alive? Perhaps at this moment as I write she is bending and twisting like a serpent, as thought it were she whom the cobra had bitten, dancing by torchlight in an open space in some far-off city of India, while women and children and intent, bare-bodied men stand around her and my father (or my uncle), white-haired and bent, sits somewhere on the edge of the circle watching her and remembers the dungeon and the hissing of the angry cobra as it glided forwards, its head raised high, its neck swelling like a scoop and the spectacle-shaped lines on the back of its hood steadily expanding and deepening in colour.

At all events I was a little baby when I was entrusted to the care of my nurse. Nanny also suckled my aunt's daughter, the bitch my wife. I grew up in the family of my aunt, the tall woman with the grey hair around her temples, in the same house as the bitch, her daughter.

Ever since I can remember I looked upon my aunt as a mother and loved her deeply. I loved her so deeply that later on I married her daughter, my foster sister, simply because she looked like her.

Or rather, I was forced to marry her. She gave herself to me only once. I shall never forget it. It happened by the bedside of her dead mother. Late at night, after everyone had gone to bed, I got up in my nightshirt and drawers and went into the dead woman's room to say goodbye to her for the last time. Two camphor candles were burning at her head. A Koran had been laid on her stomach to prevent the Devil from entering her body. I drew back the sheet which covered her and saw my aunt again, with her dignified, pleasant face, from which, it seemed, all traces of earthly concerns had been effaced. She wore an expression before which I involuntarily bowed my head and at the same time I felt that death was a normal, natural thing. The corners of her lips were fixed in a faintly ironical smile. I was about to kiss her hand and go out when, turning my head, I saw with a start that the bitch who is now my wife had come into the room. There in the presence of her dead mother she pressed herself hard against me, held me close and kissed me long and passionately on the lips. I could have sunk into the ground with shame, but I had not the strength of mind to do what I should have done. The dead woman, her teeth visible, looked as though she was mocking us – I had the impression that her expression had changed from the quiet smile she had been wearing before. Mechanically I held the girl in my arms and returned her kiss, when suddenly the curtain draped across the doorway leading to the next room was drawn aside and my aunt's husband, the bitch's father, came into the room. He was a bent old man, and he was wearing a scarf wrapped around his neck.

He burst into a hollow, grating, gooseflesh-raising peal of laughter, of a quality to make the hairs on one's body stand on end. His shoulders were shaking. And yet he did not look in our direction. I could have sunk into the ground with shame. If I had had the strength I should have slapped the dead face which was gazing mockingly at us. I was overcome with shame and fled blindly from the room. And I had the bitch to thank! The chances are that she had arranged the whole thing in advance so as to put me into a position where I should be forced to marry her.

And in fact, foster brother and sister though we were, I was obliged to marry her to save her reputation. She was not a virgin, but I was unaware of the fact, and indeed was in no position to know of it; I only learnt it later from people's gossip. When we were alone together in the bridal chamber on the first night she refused to undress, despite all my begging and praying, and would only say, "It's the wrong time of the month." She would not let me come near her but put out the light and lay down to sleep on the other side of the room from me. She was trembling like a willow tree. Anyone might have thought she had been shut up in a dungeon with a dragon. I shall probably not be believed – and indeed the thing passes belief – when I say that she did not once allow me to kiss her on the lips.

The next night also I slept on the floor as I had done the night before, and similarly on the night that followed. I could not work up the courage to do anything else. And so a considerable period went by, during which I slept on the floor on the other side of the room from my wife. Who would believe it? For two months – no, for two months and four days – I slept apart from her on the floor and could not work up the courage to come near her.

She had prepared her virginity token beforehand. I don't know – perhaps she had sprinkled the cloth with the blood of a partridge or perhaps it was a cloth she had kept from the first night of her gallantries in order to make a bigger fool of me. At the time everyone was congratulating me. They were winking at one another and I suppose they were saying to one another, "The lad took the fortress by storm last night", while I put the best face on it that I could and pretended I noticed nothing. They were laughing at me, at my blindness. I made a resolution to write the whole story down some day.

I found out later that she had lovers right and left. It may be that the reason she hated me was that a preacher, by the process of reciting a few words in Arabic over us, had placed her under my authority; perhaps she simply wanted to be free. Finally, one night I made up my mind to share her bed by force, and I carried out my resolve. After a tussle she got out of bed and left me and the only satisfaction I had was that I was able to curl up and sleep the rest of the night in her bed, which was impregnated with the warmth and odour of her body. The only time I enjoyed peaceful sleep was that night. After that she slept in a different room from me.

When I came back to the house after dark she would still be out. Or rather, I would not know whether she had returned home or not and I did not care to know, since solitude and death were my destiny. I desired at all costs to establish contact with her lovers – this is another thing that will seem incredible – and sought out everyone who I heard had caught her fancy. I put up with every sort of humiliation in order to strike up an acquaintance with them. I toadied to them, urged them to visit my wife, even brought them to the house. And what people she chose! A tripe-peddler, an interpreter of the Law, a cooked-meat vendor, the police superintendent, a shady mufti, a philosopher – their names and titles varied, but none of them was fit to be anything better than assistant to the man who sells boiled sheep's heads. And she preferred all of them to me. No one would believe me if I were to describe the abject self-abasement with which I cringed and grovelled to her and them. The reason why I behaved like this was that I was afraid my wife might leave me. I wanted my wife's lovers to teach me deportment, manners, the technique of seduction! However, as a pimp I was not a success, and the fools all laughed in my face. After all, however could I have learnt manners and deportment from the rabble? I know now that she loved them precisely because they were shameless, stupid and rotten. Her love was inseparable from filth and death. Did I really want to sleep with her? Was it her looks that had made me fall in love with her, or was it her aversion to me or her general behaviour or the deep affection I had felt for her mother since my early childhood, or was it all of these things combined? I simply do not know. One thing I do know: my wife, the bitch, the sorceress, had poured into my soul some poison which not only made me want her but made every single atom in my body desire the atoms of hers and shriek aloud its desire. I yearned to be with her in some lost island where there would be nobody but us two. I wished that an earthquake, a great storm or a thunderbolt from the sky might blast all the rabble-humanity that was there breathing, bustling and enjoying life on the far side of the wall of my room and that only she and I might remain.

But even then would she not have preferred any other living creature – an Indian serpent, a dragon – to me? I longed to spend one night with her and to die together with her, locked in her arms. I felt that this would be the sublime culmination of my existence.

While I wasted away in agony, the bitch for her part seemed to derive an exquisite pleasure from torturing me. In the end I abandoned all the activities and interests that I had and remained confined to my room like a living corpse. No one knew the secret which existed between us. Even my old nurse, who was a witness of my slow death, used to reproach me – on account of the bitch! Behind my back, around me, I heard people whispering. "How can that poor woman put up with that crazy husband of hers?" And they were right, for my abasement had gone beyond all conceivable limits.

I wasted away from day to day. When I looked at myself in the mirror my cheeks were crimson like the meat that hangs outside butchers' shops. My body was glowing with heat and the expression of my eyes was languid and depressed.

I was pleased with the change in my appearance. I had seen the dust of death sprinkled over my eyes, I had seen that I must go.

At last they sent word to the doctor, the rabble doctor, the family doctor who, in his own words, had "brought us all up". He came into the room in an embroidered turban and with a beard three hand's-breadths long. It was his boast that he had in his time given my grandfather drugs to restore his virility, administered grey powders to me and forced cassia down the throat of my aunt. He sat down by my bedside and, after feeling my pulse and inspecting my tongue, gave his professional advice: I was to go onto a diet of ass's milk and barley water and to have my room fumigated twice a day with mastic and arsenic. He also gave my nurse a number of lengthy prescriptions consisting of herbal extracts and weird and wonderful oils – hyssop, olive oil, extract of liquorice, camphor, maidenhair, camomile oil, oil of bay, linseed, fir-tree nuts and suchlike trash.

My condition grew worse. Only my old grey-haired nurse, who was *her* nurse also, attended me, bringing me my medicine or sitting beside my bed, dabbing cold water on my forehead. She would talk about the time when the bitch and I were children. For example, she told me how my wife from early childhood had a habit of biting the nails of her left hand and would sometimes gnaw them to the quick. Sometimes she would tell me stories and then I would feel that my life had reversed its course and I had become a child again, for the stories were intimately associated with my memories of those days. I remember quite plainly that when I was very little and my wife and I used to sleep together in the one cradle, a big double cradle, my nurse used to tell the same stories. Some things in these stories which then used to strike me as far-fetched now seem perfectly natural and credible to me.

My morbid condition had created within me a new world, a strange indistinct world of shapes and colours and desires of which a healthy person could have no conception. In these circumstances the crowding incidents of my nurse's tales struck an echo which filled me with an indescribable delight and agitation. I felt that I had become a child again. At this very moment as I write I experience those sensations. They belong, all of them, to the present. They are not an element of the past.

It would seem that the behaviour, thoughts, aspirations and customs of the men of past ages, as transmitted to later generations by the medium of such stories, are among the essential components of human life. For thousands of years people have been saying the same words, performing the same sexual act, vexing themselves with the same childish worries. Is not life from beginning to end a ludicrous story, an improbable, stupid yarn? Am I not now writing my own personal piece of fiction? A story is only an outlet for frustrated aspirations, for aspirations which the storyteller conceives in accordance with a limited stock of spiritual resources inherited from previous generations.

If only I could have slept peacefully as I did in the days when I was an innocent child! Then I slept tranquil and easy. Now when I awoke my cheeks were crimson like the meat which hangs in front of butchers' shops, my body was burning hot and I coughed – how deep and horrible my cough was! It was impossible to imagine from what remote cavity of my body it proceeded. It resembled the coughing of the horses that bring the sheep carcasses each morning to the butcher's shop opposite my window.

I remember well, the room was quite dark. I lay still for several minutes in a state of semi-consciousness. I used to talk to myself before I fell asleep. On this occasion I was convinced that I had become a child again and that I was lying in the cradle. I sensed that there was someone near me. Everyone in the house had long been in bed. It was the hour just before dawn, the time when, as sick people know, one's being seems to transcend the boundaries of the world. My heart was beating hard but I experienced no fear. My eyes were open but I could see no one, for the darkness was intense. Several minutes passed. An idea, a sick man's idea, came into my mind. I said to myself, "Perhaps it is she!" At the same moment I felt a cool hand laid on my burning forehead.

I shuddered. Two or three times I wondered if it was the hand of Ezraïl.* Then I fell asleep. When I awoke in the morning my nurse said to me, "My daughter" – she meant the bitch, my wife – "came to your bedside and took your head in her lap and rocked you like a baby." Apparently a maternal feeling had suddenly awakened in her. I wish I could have died at that moment. Perhaps the child she was pregnant with had died. Had she had her baby? I did not know.

Lying in this room of mine, which was steadily shrinking and growing dark like the grave, I had watched the door throughout my waking hours in the hope that my wife would come to me. But she never did. Was not she to blame for the condition I was in? For three years, or rather for two years and four months – although, what do days and months matter? To me they mean nothing; time has no meaning for one who is lying in the grave – this room has been the tomb of my existence, the tomb of my mind. All the bustle, noise and pretence that filled the lives of other people, the rabble-people who, body and soul, are turned out of the one mould, had become foreign and meaningless to me. Ever since I had been confined to my bed I had been living in a strange unimaginable world in which I had no need of the world of the rabble. It was a world which existed within me, a world of unknowns, and I felt an inner compulsion to probe and investigate every nook and cranny of it.

During the night, at the time when my being hovered on the boundary of the two worlds, immediately before I sank into a deep, blank sleep, I used to dream. In the course of a single second I lived a life which was entirely distinct from my waking life. I breathed a different atmosphere in some far-off region. It was probably that I wished to escape from myself and to change my destiny. When I shut my eyes my own real world was revealed to me. The images that I saw had an independent life of their own. They faded and reappeared at will and my volition appeared to exercise no control over them. This point, however, is not certain. The scenes which passed before my eyes were no ordinary dream, for I was not yet asleep. In silence and tranquillity I distinguished the various images and compared them with one another. It seemed to me that until now I had not known myself and that the world as I had conceived it hitherto had lost all significance and validity and had been replaced by the darkness of night. For I had not been taught to gaze at and to love the night.

I am not sure whether or not I had control of my arms at such times. I felt however that if once I were to leave my hand to its own resources it would begin to function spontaneously, impelled by some mysterious motive force of its own, without my being able to influence or master its movements, and that if I had not constantly kept careful watch of my body and automatically controlled it, it would have been capable of doing things which I did not in the least expect.

A sensation which had long been familiar to me was this: that I was slowly decomposing while I yet lived. My heart had always been at odds not only with my body but with my mind, and there was absolutely no compatibility between them. I had always been in a state of decomposition and gradual disintegration. At times I conceived thoughts which I myself felt to be inconceivable. At other times I experienced a feeling of pity for which my reason reproved me. Frequently when talking or engaged in business with someone I would begin to argue on this or that subject while all my feelings were somewhere else and I was thinking of something quite different and at the same time reproaching myself. I was a crumbling, decomposing mass. It seemed to me that this was what I had always been and always would be, a strange compound of incompatible elements...

A thought which I found intolerably painful was this: whereas I felt that I was far removed from all people whom I saw and among whom I lived, yet at the same time I was related to them by an external similarity which was both remote and close. My surprise at the fact was diminished by the knowledge that my physical needs were the same as theirs. The point of resemblance which tortured me more than any other was the fact that the rabble-men were attracted as I was to the bitch, my wife, she feeling a stronger appetite for them than for me. I am certain that there was something lacking in the make-up of one of us.

I call her "the bitch" because no other name would suit her so well. I do not like to say simply "my wife", because the man-wife relationship did not exist between us and I should be lying to myself if I called her so. From the beginning of time I have called her "the bitch", and the word has had a curious charm for me. If I married her it was because she made the first advances. She did so by design and fraud. No, she had no kindness for me. How could she ever have felt kindness for anyone? A sensual creature who required one man to satisfy her lust, another to play the gallant and another to satisfy her need to inflict pain.

Not that I think she restricted herself to this trinity, but at any rate I was the one she selected to torture. To tell the truth she could not have chosen a better subject. For my part I married her because she looked like her mother and because she had a faint, remote resemblance to me. And by this time not merely did I love her but every atom in my body desired her. And more than any other part of me, my loins – for I refuse to hide real feelings behind a fanciful veil of "love", "fondness" and suchlike theological terms: I have no taste for literary *huzvaresh*.* I felt as though both of us had pulsating in our loins a kind of radiation or aureole like those which one sees depicted around the heads of the prophets and that my sickly, diseased aureole was seeking hers and striving with all its might towards it.

When my condition improved I made up my mind to go away, to go somewhere where people would never find me again, like a dog with distemper who knows that he is going to die or like the birds that hide themselves when the time to die has come. Early one morning I rose, dressed, took a couple of cakes that were lying on the top shelf and, without attracting anyone's attention, fled from the house. I was running away from my own misery. I walked aimlessly along the streets, I wandered without set purpose among the rabble-men as they hurried by, an expression of greed on their faces, in pursuit of money and sexual satisfaction. I had no need to see them since any one of them was a sample of the lot. Each and every one of them consisted only of a mouth and a wad of guts hanging from it, the whole terminating in a set of genitals.

I felt that I had suddenly become lighter and more agile. My leg muscles were functioning with a suppleness and speed which until then I could not have imagined to be possible. I felt that I had escaped from all the fetters of existence and that this was my natural mode of movement. In my childhood, whenever I had slipped off the burden of trouble and responsibility, I had walked like this.

The sun was already high in the sky and the heat was intense. I found myself walking along deserted streets lined with ash-grey houses of strange, geometrical shapes – cubes, prisms, cones – with low, dark windows. One felt that these windows were never opened, that the houses were untenanted, temporary structures and that no living creature could ever have dwelt in them.

The sun, like a golden knife, was steadily paring away the edge of the shade beside the walls. The streets were enclosed between old, whitewashed walls. Everywhere were peace and stillness, as though all the elements were obeying the sacred law of calm and silence imposed by the blazing heat. It seemed as though mystery was everywhere and my lungs hardly dared to inhale the air.

All at once I became aware that I was outside the gate of the city. The sun, sucking with a thousand mouths, was drawing the sweat of my body. The desert plants looked, under the great, blazing sun, like so many patches of turmeric. The sun was like a feverish eye. It poured its burning rays from the depths of the sky over the silent, lifeless landscape. The ground and the plants gave off a peculiar smell which brought back certain moments of my childhood. Not only did it evoke actions and words from that period of my life, but for a moment I felt as though that time had returned and these things had happened only the day before. I experienced a kind of agreeable giddiness. It seemed to me that I had been born again in an infinitely remote world. This sensation had an intoxicating quality and, like an old sweet wine, affected every vein and nerve in my body. I recognized the thorn bushes, the stones, the tree stumps and the low shrubs of wild thyme. I recognized the familiar smell of the grass. Long past days of my life came back to me, but all these memories, in some strange fashion, were curiously remote from me and led an independent life of their own, in such a way that I was no more than a passive and distant witness and felt that my heart was empty now and that the perfume of the plants had lost the magic which it had had in those days. The cypress trees were more thinly spaced, the hills had grown more arid. The person that I had been then existed no longer. If I had been able to conjure him up and to speak to him he would not have listened to me and, if he had, would not have understood what I said. He was like someone whom I had known once, but he was no part of me.

The world seemed to me like a forlorn, empty house and my heart was filled with trepidation, as though I were now obliged to go barefoot and explore every room in that house: I would pass through room after room, but when I reached the last of all and found myself face to face with "the bitch" the doors behind me would shut of their own accord and only the quivering, blurred shadows of the walls would stand guard, like black slaves, around me.

I had nearly reached the river Suran when I found myself at the foot of a barren, stony hill. Its lean, hard contours put me in mind of my nurse; there was an indefinable resemblance between them. I skirted the hill and came upon a small, green enclosure surrounded on every side by hills. The level ground was covered with vines of morning glory, and on one of the hills stood a lofty castle built of massive bricks.

I suddenly realized that I was tired. I walked up to the Suran and sat down on the fine sand on its bank in the shade of an old cypress tree. It was a peaceful, lonely spot. I felt that no one until then had ever set foot there. All at once I saw a little girl appear from behind the cypress trees and set off in the direction of the castle. She was wearing a black dress of very fine, light material, apparently silk. She was biting the nail of one of the fingers of her left hand, and she glided by with an unconstrained, carefree air. I had the feeling that I had seen her before and knew who she was but could not be sure. Suddenly she vanished. Where she had gone, the distance between us and the glare of the sun prevented me from making out.

I remained petrified, unable to make the slightest movement. I was quite sure that I had seen her with my own two eyes walk past and then disappear. Was she a real being or an illusion? Had I seen her in a dream or waking? All my attempts to call her face to mind were vain. I experienced a peculiar tremor down my spine. It occurred to me that this was the hour of the day when the shadows of the castle upon the hill returned to life, and that this little girl was one of the old-time inhabitants of the ancient city of Rey.

The landscape before my eyes all at once struck me as familiar. I remembered that once in my childhood on the thirteenth day of Nouruz I had come here with my mother-in-law and "the bitch". That day we ran after each other and played for hours on the far side of these same cypress trees. Then we were joined by another band of children – who they were, I cannot quite remember. We played hide-and-seek together. Once when I was running after the bitch on the bank of the Suran her foot slipped and she fell into the water. The others pulled her out and took her behind the cypress tree to change her clothes. I followed them. They hung up a woman's veil as a screen in front of her but I furtively peeped from behind a tree and saw her whole body. She was smiling and biting the nail of the index finger of her left hand. Then they wrapped her up in a white cloak and spread out her fine-textured black silk dress to dry in the sun.

I stretched myself out at full length on the fine sand at the foot of the old cypress tree. The babbling of the water reached my ears like the staccato, unintelligible syllables murmured by a man who is dreaming. I automatically thrust my hands into the warm, moist sand. I squeezed the warm, moist sand in my fists. It felt like the firm flesh of a girl who has fallen into the water and who has changed her clothes.

I do not know how long I spent thus. When I stood up I began automatically to walk. The whole countryside was silent and peaceful. I walked on, completely unaware of my surroundings. Some force beyond my control compelled me to keep moving. All of my attention was concentrated on my feet. I did not walk in the normal fashion but glided along as the girl in black had done.

When I came to myself I found that I was back in the city and standing before my father-in-law's house. His little son, my brother-in-law, was sitting on the stone bench outside. He and his sister were like two halves of the one apple. He had slanting Turkoman eyes, prominent cheekbones, a complexion the colour of ripe wheat, sensual nostrils and a strong, thin face. As he sat there he was holding the index finger of his left hand to his lips. I automatically went up to him, put my hand into my pocket, took out the two cakes, gave them to him and said, "These are for you from Mummy" – he used to call my wife "Mummy" for want of a real mother. He took the cakes with some hesitation and looked at them with an expression of surprise in his Turkoman eyes. I sat down beside him on the bench. I set him on my lap and pressed him to me. His body was warm and the calves of his legs reminded me of my wife's. He had the same unconstrained manner as she. His lips were like his father's, but what in the father aroused my aversion I found charming and attractive in the boy. They were half open, as though they had only just broken away from a long, passionate kiss. I kissed him on his half-open mouth, which was so much like my wife's. His lips tasted like the stub end of a cucumber: they were acrid and bitter. The bitch's lips, I thought, must have the same taste.

At that moment I caught sight of his father, the bent old man with the scarf around his neck, coming out of the doorway. He passed by without looking in my direction. He was laughing convulsively. It was a horrible laugh, of a quality to make the hairs on one's body stand on end, and he laughed so that his shoulders shook. I could have sunk into the ground with shame. It was shortly before sunset. I stood up, wishing that I could somehow escape from myself. Mechanically, I took the direction that led to my own house. I saw nothing and nobody in the street. It seemed to me that I was walking through a strange, unknown city. Around me were weird isolated houses of geometrical shapes, with forlorn, black windows. One felt that no creature with the breath of life in it could ever have dwelt in them. Their white walls gave off a sickly radiance. A strange, an unbelievable thing was this: whenever I stopped, my shadow fell long and black on the wall in the moonlight, but it had no head. I had heard people say that if anyone cast a headless shadow on a wall that person would die before the year was out.

Overcome with fear, I went into my house and shut myself up in my room. At the same moment I began to bleed from the nose. After losing a great quantity of blood I collapsed upon my bed. My nurse came in to see to me.

Before I went to sleep I looked at myself in the mirror. My face was ravaged, lifeless and indistinct, so indistinct that I did not recognize myself. I got into bed, pulled the quilt over my head, huddled myself up and, with eyes closed, pursued the course of my thoughts. I was conscious of the strands which had been woven by a dark, gloomy, fearful and delightful destiny; I moved in the regions where life and death fuse together and perverse images come into being and ancient, extinct desires, vague, strangled desires, again come to life and cry aloud for vengeance. For that space of time I was severed from nature and the phenomenal world and was prepared to accept effacement and dissolution in the everlasting flux. I murmured again and again, "Death, death... where are you?" The thought of death soothed me and I fell asleep.

In my sleep I dreamt. I was in the Mohammadiyye square. A tall gallows tree had been erected there and the body of the old odds-and-ends man whom I used to see from my window was hanging from its arm. At its foot were several drunken policemen drinking wine. My mother-in-law, in a state of great excitement, with the expression which I see on my wife's face when she is badly upset – bloodless lips, staring, wild eyes – was dragging me by the arm through the crowd, gesticulating to the red-clad hangman and shouting, "String this one up too!" I awoke in terror. I was glowing like a furnace, my body was streaming with sweat and my cheeks were burning. In order to get the nightmare out of my mind I rose, drank some water and dabbed my head and face. I went back to bed but could not fall asleep.

Lying there in the transparent darkness I gazed steadily at the water jug that stood on the topmost shelf. I had an irrational fear that it was going to fall and decided that so long as it stood there I should be unable to fall asleep. I got up, intending to put the jug in a safe place, but by some obscure impulsion that had nothing to do with me my hand deliberately nudged it so that it fell and was smashed to pieces. I was able to close my eyes at last but I had the feeling that my nurse had come into the room and was looking at me. I clenched my fists under the quilt but in fact nothing out of the ordinary happened. In a state of semi-consciousness I heard the street door open and recognized the sound of my nurse's steps as, shuffling her slippers along the ground, she went to buy bread and cheese for breakfast. Then came the far-off cry of a street vendor, "Mulberries for your bile!" No, life, wearisome as ever, had begun again. The light was growing brighter. When I opened my eyes a patch of sunlight reflected from the surface of the tank outside my window was flickering on the ceiling.

I felt that the dream of the night had receded and faded like one seen years before during my childhood. My nurse brought me my breakfast. Her face was like a reflection in a distorting mirror, it was so lean and drawn and seemed to have acquired such an unnatural, comical shape. One might have thought that it had been stretched out by some heavy weight fastened to the chin.

Although Nanny knew that narghile smoke was bad for me, nonetheless she used to bring a narghile with her when she came into my room. The fact is that she never felt quite herself until she had had a smoke. With all her chit-chat about her family affairs, about her son and her daughter-in-law, she had made me a participant in her intimate life. Stupid as it may seem, I would sometimes find myself ruminating idly about the doings of the members of my nurse's family. For some reason all activity, all happiness on the part of other people, made me feel like vomiting. I was aware that my own life was finished and was slowly and painfully guttering out. What earthly reason had I to concern myself with the lives of the fools, the rabble-people who were fit and healthy, ate well, slept well, and copulated well and who had never experienced a particle of my sufferings or felt the wings of death every minute brushing against their faces?

Nanny treated me like a child. She tried to pry into every cranny of my mind. I was still shy of my wife. Whenever she came into the room I would cover up the phlegm which I had spat into the basin; I would comb my hair and beard and set my nightcap straight on my head. But I had no trace of shyness with nurse. How had that woman, who was so utterly different from me, managed to occupy so large a zone of my life? I remember how in the winter time they used to set up a *korsi** in this same room above the cistern. My nurse and I and the bitch would go to sleep around the *korsi*. When I opened my eyes in the transparent darkness the design on the embroidered curtain that hung in the doorway opposite me would come to life. What a strange, disquieting curtain it was! On it was depicted a bent old man like an Indian fakir with a turban on his head. He was sitting under a cypress tree, holding a musical instrument that resembled a sitar. Before him stood a beautiful young girl, such a girl as I imagined Bugam Dasi, the Indian temple dancer, to have been. Her hands were bound and it seemed that she was

68

obliged to dance before the old man. I used to think to myself that perhaps this old man had been shut up in a dungeon with a cobra and that it was this experience that had bent him double and turned his hair and beard white. It was a gold-embroidered Indian curtain such as my father (or my uncle) might have sent from abroad. Whenever I happened to gaze for a long time at the design upon it I would become frightened and, half-asleep as I was, would wake up my nurse. She, with her bad breath and her coarse black hair against my face, would hold me close to her.

When I awoke in the morning she looked exactly the same to me as she did on those days, except that the lines of her face were deeper and harder.

I often used to recall the days of my childhood in order to forget the present, in order to escape from myself. I tried to feel as I did in the days before I fell ill. Then I would have the sensation that I was still a child and that inside me there was a second self which felt sorry for this child who was about to die. In my moments of crisis one glimpse of my nurse's calm, pallid face with its deep set, dim, unmoving eyes, thin nostrils, and broad, bony forehead, was enough to revive in me the sensations of my childhood. Perhaps she emitted some mysterious radiation which created this peace of mind in me.

On her forehead there was a fleshy birthmark with hairs sprouting from it. I do not remember having noticed it before today. Previously when I looked at her face I did not scrutinize it so closely.

Although Nanny had changed outwardly her ideas remained what they had always been. The only difference was that she evinced a greater fondness for life and seemed afraid of death, in which she reminded me of the flies which take refuge indoors at the beginning of the autumn. I on the other hand changed with every day and every minute. It seemed to me that the passage of time had become thousands of times more rapid in my case than in that of other people and that the alterations I daily observed in myself should normally have been the work of years, whereas the satisfaction I should have derived from life tended, on the contrary, towards zero and perhaps even sank below zero. There are people whose death agonies begin at the age of twenty, while others die only at the very end, calmly and peacefully, like a lamp in which all the oil has been consumed.

When my nurse brought me my dinner at midday I upset the soup bowl and began to shriek at the top of my voice. Everyone in the house came running to my room and gathered at the door. The bitch came along with the rest but she soon went away again. I had a look at her belly. It was big and swollen. No, she had not had the baby yet. Someone went to fetch the doctor. I was delighted at the thought that at any rate I had given the fools trouble.

The doctor came, with his beard three hand's-breadths long, and prescribed opium for me. What a marvellous remedy for the pains of my existence! Whenever I smoked opium my ideas acquired grandeur, subtlety, magic and sublimity and I moved in another sphere beyond the boundaries of the ordinary world. My thoughts were freed from the weight of material reality and soared towards an empyrean of tranquillity and silence. I felt as though I were borne on the wings of a golden bat and ranged through a radiant, empty world with no obstacle to block my progress. So profound and delicious was the sensation I experienced that the delight it gave me was stronger than death itself.

When I stood up from beside my brazier I went over to the window facing onto the courtyard of our house. My nurse was sitting in the sun cleaning some vegetables. I heard her say to her daughter-in-law, "We all feel very sorry for him. I only wish God would put him out of his misery." So the doctor, apparently, had told them I was not going to get better.

It did not surprise me at all. What fools all these people were! When she brought me my medicine an hour later her eyes were red and swollen with weeping. She forced a smile when she saw me. They used to play-act in front of me, they all used to play-act in front of me, and how clumsily they did it! Did they suppose I did not know, myself? But why was this woman of all people so fond of me? Why did she feel that she had a share in my sufferings? All that had happened was that someone had come to her one day and given her money, and she had thrust her wrinkled black nipples, like little buckets, between my lips – and I wish that the canker had eaten them away! Whenever I saw them now I felt like vomiting to think that at that time I had greedily sucked out their life-giving juice while the warmth of our two bodies blended together. She had handled me all over when I was little and it was for this reason that she still treated me with that peculiar boldness that you find only in widows. Just because at one time she used to hold me over the latrine she still looked on me as a child. Who knows? Perhaps she had used me as women use their adoptive sisters...

Even now she missed nothing whenever she helped me to do the things which I could not do on my own. If the bitch my wife had shown any interest in me I should never have let Nanny come near me in her presence, because I felt that my wife had a wider range of ideas and a keener aesthetic sense than my nurse had. Or perhaps this bashfulness of mine was merely the result of my obsession.

At any rate I was not shy of my nurse, and she was the only one who looked after me. I suppose she thought it was all a matter of destiny and that it was her star that had saddled her with this responsibility. In any case she made the most of my illness and confided all her family troubles and joys to me, kept me posted on current quarrels and feuds and in general revealed all the simplicity, the cunning and the avarice which went into her make-up. She told me what a trial her daughter-in-law was to her and spoke with such feeling on the subject that one would have thought that the younger woman was a rival wife who had stolen a portion of her son's love for her. Obviously the daughter-in-law was good-looking. I saw her once in the courtyard from my window. She had grey eyes, fair hair and a small, straight nose.

Sometimes my nurse would talk about the miracles performed by the prophets. Her purpose in so doing was to entertain me but the only effect was to make me envy her the pettiness and stupidity of her ideas. Sometimes she retailed pieces of gossip. For example, she told me a few days ago that her daughter (meaning the bitch) had made a set of clothes for the baby – her baby. After which she began to console me in a way that suggested she knew the truth. Sometimes she would fetch me home-made remedies from the neighbours or she would consult magicians and fortune-tellers about my case. On the last Wednesday of the year she went to see one of her fortune-tellers and came back with a bowl of onions, rice and rancid oil. She told me she had begged this rubbish from the fortune-teller in the hope that it would help me to get better.* On the following days she gave it to me in small portions in my food without my knowledge. She also made me swallow at regular intervals the various concoctions prescribed by the doctor: hyssop, extract of liquorice, camphor, maidenhair, camomile, oil of bay, linseed, fir-tree nuts, starch, grey powders, and heaven knows how many more varieties of trash.

A few days ago she brought me a prayer book with half an inch of dust on it. I had no use, not only for prayer books, but for any sort of literature that expressed the notions of the rabble. What need had I of their nonsense and lies? Was not I myself the result of a long succession of past generations which had bequeathed their experience to me? Did not the past exist within me? As for mosques, the muezzin's call to prayer, the ceremonial washing of the body and rinsing of the mouth, not to mention the pious practice of bobbing up and down in honour of a high and mighty Being, the omnipotent Lord of all things, with whom it was impossible to have a chat except in the Arabic language – these things left me completely cold.

Earlier, in the days before I fell ill, I had been to the mosque a number of times, always more or less unwillingly. On these occasions I had tried to enter into a community of feeling with the people around me. But my eye would rest on the shining, patterned tiles on the wall and I would be transported into a delightful dream world. Thereby I unconsciously provided myself with a way of escape. During the prayers I would shut my eyes and cover my face with my hand and in this artificial night of my own making I would recite the prayers like the meaningless sounds uttered by someone who is dreaming. The words were not spoken from the heart. I found it pleasanter to talk to a friend or acquaintance than to God, the high and mighty One. God was too important a personage for me.

When I was lying in my warm, damp bed these questions did not interest me one jot and at such a time it did not matter to me whether God really existed or whether He was nothing but a personification of the mighty ones of this world, invented for the greater glory of spiritual values and the easier spoliation of the lower orders, the pattern of earthly things being transferred to the sky. All that I wanted to know was whether or not I was going to live through to the morning. In face of death I felt that religion, faith, belief were feeble, childish things of which the best that could be said was that they provided a kind of recreation for healthy, successful people. In face of the frightful reality of death and of my own desperate condition, all that had been inculcated into me on the subject of Judgement Day and rewards and penalties in a future life seemed an insipid fraud, and the prayers I had been taught were completely ineffective against the fear of death.

No, the fear of death would not let me go. People who have not known suffering themselves will not understand me when I say that my attachment to life had grown so strong that the least moment of ease compensated for long hours of palpitation and anguish.

I saw that pain and disease existed and at the same time that they were void of sense and meaning. Among the men of the rabble I had become a creature of a strange, unknown race, so much so that they had forgotten that I had once been part of their world. I had the dreadful sensation that I was not really alive or wholly dead. I was a living corpse, unrelated to the world of living people and at the same time deprived of the oblivion and peace of death.

It was night when I stood up from beside my opium brazier. I looked out of the window. A single black tree was visible beside the shuttered butcher's shop. The shadows had merged into one black mass. I felt as though everything in the world was hollow and provisional. The pitch-black sky reminded me of an old black tent in which the countless shining stars represented holes. As I watched I heard from somewhere the voice of a muezzin, although it was not the time for the call to prayer. It sounded like the cry of a woman – it could have been the bitch – in the pangs of childbirth. Mingled with the cry was the sound of a dog howling. I thought to myself, "If it is true that everyone has his own star in the sky mine must be remote, dark and meaningless. Perhaps I have never had a star at all."

Just then the voices of a band of drunken policemen rose loud from the street. As they marched by they were joking obscenely among themselves. Then they began to sing in chorus:

> Come, let us go and drink wine;
> Let us drink wine of the Kingdom of Rey.
> If we do not drink now, when should we drink?

In terror I shrank back from the window. Their voices resounded strangely through the night air, gradually growing fainter and fainter. No, they were not coming for me, they did not know... Silence and darkness settled down upon the world again. I did not light my oil lamp. It was more pleasant to sit in the dark, that dense liquid which permeates everything and every place. I had grown accustomed to the dark. It was in the dark that my lost thoughts, my forgotten fears, the frightful, unbelievable ideas that had been lurking in some unknown recess of my brain, used to return to life, to move about and to grimace at me. In the corners of my room, behind the curtains, beside the door, were hosts of these ideas, of these formless, menacing figures.

There, beside the curtain, sat one fearful shape. It never stirred, it was neither gloomy nor cheerful. Every time I came back to my room it gazed steadily into my eyes. Its face was familiar to me. It seemed to me that I had seen that face at some time in my childhood. Yes, it was on the thirteenth day of Nouruz. I was playing hide-and-seek with some other children on the bank of the river Suran when I caught sight of that same face amid a crowd of other, ordinary faces set on top of funny, reassuring little bodies. It reminded me of the butcher opposite the window of my room. I felt that this shape had its place in my life and that I had seen it often before. Perhaps this shadow had been born along with me and moved within the restricted circuit of my existence...

As soon as I stood up to light the lamp the shape faded and disappeared. I stood in front of the mirror and stared at my face. The reflection that I saw was unfamiliar to me. It was a weird, frightening image. My reflection had become stronger than my real self and I had become like an image in a mirror. I felt that I could not remain alone in the same room with my reflection. I was afraid that if I tried to run away he would come after me. We were like two cats face to face, preparing to do battle. But I knew that I could create my own complete darkness with the hollow of my palm and I raised my hand and covered my eyes. The sensation of horror as usual aroused in me a feeling of exquisite, intoxicating pleasure which made my head swim and my knees give way and filled me with nausea. Suddenly I realized that I was still standing. The circumstances struck me as odd, even inexplicable. How could it have come about that I was standing on my feet? It seemed to me that if I were to move one of my feet I should lose my balance. A kind of vertigo took possession of me. The earth and everything upon it had receded infinitely far from me. I wished vaguely for an earthquake or a thunderbolt from the sky which would make it possible for me to be born again in a world of light and peace.

When at last I went back to bed, I said to myself, "Death... death..." My lips were closed, yet I was afraid of my voice. I had quite lost my previous boldness. I had become like the flies which crowd indoors at the beginning of the autumn, thin, half-dead flies which are afraid at first of the buzzing of their own wings and cling to some one point of the wall until they realize that they are alive; then they fling themselves recklessly against door and walls until they fall dead around the floor.

As my eyes closed a dim, indistinct world began to take shape around me. It was a world of which I was the sole creator and which was in perfect harmony with my vision of reality. At all events it was far more real and natural to me than my waking world and presented no obstacle, no barrier, to my ideas. In it time and place lost their validity. My repressed lusts, my secret needs, which had begotten this dream, gave rise to shapes and to happenings which were beyond belief but which seemed natural to me. For a few moments after waking up I had no sense of time or place and doubted whether I really existed. It would seem that I myself created all my dreams and had long known the correct interpretation of them.

A great part of the night had passed by the time I fell asleep. All at once I found myself wandering free and unconstrained through an unknown town, along streets lined with weird houses of geometrical shapes – prisms, cones, cubes – with low, dark windows and doors and walls overgrown with vines of morning glory. All the inhabitants of the town had died by some strange death. Each and every one of them was standing motionless with two drops of blood from his mouth congealed upon his coat. When I touched one of them his head toppled and fell to the ground.

I came to a butcher's shop and saw there a man like the odds-and-ends man in front of our house. He had a scarf wrapped around his neck and held a long-bladed knife in his hand and he stared at me with red eyes from which the lids seemed to have been cut off. I tried to take the knife from his hand. His head toppled and fell to the ground. I fled in terror. As I ran along the streets everyone I saw was standing motionless. When I reached my father-in-law's house my brother-in-law, the bitch's little brother, was sitting on the stone bench outside. I put my hand into my pocket, took out a pair of cakes and tried to put them into his hand, but the moment I touched him his head toppled and fell to the ground. I shrieked aloud and awoke.

The room was still half dark. My heart was beating hard. I felt as if the ceiling were weighing down upon my head and the walls had grown immensely thick and threatened to crush me. My eyes had become dim. I lay for some time in terror, counting and recounting the uprights of the walls. I had hardly shut my eyes when I heard a noise. It was Nanny, who had come to tidy up the room. She had laid breakfast for me in a room in the upper storey. I went upstairs and sat down by the sash window. From up there the old odds-and-ends man in front of my window was out of sight but I could see the butcher over on the left. His movements which, seen from my own window, seemed heavy, deliberate and frightening, now struck me as helpless, even comical. I felt that this man had no business to be a butcher at all and was only acting a part. A man led up the two gaunt, black horses with their deep, hollow cough. Each of them had a pair of sheep carcasses slung across its back. The butcher ran his greasy hand over his moustache and appraised the carcasses with a buyer's eye. Then, with an effort, he carried two of them across and hung them from the hook at the entrance to the shop. I saw him pat their legs. I have no doubt that when he stroked his wife's body at night he would think of the sheep and reflect how much he could make if he were to kill his wife.

When the tidying up was finished I went back to my room and made a resolution, a frightful resolution. I went into the little closet off my room and took out a bone-handled knife which I kept in a box there. I wiped the blade on the skirt of my kaftan and hid it under the pillow. I had made this resolution a long time before but there had been something just now in the movements of the butcher as he cut up the legs of the sheep, weighed out the meat and then looked around with an expression of self-satisfaction which somehow made me want to imitate him. This was a pleasure that I too must experience. I could see from my window a patch of perfect, deep blue in the midst of the clouds. It seemed to me that I should have to climb a very long ladder to reach that patch of sky. The horizon was covered with thick, yellow, deathly clouds which weighed heavily upon the whole city.

It was horrible, delicious weather. For some reason which I cannot explain I crouched down to the floor. In this kind of weather I always tended to think of death. But it was only now, when death, his face smeared with blood, was clutching my throat with his bony hands, that I made up my mind. I made up my mind to take the bitch with me, to prevent her from saying when I had gone, "God have mercy on him, his troubles are over."

A funeral procession passed by in front of my window. The coffin was draped with black and a lit candle stood upon it. My ear caught the cry "*La elaha ell' Allah*".* All the tradespeople and the passers-by left whatever they were doing and walked seven paces after the coffin. Even the butcher came out, walked the regulation seven paces after the coffin and returned to his shop. But the old pedlar man did not stir from his place beside his wares. How serious everybody suddenly looked! Doubtless their thoughts had turned abruptly to the subject of death and the afterlife. When my nurse brought me my medicine I observed that she looked thoughtful. She was fingering the beads of a large rosary and was muttering some formula to herself. Then she took up her position outside my door, beat her breast and recited her prayers in a loud voice:

"My God! My Go-o-o-d!"

Anyone might have thought it was my business to pardon the living! All this buffoonery left me completely cold. It actually gave me a certain satisfaction to think that, for a few seconds at any rate, the rabble-men were undergoing, temporarily and superficially it is true, something of what I was suffering. Was not my room a coffin? This bed that was always unrolled, inviting me to sleep, was it not colder and darker than the grave? The thought that I was lying in a coffin had occurred to me several times. At night my room seemed to contract and to press against my body. May it not be that people have this same sensation in the grave? Is anything definite known about the sensations we may experience after death? True, the blood ceases to circulate and after the lapse of twenty-four hours certain parts of the body begin to decompose. Nevertheless the hair and the nails continue to grow for some time after death. Do sensation and thought cease as soon as the heart has stopped beating or do they continue a vague existence, alimented by the blood still remaining in the minor blood vessels? The fact of dying is a fearful thing in itself but the consciousness that one is dead would be far worse. Some old men die with a smile on their lips like people passing from sleep into a deeper sleep or like a lamp burning out. What must be the sensations of a young, strong man who dies suddenly and who continues for some time longer to struggle against death with all the strength of his being?

I had many times reflected on the fact of death and on the decomposition of the component parts of my body, so that this idea had ceased to frighten me. On the contrary, I genuinely longed to pass into oblivion and non-being. The only thing I feared was that the atoms of my body should later go to make up the bodies of rabble-men. This thought was unbearable to me. There were times when I wished I could be endowed after death with large hands with long, sensitive fingers: I would carefully collect together all the atoms of my body and hold them tightly in my hands to prevent them, my property, from passing into the bodies of rabble-men.

Sometimes I imagined that the visions I saw were those which appeared to everyone who was at the point of death. All anxiety, awe, fear and will to live had subsided within me and my renunciation of the religious beliefs which had been inculcated into me in my childhood had given me an extraordinary inner tranquillity. What comforted me was the prospect of oblivion after death. The thought of an afterlife frightened and fatigued me. I had never been able to adapt myself to the world in which I was now living. Of what use would another world be to me? I felt that this world had not been made for me but for a tribe of brazen, money-grubbing, blustering louts, sellers of conscience, hungry of eye and heart – for people, in fact, who had been created in its own likeness and who fawned and grovelled before the mighty of earth and heaven as the hungry dog outside the butcher's shop wagged his tail in the hope of receiving a fragment of offal. The thought of an afterlife frightened and fatigued me. No, I had no desire to see all these loathsome worlds peopled with repulsive faces. Was God such a parvenu that He insisted on my looking over His collection of worlds? I must speak as I think. If I had to go through another life, then I hoped that my mind and senses would be numb. In that event I could exist with effort and weariness. I would live my life in the shadow of the columns of some lingam temple. I would retire into some corner where the light of the sun would never strike my eyes and the words of men and the noise of life never grate upon my ears.

I retired as deep as I could into the depths of my own being like an animal that hides itself in a cave in the wintertime. I heard other people's voices with my ears; my own I heard in my throat. The solitude that surrounded me was like the deep, dense night of eternity, that night of dense, clinging, contagious darkness which awaits the moment when it will descend upon silent cities full of dreams of lust and rancour. From the viewpoint of this throat with which I had identified myself I was nothing more than an insane abstract mathematical demonstration. The pressure which, in the act of procreation, holds together two people who are striving to escape from their solitude is the result of this same streak of madness which exists in every person, mingled with regret at the thought that he is slowly sliding towards the abyss of death...

Only death does not lie.

The presence of death annihilates all superstitions. We are the children of death and it is death that rescues us from the deceptions of life. In the midst of life he calls us and summons us to him. At an age when we have not yet learnt the language of men, if at times we pause in our play it is that we may listen to the voice of death... Throughout our life death is beckoning to us. Has it not happened to everyone suddenly, without reason, to be plunged into thought and to remain immersed so deeply in it as to lose consciousness of time and place and the working of his own mind? At such times one has to make an effort in order to perceive and recognize again the phenomenal world in which men live. One has been listening to the voice of death.

Lying in this damp, sweaty bed, as my eyelids grew heavy and I longed to surrender myself to non-being and everlasting night, I felt that my lost memories and forgotten fears were all coming to life again: fear lest the feathers in my pillow should turn into dagger blades or the buttons on my coat expand to the size of millstones; fear lest the breadcrumbs that fell to the floor should shatter into fragments like pieces of glass; apprehension lest the oil in the lamp should spill during my sleep and set fire to the whole city; anxiety lest the paws of the dog outside the butcher's shop should ring like horses' hoofs as they struck the ground; dread lest the old odds-and-ends man sitting behind his wares should burst into laughter and be unable to stop; fear lest the worms in the foot bath by the tank in our courtyard should turn into Indian serpents; fear lest my bedclothes should turn into a hinged gravestone above me and the marble teeth should lock, preventing me from ever escaping; panic fear lest I should suddenly lose the faculty of speech and, however much I might try to call out, nobody should ever come to my aid...

I used to try to recall the days of my childhood but when I succeeded in doing so and experienced that time again it was as grim and painful as the present.

Other things which brought their contribution of anxiety and fear were my coughing, which sounded like that of the gaunt, black horses in front of the butcher's shop; my spitting, and the fear lest the phlegm should some day reveal a streak of blood, the tepid, salty liquid which rises from the depths of the body, the juice of life, which we must vomit up in the end; and the continuous menace of death, which smashes for ever the fabric of the mind and passes on.

Life as it proceeds reveals, coolly and dispassionately, what lies behind the mask that each man wears. It would seem that everyone possesses several faces. Some people use only one all the time, and it then, naturally, becomes soiled and wrinkled. These are the thrifty sort. Others look after their masks in the hope of passing them on to their descendants. Others again are constantly changing their faces. But all of them, when they reach old age, realize one day that the mask they are wearing is their last and that it will soon be worn out, and then, from behind the last mask, the real face appears.

The walls of my room must have contained some virus that poisoned all my thoughts. I felt sure that before me some murderer, some diseased madman, had lived in it. Not only the walls of the room itself, but the view from the window, the butcher, the old odds-and-ends man, my nurse, the bitch and everyone whom I used to see, even the bowl from which I ate my barley broth and the clothes that I wore – all these had conspired together to engender such thoughts in my brain.

A few nights ago when I took off my clothes in a cubicle at the bathhouse my thoughts took a new direction. As the attendant poured water over my head I felt as though my black thoughts were being washed away. I observed my shadow on the steamy wall of the bathhouse. I saw that I was as frail and thin as I had been ten years earlier, when I was a child. I remembered distinctly that my shadow had fallen then in just the same way on the wet wall of the bathhouse. I looked down at my body. There was something lascivious and yet hopeless in the look of my thighs, calves and loins. Their shadow too had not changed since ten years before, when I was only a child. I felt that my whole life had passed without purpose or meaning like the flickering shadows on the bathhouse wall. Other people were massive, solid, thick-necked. Doubtless the shadows they cast on the steamy wall of the bathhouse were bigger and denser and left their imprint for some moments after they had gone, whereas mine was effaced instantaneously. When I had finished dressing after the bath my gestures and thoughts seemed to change again. It was as though I had entered a different world, as though I had been born again in the old world that I detested. At all events I could say that I had acquired a new life, for it seemed a miracle to me that I had not dissolved in the bath like a lump of salt.

My life appeared to me just as strange, as unnatural, as inexplicable, as the picture on the pen case that I am using this moment as I write. I feel that the design on the lid of this pen case must have been drawn by an artist in the grip of some mad obsession. Often when my eye lights on this picture it strikes me as somehow familiar. Perhaps this picture is the reason why… Perhaps it is this picture that impels me to write. It represent a cypress tree at the foot of which is squatting a bent old man like an Indian fakir. He has a long cloak wrapped about him and he is wearing a turban on his head. The index finger of his left hand is pressed to his lips in a gesture of surprise. Before him a girl in a long black dress is dancing. Her movements are not those of ordinary people – she could be Bugam Dasi. She is holding a flower of morning glory in her hand. Between them runs a little stream.

I was sitting beside my opium brazier. All my dark thoughts had dissolved and vanished in the subtle heavenly smoke. My body was meditating, my body was dreaming and gliding through space. It seemed to have been released from the burden and contamination of the lower air and to be soaring in an unknown world of strange colours and shapes. The opium had breathed its vegetable soul, its sluggish, vegetable soul, into my frame, and I lived and moved in a world of vegetable existence. But as, with my cloak over my shoulders, I drowsed beside the leather ground sheet on which my brazier stood, the thought of the old odds-and-ends man for some reason came to my mind. He used to sit huddled up beside his wares in the same posture as I was then in. The thought struck me with horror. I rose, threw off the cloak and stood in front of the mirror. My cheeks were inflamed to the colour of the meat that hangs in front of butchers' shops. My beard was dishevelled. And yet there was something immaterial, something fascinating, in the reflection I saw. The eyes wore an expression of weariness and suffering like those of a sick child. It was as though everything that was heavy, earthy and human in me had melted away. I was pleased with my face. I inspired in myself a certain voluptuous satisfaction. As I looked into the mirror I said to myself, "Your pain is so profound that it has settled in the depths of your eyes... and, if you weep, the tears will come from the very depths of your eyes or they will not come at all." Then I said, "You are a fool. Why don't you put an end to yourself here and now? What are you waiting for? What have you to hope for now? Have you forgotten the bottle of wine in the closet? One gulp, and there's an end of everything... Fool!... You are a fool!... Here I am, talking to the air!"

The thoughts which came into my mind were unrelated to one another. I could hear my voice in my throat but I could not grasp the meaning of the words. The sounds were mingled in my brain with other sounds. My fingers seemed bigger than normal, as always when the fever was on me. My eyelids felt heavy, my lips had grown thick. I turned round and saw my nurse standing in the doorway. I burst out laughing. My nurse's face was motionless. Her lustreless eyes were fixed on me but they were empty of surprise, irritation or sadness. Generally speaking, it is ordinary stupid conduct that makes one laugh, but this laughter of mine arose from a deeper cause. The vast stupidity that I saw before me was part of the general inability of mankind to unravel the central problems of existence and that thing which for her was shrouded in impenetrable darkness was a gesture of death itself.

She took the brazier and walked with deliberation out of the room. I wiped the sweat from my forehead. My hands were covered with white flecks. I leant against the wall, pressing my head to the bricks, and began to feel better. After a little I murmured the words of a song which I had heard somewhere or other:

Come, let us go and drink wine;
Let us drink wine of the Kingdom of Rey.
If we do not drink now, when should we drink?

When the crisis was coming upon me I could always feel its approach in advance and was filled with an extraordinary uneasiness and depression as though a cord had been tied tightly around my heart. My mood was like the weather before the storm breaks. At such times the real world receded from me and I lived in a radiant world incalculably remote from that of earth.

Then I was afraid of myself and of everyone else. I suppose this condition of mine was due to my illness, which had sapped my mental strength. The sight of the old odds-and-ends man and the butcher through the window filled me with fear. There was something frightening in their gestures and in their faces. My nurse told me a frightful thing. She swore by all the prophets that she had seen the odds-and-ends man come to my wife's room during the night and that from behind the door she had heard the bitch say to him, "Take your scarf off." It does not bear thinking of. Two or three days ago when I shrieked out and my wife came and stood in the doorway, I saw, I saw with my own eyes, that her lips bore the imprint of the old man's dirty, yellow, decayed teeth, between which he used to recite the Arabic verses of the Koran. And, now I came to think of it, why was it this man had been hanging about outside our house ever since I had got married? Was he one of the bitch's lovers? I remember I went over that same day to where the old man was sitting beside his wares and asked him how much he wanted for his jar. He looked at me over the folds of the scarf that muffled his face. Two decayed teeth emerged from under the harelip and he burst into laughter. It was a grating, hollow laugh, of a quality to make the hairs on one's body stand on end. He said, "Do you usually buy things without looking at them? This jar's not worth bothering about. Take it, young man. Hope it brings you luck." I put my hand into my pocket and took out two *dirhems* and four *peshiz** which I laid on the corner of the canvas sheet. He burst into laughter again. It was a grating laugh, of a quality to make the hairs on one's body stand on end. I could have sunk into the ground with shame. I covered my face with my hands and walked back to the house.

From all the articles laid out before him came a rusty smell as of dirty discarded objects which life had rejected. Perhaps his aim was to show people the discarded things of life and to draw attention to them. After all, was he not old and discarded himself? All the articles in his collection were dead, dirty and unserviceable. But what a stubborn life was in them and what significance there was in their forms! These dead objects left a far deeper imprint upon my mind than living people could ever have done.

But Nanny had told me this story about him and had passed it on to everyone else... With a dirty beggar! My nurse told me that my wife's bed had become infested with lice and she had gone to the baths. I wonder how her shadow looked on the steamy wall of the bathhouse. No doubt it was a voluptuous shadow with plenty of self-confidence. All things considered, my wife's taste in men did not offend me this time. The old odds-and-ends man was not a commonplace, flat, insipid creature like the stud males that stupid randy women usually fall for. The old man with his ailments, with the rind of misfortune that encrusted him, and the misery that emanated from him was, probably without realizing it himself, a kind of small-scale exhibition organized by God for the edification of mankind. As he sat there with his squalid collection of wares on the ground in front of him, he was a sample and a personification of the whole creation.

Yes, I had seen on my wife's face the mark of the two dirty, decayed teeth between which he used to recite the Arabic verses of the Koran. This was the same wife who would not let me come near her, who scorned me, and whom I loved in spite of everything, in spite of the fact that she had never once allowed me to kiss her on the lips.

The sun was setting. From somewhere came the high-pitched, plaintive sound of a kettle drum. It was a sound expressive of entreaty and supplication, which awoke in me all my ancestral superstitions and, with them, my fear of the dark. The crisis, the approach of which I had felt in advance and which I was expecting from moment to moment, came upon me. My whole body was filled with burning heat and I felt that I was suffocating. I collapsed onto my bed and shut my eyes. It seemed to me in my feverish condition that everything had expanded and had lost all distinctness of outline. The ceiling, instead of sinking, had risen. I felt oppressed by the weight of my clothes. For no reason I stood up and sat down again upon my bed, murmuring to myself, "The thing has reached the limit... This is beyond endurance..." Then I stopped abruptly. After a little I began again slowly and distinctly, in an ironical tone of voice: "The thing has..." I stopped, and added, "I am a fool." I paid no attention to the meaning of the words I uttered. I was merely amusing myself with the vibration of my voice in the air. Perhaps I was talking to my shadow in order to dispel my loneliness.

And then I saw an incredible thing. The door opened and the bitch came into the room. So then, she used to think of me at times and in spite of everything I still had reason to feel grateful to her. She knew that I was still alive, that I was suffering, that I was slowly dying. In spite of everything I still had reason to feel grateful to her. I only wondered whether she knew that I was dying because of her. If she did know that I would die perfectly happy. At that moment I was the happiest man on the face of the earth. Merely by coming into the room the bitch had driven away all my evil thoughts. Some sort of radiation emanated from her, from her movements, and brought me relief. On this occasion she was in better health than when I had last seen her. She was plump and comfortable-looking. She had on a cloak of Tus material. Her eyebrows were plucked and were stained with indigo. She was wearing a beauty spot and her face was made up with rouge, ceruse and kohl. In a word she was turned out to perfection. She appeared to be well pleased with life. She was unconsciously holding the index finger of her left hand to her lips. Was this the same graceful creature, was this the slim, ethereal girl who, in a black pleated dress, had played hide-and-seek with me on the bank of the Suran, the unconstrained, childlike, frail girl whose ankles, appearing from under her skirt, had so excited me? Until this moment, when I had looked at her I had not seen her as she really was. Now it was as though a veil had fallen from my eyes. For some reason the thought of the sheep hanging by the door of the butcher's shop occurred to me. She had become for me the equivalent of a lump of butcher's meat. Her old enchantment had gone. She had become a comfortable, solid woman with a head full of commonplace, practical ideas – a genuine woman. I realized with affright that my wife was now a grown-up while I had remained a child. I actually felt ashamed in her presence, under her gaze. This woman who yielded her body to everyone but me while I consoled myself with fanciful memories of her childhood, when her face was simple and innocent and wore a dreamy, fleeting expression, this woman whose face still bore the tooth-marks of the old odds-and-ends man in the square – no, this was not the same person as I had known.

She asked me in a sarcastic tone, "How are you feeling?"

I replied, "Aren't you perfectly free? Don't you do everything you feel like doing? What does my health matter to you?"

She left the room, slamming the door behind her. She did not turn to look at me. It seems as though I have forgotten how to talk to the people of this world, to living people. She, the woman who I had thought was devoid of all feelings, was offended at my behaviour! Several times I thought of getting up and going to her to fall at her feet, weeping and asking her to forgive me. Yes, weeping; for I thought that if only I could weep I should find relief. Some time passed; whether it was to be measured in minutes, hours or centuries I do not know. I had become like a madman and I derived an exquisite pleasure from the pain I felt. It was a pleasure which transcended human experience, a pleasure which only I was capable of feeling and which the gods themselves, if they existed, could not have experienced to such a degree. At that moment I was conscious of my superiority. I felt my superiority to the men of the rabble, to nature and to the gods – the gods, that product of human lusts. I had become a god. I was greater than God, and I felt within me the eternal, infinite flux...

She came back. So then she was not as cruel as I had thought. I rose, kissed the hem of her dress and fell at her feet, weeping and coughing. I rubbed my face against her leg and several times I called her by her real name. It seemed to me that the sound of her real name had a peculiar ring. And at the same time in my heart, in the bottom of my heart, I said, "Bitch... bitch!" I kissed her legs; the skin tasted like the stub end of a cucumber, faintly acrid and bitter. I wept and wept. How much time passed so I do not know. When I came to myself she had gone. It may be that the space of time in which I had experienced all the pleasures, the caresses and the pain of which the nature of man is susceptible had not lasted more than a moment. I was alone, in the same posture as when I used to sit with my opium pipe beside the brazier, sitting by my smoky oil lamp like the old odds-and-ends man behind his wares. I did not budge from my place but sat watching the smoke of the lamp. Particles of soot from the flame settled on my hands and face like black snow. My nurse came in with my supper, a bowl of barley broth and a plate of greasy chicken pilaff. She uttered a scream of terror, dropped the tray and ran out of the room. It pleased me to think that I was able at any rate to frighten her. I rose to my feet, snuffed the lamp wick and stood in front of the mirror. I smeared the particles of soot over my face. How frightful was the face that I saw! I pulled down my lower eyelids, released them, tugged at the corners of my mouth, puffed out my cheeks, pulled the tip of my beard upwards and twisted it out to the sides and grimaced at myself. My face had a natural talent for comical and horrible expressions. I felt that they enabled me to see with my own eyes all the weird shapes, all the comical, horrible, unbelievable images which lurked in the recesses of my mind. They were all familiar to me, I felt them within me, and yet at the same time they struck me as comical. All of these grimacing faces existed inside me and formed part of me: horrible, criminal, ludicrous masks which changed at a single movement of my fingertip. The old Koran-reader, the butcher, my wife – I saw all of them within me. They were reflected in me as in a mirror; the forms of all of them existed inside me but none of them belonged to me. Were not the substance and the expressions of my face the result of a mysterious sequence of impulses, of my ancestors' temptations, lusts and despairs? And I who was the custodian of the heritage, did I not, through some mad, ludicrous feeling, consider it my duty, whether I liked it or not, to preserve this stock of facial expressions? Probably my face would be released from this responsibility and would assume its own natural expression only at the moment of my death... But even then would not the expressions which had been incised on my face by a sardonic resolve leave their traces behind, too deeply engraved to be effaced? At all events I now knew what possibilities existed within me, I appreciated my own capabilities.

Suddenly I burst into laughter. It was a harsh, grating, horrible laugh which made the hairs on my body stand on end. For I did not recognize my own laughter. It seemed to come from someone other than me. I felt that it had often reverberated in the depths of my throat and that I had heard it in the depths of my ears. Simultaneously I began to cough. A clot of bloody phlegm, a fragment of my inside, fell onto the mirror. I wiped it across the glass with my fingertip. I turned round and saw Nanny staring at me. She was horror-stricken. She was holding in her hand a bowl of barley broth which she had brought me, thinking that I might now be able to eat my supper. I covered my face with my hands and ran behind the curtain which hung across the entrance to the closet.

Later, as I was falling asleep, I felt as though my head was clamped in a fiery ring. The sharp exciting perfume of sandalwood oil with which I had filled my lamp penetrated my nostrils. It contained within it the odour of my wife's legs, and I felt in my mouth the faintly bitter taste of the stub end of a cucumber. I ran my hand over my body and mentally compared it – thighs, calves, arms and the rest – with my wife's. I could see again the line of her thigh and buttocks, could feel the warmth of her body. The illusion was far stronger than a mere mental picture; it had the force of a physical need. I wanted to feel her body close to mine. A single gesture, a single effort of the will would have been enough to dispel the voluptuous temptation. Then the fiery ring around my head grew so tight and so burning hot that it sank deep into a mysterious sea peopled with terrifying shapes.

It was still dark when I was awakened by the voices of a band of drunken policemen who were marching along the street, joking obscenely among themselves. They sang in chorus:

Come, let us go and drink wine;
Let us drink wine of the Kingdom of Rey.
If we do not drink now, when should we drink?

I remembered – no, I had a sudden flash of inspiration: I had some wine in the closet, a bottle of wine which contained a portion of cobra venom. One gulp of that wine, and all the nightmares of life would fade as though they had never been… But what about the bitch?… The word intensified my longing for her, brought her before me full of vitality and warmth. What better could I do than give her a glass of that wine and drink off another myself? Then we should die together in a single convulsion. What is love? For the rabble-men it is an obscenity, a carnal, ephemeral thing. The rabble-men must needs express their love in lascivious songs, in obscenities and in the foul phrases they are always repeating, drunk or sober – "shoving the donkey's hoof into the mud", "giving the ground a thump", and so forth. Love for her meant something different to me. True, I had known her for many years. Her strange, slanting eyes, small, half-open mouth, husky, soft voice – all of these things were charged with distant, painful memories and in all of them I sought something of which I had been deprived, something that was intimately connected with my being and which had been taken from me.

Had I been deprived of this thing for all time to come? The fear that it might be so aroused in me a grimmer feeling. The thought of the other pleasure, the one which might compensate me for my hopeless love, had become a kind of obsession. For some reason the figure of the butcher opposite the window of my room occurred to me. I remembered how he would roll up his sleeves, utter the sacred formula "*besmellah*"* and proceed to cut up his meat. His expression and attitude were always present to my mind. In the end I too came to a decision, a frightful decision. I got out of bed, rolled up my sleeves and took out the bone-handled knife which I had hidden underneath my pillow. I stooped and threw a yellow cloak over my shoulders and muffled my neck and face in a scarf. I felt that as I did so I assumed an attitude of mind which was a cross between that of the butcher and that of the old odds-and-ends man.

Then I went on tiptoe towards my wife's room. When I reached it I found that it was quite dark. I softly opened the door. She seemed to be dreaming. She cried, loudly and distinctly, "Take your scarf off." I went over to her bedside and bent down until I could feel her warm, even breath upon my face. What pleasant warmth and vitality there was in her breath! It seemed to me that if only I could breathe in this warmth for a while I should come to life again. I had thought for so long that other people's breath must be burning hot like mine. I looked around carefully to see if there was anyone else in the room, to make sure that none of her lovers was there. She was alone. I realized that all the things people said about her were mere slander. How did I know that she was not still a virgin? I was ashamed of all my unfair suspicions.

This sensation lasted only a minute. Suddenly from outside the door came the sound of a sneeze and I heard a stifled mocking laugh, of a quality to make the hairs on one's body stand on end. The sound contracted every nerve in my body. If I had not heard the sneeze and the laugh, if the man, whoever he was, had not given me pause,* I should have carried out my decision and cut her body into pieces. I should have given the meat to the butcher opposite our house to sell to his customers, and, in fulfilment of a special resolution, I myself should have given a piece of the flesh of her thigh to the old Koran-reader and gone to him on the following day and said, "Do you know where that meat you ate last night came from?" If he had not laughed, I should have done this. I should have had to do it in the dark, so that I should not have been compelled to meet the bitch's eye. Her expression of reproach would have been too much for me. Finally I snatched up a piece of cloth which was trailing from her bed and in which my foot had caught, and fled from the room. I tossed the knife up onto the roof, because it was the knife that had suggested the idea of murder to me. I got rid of a knife which was identical with the one I had seen in the butcher's hand.

When I got back to my room, I saw by the light of my oil lamp that the cloth I had taken with me was her nightdress: a soiled nightdress which had been in contact with her flesh; a soft, silk nightdress of Indian make. It smelt of her body and of champac perfume, and it still held something of the warmth of her body, something of her. I held it against my face and breathed deeply. Then I lay down, placed it between my legs and fell asleep. I had never slept as soundly as I did that night. Early in the morning I was awoken by my wife's clamours. She was lamenting the disappearance of her nightdress and kept repeating at the top of her voice, "A brand-new nightdress!" despite the fact that it had a tear in the sleeve. I would not have given it back to her to save my life. Surely I was entitled to keep an old nightdress of my own wife's.

When Nanny brought me my ass's milk, honey and bread I found that she had placed a bone-handled knife on the tray beside the breakfast things. She said she had noticed it among the old odds-and-ends man's wares and had bought it from him. Then she said, raising her eyebrows, "Let's hope it'll come in handy some day." I picked it up and examined it. It was my own knife. Then Nanny said in a querulous, offended tone, "Oh yes, my daughter" (she meant the bitch) "was saying this morning that I stole her nightdress during the night. I don't want to have to answer for anything connected with you two. Anyway, she began to bleed yesterday... I knew it was the baby... According to her, she got pregnant at the baths.* I went to her room to massage her belly during the night and I noticed her arms were all black and blue. She showed them to me and said, 'I went down to the cellar at an unlucky time, and the Good People gave me an awful pinching.'" She went on, "Did you know your wife's been pregnant for a long time?" I laughed and said, "I dare say the child'll look like the old man that reads the Koran. I suppose it gave its first leap when she was looking at the old man's face."* Nanny looked at me indignantly and went out of the room. Apparently she had not expected such a reply. I rose hastily, picked up the bone-handled knife with a trembling hand, put it away in the box in the closet and shut the lid.

No, it was out of the question that the baby should have leapt when she was looking at my face. It must have been the old odds-and-ends man.

Some time during the afternoon the door of my room opened and her little brother came in, biting his nail. You could tell the moment you saw them that they were brother and sister. The resemblance was extraordinary. He had full, moist, sensual lips, languid, heavy eyelids, slanting, wondering eyes, high cheekbones, unruly, date-coloured hair and a complexion the colour of ripe wheat. He was the image of the bitch and he had a touch of her satanic spirit. His was one of those impassive, soulless Turkoman faces which are so appropriate to a people engaged in an unremitting battle with life, a people which regards any action as permissible if it helps to go on living. Nature had shaped this brother and sister over many generations. Their ancestors had lived exposed to sun and rain, battling unceasingly with their environment, and had not only transmitted to them faces and characters modified correspondingly but had bequeathed to them a share of their stubbornness, sensuality, rapacity and hungriness. I remembered the taste of his lips, faintly bitter, like that of the stub end of a cucumber.

When he came into the room he looked at me with his wondering Turkoman eyes and said, "Mummy says the doctor said you are going to die and it'll be a good riddance for us. How do people die?"

I said, "Tell her I have been dead for a long time."

"Mummy said, 'If I hadn't had a miscarriage the whole house would have belonged to us.'"

I involuntarily burst out laughing. It was a hollow, grating laugh, of a quality to make the hairs on one's body stand on end. I did not recognize the sound of my own voice. The child ran from the room in terror.

I realized then why it was that the butcher found it pleasant to wipe the blade of his bone-handled knife on the legs of the sheep. The pleasure of cutting up the raw meat in which dead, coagulated blood had settled, like slime on the bottom of a tank, while a watery liquid dripped from the windpipes onto the ground – the yellow dog outside the shop, the severed ox head on the floor, staring dimly, and the heads of the sheep themselves with the dust of death on their eyes, they too had seen this, they too knew what the butcher felt.

I understood now that I had become a miniature God. I had transcended the mean, paltry needs of mankind and felt within me the flux of eternity. What is eternity? To me eternity meant to play hide-and-seek with the bitch on the bank of the Suran, to shut my eyes for a single moment and hide my face in the skirt of her dress.

All at once I realized that I was talking to myself and that in a strange way. I was trying to talk to myself but my lips had become so heavy that they were incapable of the least movement. Yet although my lips did not stir and I could not hear my voice I felt that I was talking to myself.

In this room which was steadily shrinking and growing dark like the grave, night had surrounded me with its fearful shadows. In the light of the smoky oil lamp my shadow, in the sheep-skin jacket, cloak and scarf that I was wearing, was stretched motionless across the wall. The shadow that I cast upon the wall was much denser and more distinct than my real body. My shadow had become more real than myself. The old odds-and-ends man, the butcher, Nanny and the bitch, my wife, were shadows of me, shadows in the midst of which I was imprisoned. I had become like a screech owl, but my cries caught in my throat and I spat them out in the form of clots of blood. Perhaps screech owls are subject to a disease which makes them think as I think. My shadow on the wall had become exactly like an owl and, leaning forwards, read intently every word I wrote. Without doubt he understood perfectly. Only he was capable of understanding. When I looked out of the corner of my eye at my shadow on the wall I felt afraid.

It was a dark, silent night like the night which had enveloped all my being, a night peopled with fearful shapes which grimaced at me from door and wall and curtain. At times my room became so narrow that I felt that I was lying in a coffin. My temples were burning. My limbs were incapable of the least movement. A weight was pressing on my chest like the weight of the carcasses they sling over the backs of horses and deliver to the butchers.

Death was murmuring his song in my ear like a stammering man who is obliged to repeat each word and who, when he has come to the end of a line, has to begin it afresh. His song

101

penetrated my flesh like the whine of a saw. He would raise his voice and suddenly fall silent.

My eyes were not yet closed when a band of drunken policemen marched by in the street outside my room, joking obscenely among themselves. Then they sang in chorus:

Come, let us go and drink wine;
Let us drink wine of the Kingdom of Rey.
If we do not drink now, when should we drink?

I said to myself, "Since the police are going to get me in the end..." Suddenly I felt within me a superhuman force. My forehead grew cool. I rose, threw a yellow cloak over my shoulders and wrapped my scarf two or three times around my neck. I bent down, went into the closet and took out the bone-handled knife which I had hidden in the box. Then I went on tiptoe towards the bitch's room. When I reached the door I saw that the room was in complete darkness. I listened and heard her voice saying, "Have you come? Take your scarf off." Her voice had a pleasant quality, as it had had in her childhood. It reminded me of the unconscious murmuring of someone who is dreaming. I myself had heard this voice in the past when I was in a deep sleep. Was she dreaming? Her voice was husky and thick. It had become like the voice of the little girl who had played hide-and-seek with me on the banks of the Suran. I stood motionless. Then I heard her say again, "Come in. Take your scarf off."

I walked softly into the dark room. I took off my cloak and scarf and the rest of my clothes and crept into her bed. For some reason I kept the bone-handled knife in my hand. It seemed to me that the warmth of her bed infused a new life into me. I remembered the pale, thin little girl with the big, strange Turkoman eyes with whom I had played hide-and-seek on the bank of the Suran, and I clasped her pleasant, moist, warm body in my arms. Clasped her? No, I sprang upon her like a savage, hungry beast and in the bottom of my heart I loathed her. To me love and hatred were twins. Her fresh, moonlight-pale body, my wife's body, opened and enclosed me within itself like a cobra coiling around its prey. The perfume of her bosom made my head swim, the flesh of the arm which encircled my neck was soft and warm. I wished that my life could cease at that moment, for the hatred, the rancour that I felt for her had vanished and I tried to hold back my tears.

Her legs somehow locked behind mine like those of a mandrake and her arms held me firmly by the neck. I felt the pleasant warmth of that young flesh. Every atom in my burning body drank in that warmth. I felt that I was her prey and she was drawing me into herself. I was filled with mingled terror and delight. Her mouth was bitter to the taste, like the stub end of a cucumber. Under the pleasant pressure of her embrace, I streamed with sweat. I was beside myself with passion.

I was dominated by my body, by each atom of my material being, and they shouted aloud their song of victory. Doomed, helpless in this boundless sea, I bowed my head in surrender before the stormy passion of the waves. Her hair, redolent of champac, clung about my face, and a cry of anguish and joy burst forth from the depths of our beings. Suddenly I felt that she was biting my lip savagely, so savagely that she bit it through. Used she to bite her nail in this way or had she realized that I was not the harelipped old man? I tried to break free from her but was unable to make the slightest movement. My efforts were useless. The flesh of our bodies had been soldered into one.

I thought to myself that she had gone mad. As we struggled, I involuntarily jerked my hand. I felt the knife, which I was still holding, sink somewhere into her flesh. A warm liquid spurted into my face. She uttered a shriek and released me. Keeping my fist clenched on the warm liquid in my hand, I tossed the knife away. I ran my other hand over her body. It was utterly cold. She was dead. And then I burst into a fit of coughing – but no, it was not coughing, it was a hollow grating laugh, of a quality to make the hairs on one's body stand on end. In terror I threw my cloak over my shoulders and hurried back to my own room. I opened my hand in the light of the oil lamp: in the palm of my hand lay her eye, and I was drenched in blood.

I went over and stood before the mirror. Overcome with horror, I covered my face with my hands. What I had seen in the mirror was the likeness, no, the exact image, of the old odds-and-ends man. My hair and beard were completely white, like those of a man who has come out alive from a room in which he has been shut up along with a cobra. My eyes were without lashes, a clump of white hairs sprouted from my chest and a new spirit had taken possession of my body. My mind and my senses were operating in a completely different way from before. A demon had awoken to life within me and I was unable to escape from him. Still holding my hands before my face, I involuntarily burst into laughter. It was a more violent laugh than the previous one had been and it made me shudder from head to foot. It was a laugh so deep that it was impossible to guess from what remote recess of the body it proceeded, a hollow laugh which came from somewhere deep down in my body and merely echoed in my throat. I had become the old odds-and-ends man.

5

T HE VIOLENCE OF MY AGITATION seemed to have awakened me from a long, deep sleep. I rubbed my eyes. I was back in my own room. It was half dark and outside a wet mist pressed against the windowpanes. Somewhere in the distance a cock crowed. The charcoal in the brazier beside me had burnt to cold ashes which I could have blown away with a single breath. I felt that my mind had become hollow and ashy like the coals and was at the mercy of a single breath.

The first thing I looked for was the flower vase of Rhages which the old hearse-driver had given me in the cemetery, but it had gone. I looked around and saw beside the door someone with a crouching shadow – no, it was a bent old man with his face partly concealed by a scarf wrapped around his neck. He was holding under his arm something resembling a jar, wrapped in a dirty handkerchief. He burst into a hollow, grating laugh, of a quality to make the hairs on one's body stand on end.

The moment that I made a move he slipped out through the doorway. I got up quickly, intending to run after him and get the jar, or whatever it was that was wrapped in the handkerchief, from him, but he was already a good way off. I went back to my room and opened the window. Down the street I could still see the old man's crouching figure. His shoulders were shaking with laughter and he held the bundle tucked under his arm. He was running with all his might and in the end he disappeared into the mist. I turned away from the window and looked down at myself. My clothes were torn and soiled from top to bottom with congealed blood. Two blister flies were circling about me, and tiny white maggots were wriggling on my coat. And on my chest I felt the weight of a woman's dead body...

Hajji Morad

(from *Buried Alive*)

(translated by Deborah Miller Mostaghel)

H AJJI MORAD SWIFTLY JUMPED OFF the platform of his shop. He gathered about him the folds of his tunic, tightened his silver belt, and stroked his henna-dyed beard. He called Hasan, his apprentice, and together they closed the shop. Then he pulled four *rials* from his large pocket and gave them to Hasan, who thanked him and with long steps disappeared whistling among the bustling crowd. Hajji threw over his shoulders the yellow cloak he had put under his arm, gave a look around, and slowly started to walk. At every footstep he took, his new shoes made a squeaking sound. As he walked, most of the shopkeepers greeted him and made polite remarks, saying, "Hello Hajji. Hajji, how are you? Hajji, won't we get to see you?…"

Hajji's ears were full of this sort of talk, and he attached a special importance to the word "Hajji". He was proud of himself and answered their greetings with an aristocratic smile.

This word for him was like a title, even though he himself knew that he had never been to Mecca. The closest he had ever come to Mecca was Karbala,* where he went as a child after his father died. In accordance with his father's will, his mother sold the house and all their possessions, exchanged the money for gold and, fully loaded, went to Karbala. After a year or two the money was spent, and they became beggars. Hajji, alone, with a thousand difficulties, had got himself to his uncle in Hamadan. By coincidence his uncle died and since he had no other heir all his possessions went to Hajji. Because his uncle had been known in the bazaar as "Hajji", the title also went to the heir along with the shop. He had no relatives in this city. He made enquiries two or three times about his mother and sister who had become beggars in Karbala, but found no trace of them.

Hajji had got himself a wife two years ago, but he had not been lucky with her. For some time there had been continual fighting and quarrelling between the two of them. Hajji could tolerate everything except the tongue-lashing of his wife, and in order to frighten her, he had become used to beating her frequently. Sometimes he regretted it, but in any case they would soon kiss and make up. The thing that irritated Hajji most was that they still had no children. Several times his friends advised him to get another wife, but Hajji wasn't a fool and he knew that taking another wife would add to his problems. He let the advice enter into one ear and come out of the other one. Furthermore, his wife was still young and pretty, and after several years they had become used to each other and, for better or worse, they somehow went through life together. And Hajji himself was still young. If God wanted it, he would be given children. That's why Hajji had no desire to divorce his wife, but at the same time, he couldn't get over his habit: he kept beating her and she became ever more obstinate. Especially since last night, the friction between them had become worse.

Throwing watermelon seeds into his mouth and spitting out the shells in front of him, he came out of the bazaar. He breathed the fresh spring air and remembered that now he had to go home: first there would be a scuffle, he would say one thing and she would answer back, and finally it would lead to his beating her. Then they would eat supper and glare at each other, and after that they would sleep. It was Thursday night, too, and he knew that tonight his wife had cooked sabzi pilau. These thoughts passed through his mind while he was looking this way and that way. He remembered his wife's words, "Go away you phoney Hajji! If you're a Hajji, how come your sister and mother have become something worse than beggars in Karbala? And me! I said no to Mashadi Hosein the moneylender when he asked for my hand only to get married to you, a good for nothing phoney Hajji!" He remembered this and kept biting his lip. It occurred to him that if he saw his wife there and then he would cut her stomach into pieces.

By this time he had reached Bayn ol'Nahrain Avenue. He looked at the willow trees which had come out fresh and green along the river. He thought it would be a good idea tomorrow, Friday, to go to Morad Bak Valley in the morning with several of his friends and their musical instruments and spend the day there. At least he wouldn't have to stay at home, which would be unpleasant for both him and his wife. He approached the alley which led to his house. Suddenly he had the impression that he had glimpsed his wife walking next to him and then straight past him. She had walked past him and hadn't paid any attention to him. Yes, that was his wife all right. Not only because like most men Hajji recognized his wife under her *chador*, but also because his wife had a special sign so that among a thousand women Hajji could easily recognize her. This was his wife. He knew it from the white trim of her *chador*. There was no room for doubt. But how come she had left home again at this time of day and without asking for Hajji's permission? She hadn't bothered to come to the shop either to say that she needed something. Where was she going? Hajji walked faster and saw that, yes, this was definitely his wife. And even now she wasn't walking in the direction of home. Suddenly he became very angry. He couldn't control himself. He wanted to grab her and strangle her. Without intending to, he shouted her name, "Shahrbanu!"

The woman turned her face and walked faster, as if she were frightened. Hajji was furious. He couldn't see straight. He was burning with anger. Now, leaving aside the fact that his wife had left home without his permission, even when he called her, she wouldn't pay any attention to him! It struck a special nerve. He shouted again.

"Hey! Listen to me! Where are you going at this time of day? Stop and listen to me!"

The woman stopped and said aloud:

"Nosy parker, what's it to you? You mule, do you know what you're saying? Why do you bother someone else's wife? Now I'll show you. Help, help! See what this drunkard wants from me. Do you think the city has no laws? I'll turn you over to the police right now. Police!"

Entrance doors opened one by one. People gathered around them and the crowd grew continually larger. Hajji's face turned red. The veins on his forehead and neck stood out. He was well known in the bazaar. A crowd had built to look at them, and the woman, who had covered her face tightly with her *chador*, was shouting, "Police!"

Everything went dark and dim before Hajji's eyes. Then he took a step back, and then stepped forwards and slapped her hard on her covered face, and said, "Don't... don't change your voice. I knew from the very beginning that it was you.

112

Tomorrow… tomorrow I'll divorce you. Now you've taken to leaving the house without bothering to get permission? Do you want to disgrace me? Shameless woman, now don't make me say more in front of these people. You people be my witness. I'm going to divorce this woman tomorrow – I've been suspicious of her for some time, but I always restrained myself. I was holding myself back, but now I've had all I can take. You be my witness, my wife has thrown away her honour. Tomorrow… you, tomorrow!…"

The woman, who was facing the people, said, "You cowards! Why don't you say anything? You let this good-for-nothing man lay hands on someone else's wife in the middle of the street? If Mashadi Hosein the moneylender were here he would show all of you. Even if I only live one more day I'll take such revenge that a dog would be better off. Isn't there anyone to tell this man to mind his own business? Who is he to associate with human beings? Go away. You'd better know who you're dealing with. Now I'm going to make you really regret it! Police!…"

Two or three mediators appeared and took Hajji aside. At this point a policeman arrived. The people stepped back. Hajji and the woman in the white-trimmed *chador* set out for police headquarters, along with two or three witnesses and mediators. On the way each of them stated his case to the policeman. People followed them to see how the business would turn out. Hajji, dripping with sweat, was walking next to the policeman in front of the people, and now he began to have doubts. He looked carefully and saw that the woman's buckled shoes and her stockings were different from his wife's. The identification she was showing the policeman was all right, too. She was the wife of Mashadi Hosein the moneylender, whom he knew.

He discovered he had made a mistake, but he had realized it too late. Now he didn't know what would happen. When they reached police headquarters the people stayed outside. The policeman had Hajji and the woman enter a room in which two officers were sitting behind a table. The policeman saluted, described what had happened, then took himself off and went to stand by the door at the end of the room. The chief turned to Hajji and said:

"What is your name?"

"Your honour, I'm your servant. My name is Hajji Morad. Everyone knows me in the bazaar."

"What is your profession?"

"I'm a rice merchant. I have a store in the bazaar. I'll do whatever you say."

"Is it true that you were disrespectful to this lady and hit her in the street?"

"What can I say? I thought she was my wife."

"Why?"

"Her *chador* has a white trim."

"That's very strange. Don't you recognize your wife's voice?"

Hajji heaved a sigh. "Oh, you don't know what a plague my wife is. My wife imitates the sound of all the animals. When she comes from the public baths she talks in the voices of other women. She imitates everyone. I thought she wanted to trick me by changing her voice."

"What impudence," said the woman. "Officer, you're a witness. He slapped me in the street, in front of a million people. Now all of a sudden he's as meek as a mouse! What impudence! He thinks the city has no laws. If Mashadi Hosein knew about it he'd give you what you deserve. To his wife, your Honour!"

The officer said, "Very well, madam. We don't need you any more. Please step outside while we settle Mr Morad's account."

Hajji said, "Oh God, I made a mistake, I didn't know. It was an error. And I have a reputation to protect."

The officer handed something in writing to the policeman. He took Hajji to another table. Hajji counted the bills for the fine with trembling hands and put them on the table. Then, accompanied by the policeman, he was taken outside in front of the police headquarters. People were standing in rows and whispering in each other's ears. They lifted Hajji's yellow cloak from his shoulders and a man with a whip in his hand came forwards and stood next to him. Hajji hung his head with shame and they whipped him fifty times in front of a crowd of spectators, but he didn't move a muscle. When it was over he took his big silk handkerchief out of his pocket and wiped the sweat from his forehead. He picked up his yellow cloak and threw it over his shoulders. Its folds dragged on the ground. With his head lowered, he set out for home, and tried to set his foot down more carefully to stifle the squeaking sound of his shoes. Two days later Hajji divorced his wife.

Three Drops of Blood

(from *Three Drops of Blood*)

(translated by Deborah Miller Mostaghel)

I T WAS ONLY YESTERDAY that they moved me to a separate room. Could it be that things are just as the supervisor had promised? That I would be fully recovered and be released next week? Have I been unwell? It's been a year. All this time, no matter how much I pleaded with them to give me pen and paper, they never did. I was always thinking to myself that if I got my hands on a pen and a piece of paper, there would be so much to write about. But yesterday they brought me a pen and some paper without me even asking for it. It was just the thing that I had wanted for such a long time, the thing that I had waited for all the time. But what was the use? I've been trying hard to write something since yesterday but there is nothing to write about. It is as if someone is holding down my hand or as if my arm has become numb. I'm focusing on the paper and I notice that the only readable thing in the messy scribbling I've left on it is this: "three drops of blood".

* * *

The azure sky; a green little garden; the flowers over the hill have blossomed and a quiet breeze is bringing over their fragrance to my room. But what's the use? I can't take pleasure in anything any more. All this is only good for poets and children and those who remain children all their lives. I have spent a year in this place. The cat's hissing is keeping me awake from night till dawn. The terrifying hissing, the heart-rending mewling, have brought me to the verge of giving up. In the morning, I've barely opened my eyes and there is the rude injection. What long days and terrifying hours I have spent here. On summer days we put on our yellow shirts and yellow trousers and come together in the cellar. Come winter we sit by the side of the garden, sun bathing. It's been a year since I've been living with these weird and peculiar people. There is no common ground between us. I am as different from them as the earth is from the sky. But their moaning, silences, insults, crying and laughter will forever turn my sleep into nightmare.

* * *

There's still an hour left until we eat our supper. It's one of those printed menus: yoghurt soup, rice pudding, rice, bread and cheese, just enough to keep us alive without starving us. Hasan's utmost wish is to eat a pot of egg soup and four hunks of bread. When it's time for him to be released they should bring him a pot of egg soup instead of pen and paper. He is one of the lucky ones here, with his short legs, stupid laugh, thick neck, bald head, and rough hands that look as if they've been made to clean sewers. Had it not been for Muhammad Ali, who stands there inspecting lunch and dinner, Hasan would have sent all of us to God. But Muhammad Ali himself is also just one of the people of this realm. No matter what they say about this place, the fact is that this is a different world to the world of normal people. We have a doctor who, I swear to God, doesn't notice anything. If I were in his place, one night I would put poison into everyone's supper and give them it to eat. Then in the morning I would stand in the garden with my hands on my hips and watch the corpses being carried out. When they first brought me here I was obsessively watching my food, fearing that they might poison me. I wouldn't touch lunch or supper unless Muhammad Ali had tasted the food first. Only then would I eat. At night I would leap awake frightened, imagining that they had come to kill me. How far away and vague that all seems now. Always the same people, the same food, the same room which is blue halfway up the wall.

It was two months ago when they threw a lunatic into that prison at the end of the courtyard. With a broken piece of marble he cut out his own stomach, pulled out his intestines and played with them. They said he was a butcher – he was used to cutting stomachs. But that other one had pulled out his own eyes with his own nails. They tied his hands behind his back. He was screaming and the blood had dried on his eyes. I know that all of this is the supervisor's fault.

Not everyone here is like this. Many of them would be unhappy if they were cured and released. For example that Soghra Sultan who is in the women's section. Two or three times she tried to escape but they caught her. She's an old woman, but she scratches plaster off the wall and rubs it on her face for powder. She even uses geraniums to make her cheeks look rosy. She thinks she's a young girl. If she was to recover and look in the mirror she would have a heart attack. Worst of all is our own Taqi, who wants to turn the world upside down. In his opinion women are the cause of men's misfortune, and to improve the world all women must be killed. He has fallen in love with Soghra Sultan.

All this is the fault of our very own supervisor. He is so crazy that he puts the rest of us to shame. With that big nose and those small eyes, like a drug addict, he always walks at the bottom of the garden under the pine tree. Sometimes he bends over and looks under the tree. Anyone who sees him would think what a poor, harmless man to have been caught with all these lunatics. But I know him. I know that there, under the tree, three drops of blood have fallen onto the ground. He has hung a cage in front of his window. The cage is empty because the cat has had his canary. So he has left the cage hanging to lure the cats to the cage and then kill them.

It was only yesterday when he followed a calico cat. As soon as the animal went up the tree towards the window, he told the guard at the door to shoot the cat. Those three drops of blood are the cat's but if anyone asked he would say they belong to the bird of truth.

Stranger than everyone else here is my friend and neighbour Abbas. It hasn't been two weeks since they brought him. He has been warming to me. He thinks he is a poet and a prophet. He says every vocation, but especially that of a prophet, depends on chance and luck. People with high foreheads, for example, have it made even if they don't know much. Whereas those with a short forehead, even if they are the wisest of all men in the world, end up like him. Abbas also thinks he is a skilful sitar player. He has put wires on a wooden board, making himself believe that he's built a string instrument. He also has composed a poem which he recites for me eight times a day. I think it is for the same poem that they sent him here. He has composed a peculiar ballad:

What a pity that once more it is night.
From head to toe the world is dark.
For everyone it has become the time of peace
Except me, whose despair and sorrow are increased.

There is no happiness in the nature of the world,
Except death there is no cure for my sorrow.
But at that corner under the pine tree
Three drops of blood have fallen free.

Yesterday we were walking in the garden. Abbas was reciting the same poem. A man and a woman and a young girl came to see him. So far they have come five times. I had seen them before and I knew them. The young girl brought a bouquet of flowers. She smiled at me. It was apparent that she liked me. She had come for me, basically. After all, Abbas's pockmarked face isn't attractive, but when the woman was talking to the doctor I saw Abbas pulling the young girl aside and kissing her.

* * *

Up to now no one has come to see me or brought me flowers. It has been a year. The last time it was Siavosh who came to see me. Siavosh was my best friend. We were neighbours. Every day we went to the Darolfonoun* together and walked back home together and discussed our homework. In leisure time I taught Siavosh to play the sitar. Rokhsare, who was Siavosh's cousin and my fiancée, would often join us. Siavosh wanted to marry Rokhsare's sister but one month before the day of the marriage ceremony, he unexpectedly fell ill. Two or three times I went to see him and to inquire how he was, but they said the doctor had strictly forbidden anyone to speak with him. No matter how much I insisted, they gave the same answer. So I stopped insisting.

I remember that day quite well. It was near the final exams. One evening, I had returned home and had dropped my books and some notebooks on the table. As I was about to change my clothes I heard the sound of a bullet being shot. The sound was so close that it frightened me because our house was behind a ditch and I had heard that there had been robberies near us. I took the revolver from the drawer and went to the courtyard and stood there, listening. Then I went up the stairs to the roof, but I didn't see anything. On my way down from the roof, I turned to look at Siavosh's house from the top. I saw him in a shirt and underpants standing in the middle of the courtyard. I said in surprise, "Siavosh, is that you?" He recognized me and said, "Come over, nobody's home." He put a finger on his lips and with his head he signalled to me to go over to him. I went down fast and knocked on the door of his house. He himself opened the door for me. With his head down and his eyes fixed on the ground, he asked me, "Why didn't you come to see me?"

"I came two or three times to see how you were, but they said that the doctor wouldn't permit it."

"They think I'm ill, but they're mistaken."

"Did you hear the bullet shot?"

He didn't answer but took my hand and led me to the foot of the pine tree where he pointed at something. I looked closely. There were three drops of fresh blood on the ground.

Then he took me to his room and closed all the doors. I sat on a chair. He turned the light on and sat opposite me on a chair in front of the table. His room was simple. It was blue, and up to the middle the walls were a darker colour. In the corner of the room there was a sitar. Several volumes of books and school notebooks had been dropped on the table. After a while Siavosh took a revolver from the drawer and showed it to me. It was one of those old revolvers with a mother-of-pearl handle. He put it in his trouser pocket and said, "I used to have a female cat – her name was Coquette. You might have seen her. She was one of those ordinary calico cats. She had two large eyes that looked as if she had black eyeliner on. The patches on her back were arranged neatly as if someone had spilt ink on a grey piece of blotting paper and then had torn the paper in the middle. Every day when I returned home from school Coquette would run up to me, miaowing. She would rub herself against me and when I sat down she would climb over my head and shoulders, rubbing her snout against my face and licking my forehead with her rough tongue, insisting that I kiss her. It's as if female cats are wilier and kinder and more sensitive than male cats. Apart from me, Coquette got along very well with the cook because he was in charge of the food. But she kept away from my grandmother who was bossy and regularly said her prayers and avoided cat hair. Coquette must have thought to herself that people were smarter than cats and that they had confiscated all the delicious food and the warm, comfortable places for themselves and in order to have a share in these luxuries, cats had to be sycophantic and flatter people a great deal.

"The only time Coquette's natural feelings would awaken and come to the surface was when she got hold of the bleeding head of a rooster. Then she would change, turning into a fierce beast. Her eyes would become bigger and sparkle. Her claws would pop out of their sheaths and with long growls she would threaten anyone who got near her. Then, as if she were fooling herself, she would start to play a game. Since with all the force of her imagination she had made herself believe that the rooster's head was a living animal, she would tap the head with her paw. Her hair would stand up, she would hide, be on the alert, and would attack again, revealing all the skill and agility of her species in repetitive jumping and attacking and retreating. After she tired of this exhibition, she would greedily finish eating the bloody head and for several minutes afterwards she would search for the rest of it. And so, for an hour or two, she would forget her artificial civilization, wouldn't go near anyone and wouldn't be charming or flattering.

"All the time during which Coquette was displaying affection she was in fact unforthcoming and brutish and wouldn't reveal her secrets. She treated our home like her own property and if a strange cat happened to enter the house, especially if the cat was a female, for hours you'd hear the sound of spitting, moaning and indignation.

"The noise that Coquette made to announce that she was ready for lunch was different to the one she made when she was being flirty. The sound of her screams when she was hungry, the cries she made during fighting, and her moaning when she was in heat all had a distinct sound and were different from each other. And their tunes would also change: first there were the heart-rending cries, second the yells of spite and vengeance, third a painful sigh drawn from the natural need to join her mate. The looks that Coquette made with her eyes appeared more meaningful than anything else and sometimes she would display emotions of such human nature that people would feel compelled to ask themselves: what thoughts and feelings exist in that woolly head, behind those green mysterious eyes?

"It was last spring when that terrible incident took place. You know that come spring, all animals become intoxicated and pair up. It is as if the spring breeze awakens crazy passion in all living beings. For the first time our Coquette was hit by the passion of love and, with shudders which moved her whole body, she would sigh with sadness. The male cats heard her sighs and welcomed her from all sides. After fighting and scuffling, Coquette chose for her mate the one who was the strongest of all and whose voice was the loudest. In animal lovemaking their special smell is very important. That's why spoilt, domesticated and clean male cats don't appeal to the females. By contrast, the cats on the walls, the thieving, skinny, wandering and hungry cats whose skin gives off the original odour of their species, are more attractive to the females. During the day, but especially at night, Coquette and her mate would bawl out their love in long cries. Her soft delicate body would writhe while the other's body would bend like a bow, and they would give happy groans. This continued until the coming of dawn. Then Coquette would enter the room with tousled hair, bruised and tired but happy.

"I didn't sleep at night because of Coquette's lovemaking. Eventually, I became very angry. One day I was working in front of this same window when I saw the lovers strutting in the garden. With the very revolver that you see I aimed at them from a distance of two or three steps. I fired the gun and a bullet hit her mate. It seemed as if his back was broken. He made a huge leap and without making a sound or groaning, he ran away through the passageway and fell at the foot of the garden wall.

"Blood had trickled all along the path he had taken. Coquette searched for a while until she found his footsteps. She smelled his blood and went straight to his dead body. For two nights and two days she kept watch by his body. Sometimes she would touch him with her paw as if to say to him, 'Get up, it's the beginning of spring. Why do you sleep in the time of love? Why don't you move? Get up, get up!' Coquette didn't know about death and didn't know that her lover was dead.

"The day after that, Coquette disappeared together with her mate's body. I searched everywhere, I asked everyone for traces of her. It was useless. Was Coquette sulking? Was she dead? Did she go to search for her love? And what happened to the body?

"One night I heard the miaowing of that same male cat. He cried until dawn. The next night was the same, but in the morning his cries had stopped. The third night I picked up the revolver again and I shot aimlessly towards the pine tree in front of my window. The glittering of his eyes was apparent in the dark. He gave a long moan and became silent. In the morning I saw that three drops of blood had fallen onto the ground under the tree. Since that night he's been coming every night and moaning in that same voice. The others sleep heavily and don't hear. No matter what I say to them they laugh at me but I know, I am certain, that this is the sound of the same cat that I shot. I haven't slept since that night. No matter where I go, no matter which room I sleep in, this damn cat moans in his frightening voice and calls for his mate.

"Today when there was no one in the house I went to the same place where the cat sits and cries every night and I aimed, since I knew where he stood from the glitter of his eyes in the dark. When the gun was empty I heard the cat's groans and three drops of blood fell from up there. You saw them with your own eyes, aren't you my witness?"

Then the door opened and Rokhsare and her mother entered the room. Rokhsare had a bouquet of flowers in her hand. I stood up and said hello, but laughing, Siavosh said, "Of course you know Mr Mirza Ahmad Khan better than I do. An introduction isn't necessary. He testifies that with his own eyes he has seen three drops of blood at the foot of the pine tree."

"Yes, I have seen them."

But Siavosh walked towards me, giving a throaty laugh. He put his hand in my trouser pocket and pulled out the revolver. Putting the pistol on the table, he said, "You know that Mirza Ahmad Khan not only plays the sitar and composes poetry well, but he is also a skilled hunter. He shoots very well." Then he signalled to me. I too stood up and said, "Yes, this afternoon I came to pick up some school notes from Siavosh. For fun we shot at the pine tree for a while, but those three drops of blood don't belong to the cat, they belong to the bird of truth. You know that according to legend the bird of truth ate three grains which belonged to the weak and the unprotected and each night he cries and cries until three drops of blood fall from his throat. Or maybe, a cat had caught the neighbour's canary and then the neighbour shot the cat and the wounded cat then passed by the tree. Now wait, I'm going to recite a new poem I have written." I picked up the sitar and tuned it in preparation for the song and then I sang this poem:

> "What a pity that once again it is night.
> From head to toe the world is dark.
> For everyone it has become the time of peace
> Except for me, whose despair and sorrow are increased.

There is no happiness in the nature of the world.
Except death there is no cure for my sorrow.
But at that corner under the pine tree
Three drops of blood have fallen on the ground."

At this point Rokhsare's mother went out of the room angrily. Rokhsare raised her eyebrows and said, "He is mad." Then she took Siavosh's hand and both of them laughed and laughed and then walked through the door and closed it on me. From behind the window I saw that when they reached the courtyard they embraced each under the lantern and kissed.

The Legalizer

(from *Three Drops of Blood*)

(translated by Deborah Miller Mostaghel)

FOUR HOURS WERE LEFT before the sunset and Pass Qale*
looked empty and quiet in the middle of the mountains.
Arranged on a table in front of a small coffeehouse were jugs
of yoghurt drink, lemonade and glasses of different colours. A
dilapidated record player and some scratchy records stood on
a bench. The coffeehouse keeper, his sleeves rolled up, shook
the bronze samovar, threw out the tea leaves, then picked up the
empty gasoline drum, to which wire handles had been attached,
and walked in the direction of the river.

The sun was shining. From below could be heard the
monotonous sound of the water, layer after layer of water
falling on each other in the riverbed, making everything seem
fresh. On one of the benches in front of the coffeehouse, a
man was lying, a damp cloth covering his face, his cloth shoes
arranged side by side next to the bench. On the opposite
bench, under the shade of a mulberry tree, two men were
sitting together. Though they hardly knew each other they
had immediately embarked on a heart-to-heart conversation.
They were so absorbed in their conversation that it seemed
as if they had known each other for years. Mashadi Shahbaz
was thin, scrawny, with a heavy moustache and eyebrows that
met in the middle. He was squatting on the edge of the bench,
and gesturing with his henna-dyed hand, saying, "Yesterday I
went to Morgh Mahale to see my cousin; he has a little garden

there. He was saying that last year he sold his apricots for thirty tomans. This year they were frostbitten and all the fruit fell off the tree. He was in a terrible condition. And his wife has been bedridden since Ramadan. It's been very costly for him."

Mirza Yadellah adjusted his glasses, sucked his pipe with an air of relaxation, stroked his greying beard, and said, "All the blessing has gone out of everything."

Shahbaz nodded in agreement and said, "How right you are. It's like the end of the world. Customs have changed. May God grant much luck to everyone – twenty-five years ago I was in the neighbourhood of the holy city of Mashad. Three kilos of butter for less than a rial, ten eggs for a rial. We bought loaves of bread as tall as a man. Who suffered from the lack of money? God bless my father – he had bought a *bandari* mule, they're fast and small, and we would ride it together. I was twenty years old. I used to play marbles in the alley with the kids from our neighbourhood. Now all the young people lose their enthusiasm easily. They turn from unripe grapes to fully-fledged raisins. Give me the days of our youth. As that fellow, God bless him, said:

> I may be old, with a trembling chin,
> But I'm worth a hundred young men."

Yadollah puffed on his pipe and said, "Every year we regret the last year."

Shahbaz nodded. "May God grant his creatures a happy ending."

Yadollah assumed a serious expression. "I'll tell you, there was a time when we had thirty mouths to feed in our house. Now every day I worry about where I'll find a few rials for my tea and tobacco. Two years ago I had three teaching jobs, I earned eight tomans a month. Just the day before yesterday, on Aide Qorban,* I went to the house of one of the wealthy people where I used to be the tutor. They told me to bless the sheep in preparation for the slaughter. The ruthless butcher lifted the poor animal up and threw it onto the ground. He was sharpening his knife. The animal struggled and pulled itself up from under the butcher's legs. I don't know what was on the ground, but I saw that the animal's eye had burst open and was bleeding. My heart was bleeding. I left on the pretext that I had a headache. All that night I saw the sheep's head before my eyes, it was covered in blood. Then a profanity slipped from my tongue and I was having blasphemous thoughts... May God strike me dumb. There's no doubt in God's goodness, but these helpless animals... it's sinful. Oh Lord, oh Providence, you know better. No matter what, man is sinful." He sat lost in thought for a moment. Then he continued, "Yes, if only I could spell out everything that is in my heart: well, but everything can't be said, God forbid. May God strike me dumb."

As if he were bored Shahbaz said, "Just think of important things."

Mirza Yadollah replied with an air of indifference, "Yes, what can we do? The world's always this way."

"Our time is over," said Shahbaz. "We're done for. We're only alive because we can't afford shrouds. What tricks haven't we played in this base world? Once in Tehran I had a grocery store. I put away six rials a day after expenses."

Mirza Yadollah interrupted his words. "You were a grocer? I don't like grocers as a group."

"Why?"

"It's a long story. But you finish what you have to say first."

Shahbaz continued talking. "Yes, I had a grocery store. I was doing all right. Little by little I was building a life for myself. To make a long story short, I married a shrew. It's been five years since my wife ruined my life. She wasn't a woman, she was a firebrand. How hard I had worked to marry and settle down: she ruined everything I had accomplished. Well, one night she came back from listening to a sermon. She insisted that she must go on pilgrimage to lighten her burden of sin. You wouldn't believe how much she harassed me... How silly I was to give my wits to that woman. In any case, man is gullible. I was strong and ruthless, but a woman got the better of me. God forbid that a woman should get under a man's skin. That very night she said, 'I don't understand these things, but I've figured it out. I don't want my dowry back, just set me free. I have a bracelet and a necklace, I'll sell them and leave. I looked for an omen and I found a good one. Either divorce me or I'll strangle your child right here by the lamp.' No matter what I did, do you think I was a match for her? For two weeks she didn't look at me. She insisted so much that I sold everything I had, collected the money and gave it to her. She took my two-year-old son and disappeared to where the Arabs play the flute. It's been five years and I don't know what happened to her."

"May she be protected from the evil of the Arabs."

"Yes, amidst those naked ignorant Arabs, the desert, the burning sun! It's as if she'd turned into water and had been soaked up by the earth. She didn't send me even a note. They're right when they say the woman is made of only one rib."

Mirza Yadollah said, "It's men's fault, they raise them that way and don't let them become worldly and experienced."

Shahbaz was wrapped up in his own words. "What's funny is that that woman was basically silly and simple-minded. I don't know what happened that suddenly she turned into a firebrand. Sometimes, when she was on her own, she would cry. I wished her tears were for her first husband—"

"You mean you were her second husband?" asked Mirza Yadollah.

"Of course," replied Shahbaz. "Now what was I saying? I forgot what I was saying."

"You mentioned her first husband."

"Yes, at first I thought she was crying for her first husband. In any case, no matter how nicely I tried to explain and make her understand, it was as if I were talking to a wall. It was as if death were out to get her. I don't know what she did with my son. Will I ever look into his eyes again? A son whom God gave me after so many prayers and offerings."

Mirza Yadollah said, "Everyone you look at has some misfortune. The heart of the matter is that people should be human, should be educated. As long as they behave like mules, we'll ride them. There was a time when I used to preach from the pulpit that whoever made a pilgrimage to the holy shrines would be forgiven and would have a place in heaven."

Shahbaz said, "You aren't a preacher, are you?"

"That was twelve years ago. You see I'm not dressed like a preacher. Now I'm a jack of all trades and master of none."

"How? I don't understand."

Mirza Yadollah moistened his lips with his tongue and said dejectedly, "A woman ruined my life also."

Shahbaz said, "Oh, these women!"

"No, this has nothing to do with women. This misfortune is my own fault. If you were in Tehran, probably you've heard the name of my father. I wasn't found under a cabbage leaf. My father was so holy that even angels obeyed him. Everyone was always extolling his virtues. When he went up to the pulpit, there wasn't even room to drop a needle. All the bigwigs were nervous around him. I'm not trying to show off. He's dead, God bless him. Whatever he was, it was his reputation. As the poet says:

> Even if your father was a learned man,
> It's nothing to you – you must do what you can.

"In any case, after my father's death I became his successor, and I examined our circumstances. He had left us a house and a handful of stuff. I was still a theology student, and I had a monthly pension of four tomans plus fifteen kilograms of wheat. In addition, during the months of *Muharram* and *Safar* we were in clover. Our bread was buttered on both sides. Since it was well known that the breath of my father, God bless him, would work miracles, one night I was brought to a sickbed to pray. I saw a girl, about eight or nine years old, hanging around. Sir, I was drawn to her at first glance. Well, that's youth, with all its ups and downs.

"Before her I had had two temporary wives, both of whom I had divorced, but this was something else. You'd have to have been me to understand. Anyway, two days later I sent a handkerchief full of nuts and dried fruit and three tomans, and I married her. At night when they brought her, she was so tiny that they carried her. I was ashamed of myself. I won't hide anything from you. For three days, whenever the girl saw me she trembled like a sparrow. Now, I was only thirty, I was in my prime. But talk about those seventy-year-old men with all kinds of diseases who marry nine-year-old girls.

"Well, what does a child understand of marriage? She thinks it's all about wearing a sequinned shawl and putting on new clothes and being patted and caressed by a husband instead of being in her father's house where she would be beaten and cursed. But she doesn't know that life isn't just a bed of roses in her husband's house either.

"In any case, it took me so much trouble to tame her. She was afraid of me. She would cry. I pleaded with her. I would say, 'For God's sake, stop embarrassing me. All right, you sleep at one end of the room, I'll sleep at the other', because I felt sorry for her. I really restrained myself not to force her. Besides, I had had a lot of experience and I could wait. In any case, she listened to my advice.

"The first night I told her a story. She fell asleep. The second night I started another story and left half of it for the next night.

"The third night I didn't say anything, until she finally said, 'You told the story up to the part where King Jamshid went hunting. Why don't you tell the rest?' And I – I couldn't contain myself for joy. I said, 'Tonight I have a headache. I can't talk loud. If you let me, I'll come a little closer.' In this manner I went closer, closer, till she gave in."

Shahbaz was amused. He wanted to say something, but when he saw Mirza Yadollah's serious face and his eyes full of tears behind his glasses, he restrained himself.

With peculiar emphasis Mirza Yadollah said, "That story goes back twelve years, twelve years! You don't know what a woman she was, so nice, so kind. She took care of all my work. Oh, now when I remember... She wore a *chador* all the time. She washed the clothes with her little hands, hung them on the line, mended my shirts and socks, cooked the food, even helped my sister. How well she behaved, how kind she was! She made everybody love her. How clever she was! I taught her how to read and write. She was reading the Koran in two months. She memorized poetry. We were together for three years, the best years of my life. As luck would have it, at that time I became the lawyer for a pretty widow who was wealthy too: well I hankered for her, all right, until it occurred to me that I should marry her. I don't know what scoundrel brought the news to my wife. Sir, may you never see such a day. This woman who was apparently so silly and dumb! I didn't know she could be so jealous. No matter how hard I tried to pull the wool over her eyes with sweet nothings, could I be a match for her? In spite of the fact that the widow owed me part of my fees, I decided not to marry her, and our relationship came to an end. But you don't know what problems my wife created for me for a month!

"Maybe she had gone mad, maybe she'd been bewitched. She had completely changed. She put her hands on her hips and said things to me which one couldn't even imagine. She said, 'I hope you're strangled with your own deceiving turban. I hope to see those spectacles on your corpse. From the very first day I realized you were not my type. May my father's pimping soul burn for having given me to you. Once I opened my eyes I saw I was being embraced by a pimp. It's three years that I've put up with your beggary. Was this my reward? May God spare us from having to deal with unprincipled people. I vow not to make a mistake like this again. You can't force me. I don't want to live with you any more. I don't want my dowry back, just let me go. I swear I'll go, I'll go and take sanctuary. Right now. Right now.'

"She said so much that I finally felt infuriated. Everything went dark before my eyes. As we were sitting at supper, I picked up the dishes and threw them into the yard. It was evening. We got up and went together to Sheik Mehdi and in his presence I divorced my wife three times.* He shook his head. The next day I was sorry, but what was the use, when being sorry wouldn't help and my wife was forbidden to me? For several days I prowled around the streets and the bazaar like a madman. I was so distracted that if an acquaintance ran into me, I couldn't return his greeting.

"I was never happy again after that. I couldn't forget her, even for a minute. I couldn't eat or sleep. I couldn't bear to be in the house: the walls cursed me. For two months I was ill in bed. All the time I was delirious I kept calling her name. When I began to recover, it was obvious that I could have had a hundred girls if I was interested. But she was something else. Finally I resolved that no matter what it took, I would marry her again. The time during which she couldn't remarry came to an end. I tried everything, but I saw it wasn't any use. I sold everything I had, even the junk: I got together eighteen tomans. There wasn't any other choice except to find a legalizer, someone who would marry my wife and then divorce her, so that after the one hundred day waiting period, I could remarry her.

"There was a clownish good-for-nothing grocer in our neighbourhood. Even if seven dogs licked his face, it wouldn't get clean. He was the kind who would cut off someone's head for an onion. I went and arranged it with him so that he would marry Robabeh, then divorce her, and I would pay all the expenses plus five tomans. And he accepted. One shouldn't be fooled by people – that bastard, that good-for-nothing..."

Shahbaz, pale, hid his face in his hands and said, "He was a grocer? What was his name? What kind of grocer was he? What neighbourhood was he from? No... No... Nothing like that could happen."

But Mirza Yadollah was so involved in what he was saying, and the past events had become so vivid to him, that he didn't stop.

"That damn grocer married my wife. You don't know how hard I took it. A woman who had been mine for three years. If someone had mentioned her name I would have torn him apart. Think of it: now, with my own help, she had to become the wife of that damned illiterate grocer. I said to myself, 'Maybe this is the revenge of my temporary wives, who cried when I divorced them.' Anyway, early the next morning I went to the grocer's house. He kept me waiting for an hour, which seemed a century to me. When he came I said to him, 'Stick to your bargain, divorce Robabeh, and you've made five tomans.' I can still picture his devilish face. He laughed and said, 'She's my wife, I wouldn't sell a hair on her head for a thousand tomans.' My eyes were blasting lightning!"

Shahbaz trembled and said, "No, something like that couldn't happen. Tell me the truth. God!..."

Mirza Yadollah said, "Now do you see that I was right? Now do you understand why I can't stand grocers? When he said he wouldn't give up a hair of her head for a thousand tomans, I understood that he wanted to get more money. But who had the time to bargain? I was hurting. I was horrified. I was so upset, and I was so sick and tired of life, that I didn't answer him. I gave him a look which was worse than any curse. From there I went directly to a second-hand store. I sold my robe and my cloak and bought a buckram robe. I put on a felt hat, adjusted my shoes, and set out. Since then I've been wandering from one town to the next, from one village to another, like a bewildered vagabond. It's been twelve years. I couldn't stay in one place any longer. Sometimes I work as a storyteller, sometimes as a teacher. I write letters for people, I recite the *Shahnameh* in teahouses, I play the flute. I enjoy seeing the world and its people. I want to spend my life just like this. One gets a lot out of it. In any case, we're old. We're flogging a dead horse. We've got one foot in this world and one in the next. It's too bad that we can't take advantage of the experience we've gained. How well the poet said it:

> A wise and skilful man
> Should live not once, but twice:
> At first to gain experience,
> Then to follow his own advice."

At this point Mirza Yadollah grew tired. It was as if his jaws stopped working because he had thought and spoken more than usual. He reached out and took his pipe, staring at the ricer and listening to the faint muffled melody which came from beyond the mountain.

Shahbaz raised his head from his hands. He sighed and said, "Every pair of actions requires a third to be complete!"

Mirza Yadollah was confused and didn't notice.

Shahbaz said louder, "She's sure to turn yet another wealthy man into a destitute tramp."

Yadollah came to himself and said, "Who?"

"That bitch Robabeh."

Mirza Yadollah's eyes popped out. Shocked, he asked, "What do you mean?"

Mashadi Shahbaz gave a forced laugh. "It's true that life really changes man. His face becomes wrinkled, his hair turns white, his teeth fall out. His voice changes. You didn't recognize me and I didn't recognize you."

Mirza Yadollah asked, "What?"

"Didn't Robabeh have a pockmark on her face? Didn't she blink a lot?"

Irritated, Mirza Yadollah said, "Who told you?"

Mashadi Shahbaz laughed, "Aren't you Sheikh Yadollah, the son of the late Sheikh Rasol, who lived in the alley with the public bath? You passed my store every morning. I am the legalizer, the same one."

Miraz Yadollah looked closer and said, "You're the one who has made this my life for the past twelve years? You are Shahbaz the grocer? There was a time when we would have fought it out if I had found you in these mountains. What a pity that time has tied the hands of both of us." Then he babbled to himself, "Very good, Robabeh, you've taken my revenge for me. He is wandering too, just like me." Once again he fell silent, his lips set in a painful smile.

The person sleeping on the bench opposite them rolled, sat up, yawned, and rubbed his eyes.

Mashadi Shahbaz and Mirza Yadollah glanced stealthily at each other, afraid to let their eyes meet. Two miserable enemies, with their struggles in love behind them. Now they should be thinking about death.

After a short silence, Shahbaz turned towards the coffeehouse patron and said, "Dash Akbar, bring us two cups of tea."

Whirlpool

(from *Three Drops of Blood*)

(translated by Deborah Miller Mostaghel)

HOMAYOUN WAS WHISPERING TO HIMSELF, "Is this real?... Could this be possible? So young but lying in the cold damp earth out there in the Shah Abdolazim cemetery* among thousands of other corpses... The shroud sticking to his body. Never again to see the arrival of spring or the end of autumn or suffocating sad days like today... Have the light of his eye and the song of his voice been completely turned off?... He who was so full of laughter and said such entertaining things?..."

The sky was overcast and the window was covered in a slim layer of steam. Looking out of the window you could see the neighbour's house. The neighbour's tin roof was covered with a thin coating of snow. Snowflakes were spinning slowly and neatly in the air before landing on the edge of the tin roof. Black smoke was coming out of the chimney, writhing and twisting in the grey sky and then disappearing slowly.

Homayoun was sitting in front of the gas heater together with his young wife and their little daughter, Homa. They were in the family room but unlike the past, when laughter and happiness ruled in this room on Fridays, today they all were sad and silent. Even their little daughter who usually livened things up looked dull and gloomy today. She had put a plaster-made doll next to her – the doll had a broken face – and was staring outside. It was as if she too was sensing that something was wrong, and the thing that was wrong was the fact that dear Uncle Bahram had failed to come to see them as was his habit. She was also feeling that her parents' sadness was on his account: the black clothes, the eyes red-rimmed from the lack of sleep, and the cigarette smoke which waved in the air all reinforced this suspicion.

Homayoun was staring at the fire in the gas heater, but his thoughts were elsewhere. Against his own will, his thoughts had wandered off to his schooldays in winter. Days like today, when snow was one foot high. As soon as the bell rang to announce the break, no one had a chance against him and Bahram. They always played the same game. They would roll a ball of snow on the ground until it became a big pile. Then the children would split into two groups, and use the pile as a barricade, and so snowball fights would begin. Without feeling the cold, with red hands that burned with the intensity of the cold, they would throw snowballs at each other. One day when they were busy with this game, Homayoun pressed together a handful of icy snow and threw it at Bahram, cutting his forehead. The supervisor came and hit the palm of his hand with several sharp lashes. Perhaps it was then that his friendship with Bahram started, and until recently whenever he saw the scar on Bahram's forehead he would remember the beating on the palm of his hand. In the span of eighteen years their spirit and thought had come so close together that not only did they tell each other their very private thoughts and feelings, but they perceived many of each other's unspoken inner thoughts.

The two of them had almost exactly the same thoughts, the same taste, and were almost of the same disposition. Until now there had not arisen between them the least difference of opinion or the smallest offence. Then, on the morning of the day before yesterday, Homayoun had received a phone call in the office that Bahram Mirza had killed himself. That very hour Homayoun got a droshky and went hurriedly to Bahram's bedside. He slowly pulled back the white cloth that was covering Bahram's face – it was bloodstained. His eyelashes were covered in blood, his brain had splashed on the pillow, there were bloodstains on the rug and the crying and distress of his relatives affected Homayoun as if he had been hit by a thunderbolt. Later, step by step, he walked alongside the coffin until near sunset when they buried him in the earth. He sent for a bouquet of flowers which was brought. He placed it on the grave and after the last goodbye he returned home with a heavy heart. But since that day he hadn't had a peaceful minute, he hadn't been able to sleep, and white hair had appeared on his temples. A packet of cigarettes was in front of him, and he smoked continuously.

It was the first time that Homayoun had thought deeply and reflected on the problem of death, but his thoughts led nowhere. No opinion or supposition could content him.

He was completely astonished and didn't know what to do. Sometimes a state of insanity would come over him. No matter how much he tried he couldn't forget. Their friendship had started in primary school and their lives had been almost entirely entwined. They were partners in sorrow and happiness, and every instant that he turned and looked at Bahram's picture all his past memories of Bahram would come alive and he would see him: the blond moustache, the blue, wide-set eyes, the small mouth, the narrow chin, his loud laugh and the way he cleared his throat were all before his eyes. He couldn't believe that

Bahram was dead, and that he had died so suddenly!... What self-sacrifices hadn't Bahram made for him, in the three years that he had been away on duty and Bahram had been taking care of his household! According to Homayoun's wife, Badri, "He did everything for us. We didn't have to worry about a thing."

Now Homayoun felt the burden of life, and he missed the bygone days when they would gather so intimately in this same room. They would play backgammon and would completely lose track of time. But the thing that tortured him most was the thought that since they were so close together and hid nothing from each other, why hadn't Bahram consulted with him before deciding to commit suicide? What was the cause? Had he gone crazy or had there been a family secret involved? He would ask himself this question continually. At last it seemed that an idea had occurred to him. He sought refuge with his wife, Badri, and asked her, "Have you got any suspicion? Any idea why Bahram did this?"

Badri, who was seemingly preoccupied with embroidery, raised her head and, as if she had not expected this type of question, said unwillingly, "How am I supposed to know? Didn't he tell you?"

"No... That's why I asked... I'm surprised by that too... When I came back from the trip I felt that he had changed. But he didn't say anything to me. I thought this preoccupation of his was because of his office work... Because being cooped up made him depressed, he had told me many times... But he didn't hide anything from me."

"God bless him! How lively and happy he was. This is unlike him."

"No, he pretended to be like that; sometimes he would change and be very different... When he was alone... Once when I entered his room and didn't recognize him, he had put his head between his hands and he was thinking. As soon as he saw that I was startled he laughed and made the usual jokes in order to cover up. He was a good actor!"

"Maybe there was something that he was afraid of telling you for fear of hurting you. He was probably being considerate and was thinking of you. After all, you have a wife and a child, so you have to think about getting on in life. But he..." She shook her head in a meaningful way, as if his suicide had no importance. Once more the silence obliged them to think. Homayoun felt that his wife's words were not sincere and she had said them for the sake of expediency. The same woman who eight years ago used to worship him, who had such delicate thoughts about love! He felt as if a curtain had lifted from before his eyes. His wife's attempt at consoling him had made him feel disgusted with her, especially in the face of his memories of Bahram. He became weary of his wife. She had become materialistic, wise and mature, and had started to think of wealth and worldly life and didn't want to give way to sadness and sorrow. And the reason she gave was that Bahram didn't have a wife and child. What a mean thought. Since he had deprived himself of this common pleasure, his death held no cause for regret. Was his child worth more in the world than his friend? Never! Wasn't Bahram worthy of regret? Would he find anyone else like him in the world?

That Bahram should die and this mumbling ninety-year-old, Sayyed Khanom, should live! She had come today, in the snow and cold, hobbling with a walking stick all the way from Pah Chenar,* looking for Bahram's house to eat the halva given out to invoke God's blessing. This was God's policy, and in his wife's opinion it was natural, and his wife Badri too would someday come to look like this Sayyed Khanom. Even now that she is not wearing make-up she looks different. Her appearance had changed a lot. Her voice and the expression of her eyes had changed. In the early morning when he went to work she would still be asleep. There were crow's feet around her eyes and they had lost their lustre. Probably his wife had the same feeling about him too, who knew? Hadn't he himself changed? Was he the same old kind, obedient and good-looking Homayoun? Hadn't he cheated on his wife? But why had this thought occurred to him? Was it because of the lack of sleep or the painful reminiscence about his friend?

At this point the door opened and a servant, who held the corner of her *chador* between her teeth, brought a large sealed letter, gave it to Homayoun, and left. Homayoun recognized Bahram's short, irregular handwriting on the envelope, opened it with haste, pulled out a letter and read:

Now, at 1:30 in the morning on the thirteenth day of Mehr 1311,* I, Bahram Mirza Arjanpour, of my own free will and preference, am bequeathing all my possessions to Miss Homa Mahafarid.

Bahram Arjanpour

Astonished, Homayoun reread the letter and then, in a state of amazement, let it slip through his hand.

Badri, who was watching him out of the corner of her eye, asked, "Who is the letter from?"

"Bahram."

"What does he say?"

"Do you know that he has given all his possessions to Homa?"

"What a fine man!"

This expression of surprise mixed with affability made Bahram even more disgusted with his wife. But involuntarily his glance caught Bahram's picture. Then he looked back at Homa. Suddenly something occurred to him so that he started to tremble helplessly. It was as if another curtain had fallen before his eyes: there was no doubt that his daughter resembled Bahram. She didn't look like him or her mother. Neither one of them had blue eyes. The small mouth, the narrow chin, in fact all the features on her face were just like those of Bahram. Homayoun came to understand why Bahram had loved Homa so dearly and why after his death he had bequeathed her all his possessions! Was this child whom he loved so much the result of intimacy between Bahram and his wife? And Bahram, a friend whose soul was in the same mould as his and in whom he had so much trust? His wife had been intimate with him for years without his knowing it and Bahram had deceived him all this time, had mocked him and now he had sent this will too, this insult after death. No, he couldn't tolerate all this. These thoughts passed like lightning through his mind. His head ached, his cheeks felt cold, he turned a fiery gaze on Badri and said, "What do you say, huh, why did Bahram do this? Didn't he have sisters and brothers?"

"Because he loved this child. When you were at Bandargaz,* Homa got the measles. For ten days and nights that man was a nurse at the foot of this child's bed. God bless him!"

Homayoun said angrily, "No, it isn't that simple…"

"Why isn't it that simple? Not everyone is indifferent like you are, going away and leaving your wife and child for three years.

And when you returned, you came back empty handed; you didn't even bring me a pair of stockings. People show affection through giving. To him, loving your child was the same as loving you. After all, he was not in love with Homa! And then didn't you realize that she was the apple of his eye?..."

"No, you aren't telling me the truth."

"What do you want me to say? I don't understand."

"You're feigning ignorance."

"Meaning what?... Someone else kills himself, someone else gives away his belongings and I am being held to account?"

"That much I know for sure: you're not telling everything."

"You know what? I don't understand hints and allusions. Go and get medical treatment, you're not feeling well, your mind is all over the place. What do you want from me?"

"Do you believe that I don't know?"

"If you know then why do you ask me?"

Homayoun shouted with impatience, "Enough is enough. You're mocking me!" Then he picked up Bahram's will, crumpled it and threw it in the gas heater where it flared up and turned to ashes.

Badri flung down the purple cloth she had in her hand, got up, and said, "So you're being spiteful to me, that's fine, but why can't you allow your own child some indulgence?" Homayoun got up, leant against the table and in an ironic tone said, "My child... my child?... Then why does she look like Bahram?" With his elbow he hit the inlaid frame which held Bahram's picture and it fell to the floor.

The child, who had been sulking till now, burst into a loud crying. Badri, looking pale, said in a threatening tone, "What do you mean? What are you trying to say?"

154

"I want to say that you have fooled me for eight years, mocked me. For eight years you've been a disgrace to me, not a wife…"

"To me?… To my daughter?"

Homayoun showed the picture with an angry laugh and said, breathing heavily, "Yes, your daughter… your daughter… Pick her up and have a look at her. I want to say that now my eyes are opened, I understand why he left everything to her, he was a kind father. But you – it's been eight years that…"

"That I've been in your house, that I've suffered every kind of hardship, that I put up with your misfortunes, that I took care of your household for three years when you weren't here, then, later, I found out that you had fallen in love with a Russian slut in Bandargaz, and now I get this reward. You can't find any excuse so you say my child looks like Bahram. But I can no longer put up with this. I won't stay in this house for another minute. Come darling… let's go."

Homa, pale and in a state of fright, was trembling and watching this strange and unprecedented quarrel between her father and her mother. Crying, she took hold of her mother's skirt and the two of them went towards the door. Near the door Badri took a key chain from her pocket and threw it heavily so that it rolled in front of Homayoun's feet. The sounds of Homa's crying and of footsteps in the hall became faint. Ten minutes later the sound of the wheels of a droshky was heard carrying them off in the snow and cold. Homayoun stood astonished and giddy in his place. He was afraid to lift his head: he didn't want to believe that these events were real. He was asking himself if he had gone crazy or was having a nightmare. At any rate, the thing that was evident was that this house and this life had become unbearable for him, and his daughter Homa, whom he loved so much, he couldn't see any more. He couldn't kiss her and caress her. The memories of his friend had become stained. Worse than everything else was that, unbeknown to him, for eight years his wife had been cheating on him with his only friend and had polluted the heart of his family. All of this hidden from him, without his knowing it! They had all been very good actors. He was the only one who had been fooled, and ridiculed. Suddenly he became completely weary of his life, he was disillusioned with everything and everyone. He felt limitlessly alone and alienated. He had no other choice but to be sent on a bureaucratic mission to a distant city or to a port in the south and pass the rest of his life there, or else do away with himself: go somewhere he wouldn't see anyone, wouldn't hear anyone's voice, sleep in a ditch and never wake again. Because for the first time he felt that between him and all the people who were around him a frightening whirlpool existed that he hadn't perceived until now.

He lit a cigarette and took several paces. Once again he leant against the table. Outside the window snowflakes were landing on the edge of the tin roof neatly, slowly, and heedlessly, as if they were dancing to the tune of mysterious music. Without intending to, he remembered the happy and wholesome days when he and his father and mother would go to their village in Iraq. During the days he would sleep by himself on the grass under the shade of the trees, the same place where Shir Ali would smoke his pipe and sit on the wheel of the threshing machine. Shir Ali's daughter, who had a red *chador*, would spend long hours there waiting for her father. The threshing machine with its plaintive sound would crush the golden stalks of wheat. The cows with long horns and wide foreheads whose necks had been scarred by the yoke walked in circles until nightfall. Now his condition was like that of those cows. Now he knew what these animals had been feeling. He too had passed his life with closed eyes, in an endless circle, like a horse on a treadmill, like those cows that crushed the stalks of wheat. He remembered the monotonous hours when he sat behind a desk in the small customs room and continually scribbled out the same papers. Sometimes his colleague would look at his watch and yawn, but he would carry on, writing the same numbers in their proper columns. He would check, add, turn the notebooks inside out – but at that time he had something to be happy about. He knew that although his vision, his thought, his youth, and his strength were diminishing bit by bit, he still had something to keep him happy. He knew that when he returned home at night and saw Bahram, his daughter and his wife smiling, his tiredness would disappear. But now he was disgusted with all three of them. It was the three of them who had brought him to such a pass.

As if he had made a sudden decision, he went to his desk and sat down. He pulled out a drawer and took out a small pistol that he always carried when he was travelling. He checked it. The bullets were in their place. He looked inside the cold black barrel and moved the pistol slowly towards his temple, but then remembered Bahram's bloody face. Finally he put it away in the pocket of his trousers.

He got up again. In the hall he put on his overcoat and galoshes. He picked up the umbrella too and left the house. The alley was empty. Snowflakes were whirling slowly in the air. He set out without hesitation, although he didn't know where he was going. He just wanted to flee, to get far away from his house, from these frightening events.

He came out on a street which was cold, white and sad. Passing droshky wheels had formed furrows in the middle of the street. He was walking with long footsteps. An automobile passed him, and watery snow and mud from the street spattered on his head and face. He stood and looked at his clothes. They had been drenched in mud and it was as if they gave him consolation. As he went he came across a little boy selling matches. He called him. He bought a box of matches, but when he looked at the boy's face he saw he had blue eyes, small lips and blond hair. He remembered Bahram, his body trembled, and he continued on his way. Suddenly he stopped before the window of a shop. He went forwards and pressed his forehead against the cold glass. His hat almost fell off. Toys were arranged behind the window. He rubbed his sleeve on the glass to clean off the steam but it was useless. A big doll with a red face and blue eyes stood in front of him smiling. He stared at it for a while. He thought of how happy Homa would be if this doll belonged to her. The store owner opened the door. He started out again, and passed two more alleys. On his path a poultry seller was sitting next to his basket. Inside the basket, there had been put three hens and a rooster whose legs were tied together. Their red legs trembled from the cold. Red drops of blood had fallen near the poultry seller on the snow. A little further on, sitting in front of a house, was a boy with ringworm. The boy's arms stuck out of a torn shirt.

He noticed all this without recognizing his surroundings or route. He didn't feel the falling snow, and the closed umbrella he had picked up he held shut in his hand. He went into another empty alley and sat on the front steps of a house. The snow was falling faster. He opened his umbrella. A deep weariness had taken possession of him. His head felt heavy. His eyes slowly closed. The sound of passing voices brought him to himself. He got up. The sky had become dark. He remembered all the day's events: the boy with ringworm that he had seen in front of a house and whose arms were visible from under his torn shirt, the red, wet legs of the hens in the basket that were trembling from the cold, and the blood which had fallen on the snow. He felt a little hungry. He bought sweet bread from a bakery. He ate it as he walked and, without intending to, prowled around the alley like a shadow.

When he entered his house, it was two in the morning. He fell into the armchair. An hour later he woke up from the force of the cold, lay down on the bed in his clothes, and pulled the quilt over his head. He dreamt that in a room somewhere the same boy who was selling matches was dressed in black and was seated behind a desk on which was a big doll with blue smiling eyes, and in front of him three people were standing with their hands folded on their chests. His daughter Homa entered. She had a candle in her hand. After her a man entered who was wearing a white and bloodstained mask on his face. The man moved forwards and took the hands of Homa and the boy. Just as Homayoun wanted to go out of the door two hands came out from behind the curtain, holding pistols in his direction. Frightened, Homayoun jumped awake with a headache.

For two weeks his life passed in the same way. During the days he went to his office and only returned very late at night to sleep. Sometimes in the afternoons for no reason that he could think of he would pass near the girls' school that Homa attended. After school he would hide at the corner behind the wall, fearing he would be seen by Mashdi Ali, his father-in-law's servant. He looked the children over one by one, but he didn't see his daughter Homa among them, and life carried on in this manner until his request for a transfer was accepted and he was directed to go to the customs office in Kermanshah.

The day before leaving Homayoun made all his preparations. He even went to see that the bus was in the garage and bought the ticket. Since his suitcases were not packed he arranged to leave for Kermanshah the next morning, instead of going that very afternoon, as the garage owner had insisted.

When he entered his house he immediately went to the family room where his desk was. The room was disorganized and messy. Cold ashes had fallen in front of the gas heater. The piece of embroidered purple silk and the envelope of Bahram's will had been put on the table. He picked up the envelope and tore it down the middle, but then he saw a piece of written paper he hadn't noticed that day in his great haste. After he had put the pieces together on the table he read:

Probably this letter will come to you after my death. I know you will be surprised at this sudden decision of mine, since I did nothing without your advice, but so that there won't be any mystery between us I confess that I loved your wife Badri. I fought with myself for four years. At last I won, and I killed the demon that had awakened in me, so that I might not betray you. I give a worthless present to Homa that I hope will be accepted!

    Yours always,

        Bahram

For a while Homayoun stared around the room astonished. He no longer doubted that Homa was his own child. Could he have left without seeing Homa? He read the letter again and a third time. He put it in his pocket and left the house. On his way he entered the toy shop and without hesitation bought the big doll with the red face and blue eyes and went towards his father-in-law's house. When he got there he knocked on the door. When he saw Homayoun, Mashdi Ali the servant said with eyes full of tears, "Sir, what calamity has happened? Miss Homa!"

"What's happened?"

"Sir, you don't know how restless Miss Homa was at being away from you. I would take her to school every day. It was Sunday. Up to now that makes five days since the afternoon that she ran away from school. She had said she was going to see her dear father. We were in a frenzy. But didn't Muhammad tell you? We telephoned the police, I came to your house twice."

"What are you saying? What has happened?"

"Nothing, sir, it was evening when they brought her home. She had got lost. She got pneumonia from the terrible cold. She called you continually until the moment she died. Yesterday we took her to Shah Abdolazim. We buried her right next to Bahram Mirza's grave."

Homayoun was staring at Mashdi Ali. At this point the doll box fell from his arms. Then like a crazed man he pulled up the collar of his overcoat and went towards the garage with long strides, because he had changed his mind about packing the suitcases, and he could leave much sooner on the afternoon bus.

Fire-Worshipper

(from *Buried Alive*)

(translated by Deborah Miller Mostaghel)

F LANDON,* who had just returned from Iran, was sitting opposite one of his old friends in a room on the third floor of a Parisian guesthouse. A bottle of wine and two glasses were put on a small table between the friends and music was playing in the café below. Outside it was dark and cloudy and a light rain was falling. Flandon lifted his head from his hands, picked up a glass of wine, drained it and turned to his friend. "Do you know – there was a time when I felt that I had lost myself among those ruins, mountains, and deserts. I said to myself, 'Could it be that one day I'll return to my country? Would I be able to hear this same music that is playing now?' I wished to return some day. I wished for an hour like this when we could be alone and I could open my heart to you. But now I want to tell you something different, something that I know you won't believe: now that I've come back, I regret it. You know, I still long for Iran. It's as if I've lost something!"

On hearing this, his friend, whose face had turned red and whose eyes were wide but expressionless, jokingly hit the table with his fist and laughed out loud. "Eugene, stop joking. I know you were a painter, but I didn't know you were also a poet. So you've become tired of us? Tell me, you must have become attached to someone down there. I've heard that Eastern women are pretty."

"No, it's nothing like that. I'm not joking."

"By the way, the other day I was with your brother and the conversation turned to you. He brought several recent pictures which you had sent from Iran and we looked at them. I remember they were all pictures of ruins... Oh yes, he said one of them was a place for worshipping fire. You mean they worship fire there? The only thing I know about the country you were in is that they have good carpets: I don't know anything else. Now you describe to me everything that you've seen. You know, everything about it is new for us Parisians."

Flandon was silent a moment, then said, "You've reminded me of something. One day in Iran something took place which was very strange for me. Up to now I haven't told anyone, not even my friend Coste, who was with me. I was afraid he would laugh at me. You know that I don't believe in anything. Only once in all my life have I worshipped God sincerely, with all my heart and soul. That was in Iran, near the same fire temple you saw the picture of. One night, when I was in the south of Iran excavating at Persepolis, I had gone alone to Nagshe Rostam. There the graves of ancient Persian kings were carved into the mountain. I think you may have seen the picture. It's something like a cross that has been carved into the mountain. Above it is a picture of the king standing in front of the fire temple with his right arm raised towards the fire. Above the fire temple is Ahura Mazda, their god. Below the temple the stone has been cut in the form of a porch, and the king's tomb is located within the stone crypt. Several of those crypts can be seen there. Opposite them is the great fire temple, which is called the Kaaba of Zoroaster.

"Anyway, I remember clearly that it was near dusk. I was busy measuring this same temple. I was almost worn out with fatigue

166

and the heat. Suddenly I saw two people, whose clothes were different from ordinary Persian clothes, coming towards me. When they got closer, I saw that they were two old men. Two old but strong, lively men with sparkling eyes and striking faces. I asked them questions and it became evident that they were merchants from Yazd who had come from the north of Iran. Their religion was like that of most of the inhabitants of Yazd. In other words, they were fire-worshippers like the ancient kings of Iran. They had deliberately gone out of their way to make a pilgrimage to the ancient fire temple. They hadn't finished talking when they began to gather pieces of wood and twigs and dry leaves. They piled them up and made a small fire. I stood still, astonished, and watched them. They lit the dry wood and started to say prayers and murmur in a special language which I had not heard before. Probably it was the language of Zoroaster and the Avesta; maybe it was the same language which had been carved in cuneiform on the rocks.

"At this point, when the two fire-worshippers were busy praying in front of the fire, I lifted my head. I saw that the scene carved in the stone exactly resembled the living scene in front of me. I stood frozen in my tracks. It was as if these people on the stone exactly above the grave of Darius had come to life and after several thousand years had come down opposite me to worship the manifestation of their god: I was amazed that after this length of time, in spite of the effort expended by the Muslims to destroy and overthrow this faith, this ancient religion still had followers who, secretly but in the open air, threw themselves to the ground before the fire!

"The two fire-worshippers left and disappeared. I remained alone, but the small fire was still burning. I don't know how it happened – but I felt that I was under pressure by a religious force and tension. A heavy silence ruled there. The moon had come out from the side of the mountain like a fiery sphere of sulphur and its pale light had illuminated the body of the great fire temple. Time seemed to have gone backwards two or three thousand years. I had forgotten my nationality, personality, and surroundings. I looked at the ashes in front of which those two mysterious old men had fallen down in worship and praise. Blue smoke was slowly rising from the spot in the shape of a column and was spiralling in the air. The shadow of broken stones, the blurred horizon, the stars which shone above my head and winked to each other, the display of the quiet and splendour of the plain among these mysterious ruins and ancient fire temples – it was as if the surroundings, the souls of all the dead, and the power of their thought, which was aloft over the crypt and the broken stones, had forced or inspired me, because things were no longer in my hands. I, who had no belief in anything, fell involuntarily to my knees before these ashes from which the blue smoke rose, and worshipped them: I didn't know what to say but I didn't need to murmur anything. Perhaps less than a minute passed before I came to myself again, but I worshiped the manifestation of Ahura Mazda – perhaps in the same way the ancient kings of Iran worshipped fire. In that moment I was a fire-worshipper. Now, think whatever you like about me. Maybe it was just because mankind is weak and is not capable…"

Abji Khanom

(from *Buried Alive*)

(translated by Deborah Miller Mostaghel)

A BJI KHANOM WAS MAROKH'S OLDER SISTER, but anyone who didn't know the family would have found it hard to believe that they were sisters. Abji Khanom was tall, lanky, swarthy, with thick lips and coarse black hair. She was altogether ugly. Marokh, on the other hand, was petite, fair, with a small nose and chestnut hair. Her eyes were alluring, and every time she laughed dimples appeared. They were very different from each other with regard to behaviour and habit too. Ever since she was a child, Abji Khanom had been fussy and quarrelsome and didn't get along with people. She would even sulk at her mother for two or three months at a time. Her sister, by contrast, was tactful and appealing. She was always good natured and laughing. Naneh Hasan, their neighbour, had nicknamed her "Miss Favourite". Even her mother and father loved Marokh more, since she was the youngest child and their dear darling.

Abji Khanom's mother used to hit her when she was a child. She would nag her and make a fuss but publicly, in front of the neighbours and other people, she would pretend that she felt sorry for Abji Khanom. She would cross her hands and say, "What can I do with this bad luck, eh? Who will marry such an ugly girl? I am afraid she will remain at home. A girl who has no wealth, no beauty, and no accomplishment. Who is the miserable person who will marry her?" Words like this had been repeated in the presence of Abji Khanom so many

171

times that she too had totally lost hope, and had given up on the idea of finding a husband. She spent most of her time praying and fulfilling religious duties. She had completely given up on marriage, since no husband had appeared for her. Once they wanted to give her to Kalb Hosein, the apprentice carpenter, but he didn't want her. Nonetheless, every time Abji Khanom met people, she would tell them, "I had a proposal but I turned it down. Today's husbands are all immoral drunkards, better dead than alive. I shall never get married."

She spoke like this on the surface, but it was evident that in her heart she liked Kalb Hosein and was very eager to get married. But since from the age of five she had been told that she was ugly and no one would marry her, and since she knew she had no share in the pleasures of this world, she wanted at least to receive the wealth of the other world by the power of prayer and worship. In this way she had found comfort for herself. Yes, why should she regret that she had no share in the pleasures of this transitory world? After all, the eternal world, the hereafter, would be all hers. Then all the attractive people, including her sister and everybody else, would wish they were her. When the months of Muharri and Safar* arrived, this was Abji Khanom's time to show off. There was no preaching at which she was not at the head of the crowd. In the passion plays* she would take a place for herself an hour before noon. All the preachers knew her and were very eager that Abji Khanom should be at the foot of their pulpits so that the crowd would get worked up from her crying groans and screams. She had memorized most of the sermons. She had heard the sermons so many times and she knew so many religious problems that most of the neighbours would come to her and ask about their mistakes.

Early in the morning, she was the one in charge of waking up the household. First she would go to her sister's bed and kick her, saying, "It's almost noon. When are you going to get up and say your prayers?" The poor girl would get up, sleepily wash and stand up to say her prayers. The morning call to prayer, the cry of the rooster, the dawn breeze, the murmur of prayers, gave Abji Khanom a special feeling, a spiritual feeling, and she felt proud before her conscience. She would say to herself, "If God doesn't take me to heaven then whom will He take?" The rest of the day also, after doing some insignificant housework and fussing about this and that, she would take in her hand a long rosary, whose black colour had turned yellow from being handled so much, and recite the beads. Now her only wish was that, by whatever means, she could go on a pilgrimage trip to Karbala and stay there.

But her sister didn't show any special religious zeal and did all of the housework. Then when she was fifteen she went to work as a maid. Abji Khanom was twenty-two, but she was stuck at home and secretly envied her sister. During the year and a half that Marokh went away to work as a maid, not even once had Abji Khanom tried to visit her or asked how she was. When Marokh came home every two weeks to see her family, Abji Khanom would either quarrel with someone or go and pray, stretching it out for two or three hours. Also, later when everyone was sitting together, she would make sarcastic remarks to her sister and would begin lecturing her about prayers, fasting, cleanliness and scepticism. For example, she would say, "From the time when these modern, mincing women appeared, bread became more expensive... Whoever doesn't cover her face will be suspended by the hair in hell. Whoever talks behind someone's back will have her head as big as a mountain and her neck as thin as a hair. In hell there are such snakes that people take shelter with dragons." And she would go on in this vein. Marokh had felt that her sister was jealous but she pretended that she didn't notice.

One day towards evening, Marokh came home and talked quietly with her mother for a while and then left. Abji Khanom had gone to the entrance of the opposite room and had sat, puffing on a water pipe, but because of her jealousy she didn't ask her mother what her sister's conversation had been about and her mother said nothing about it either. In the evening when her father, with his egg-shaped hat on which whitewash had dried, came home from bricklaying, he changed his clothes, took his tobacco pouch and his pipe, and went up on the roof. Abji Khanom, leaving her work as it was, went with her mother and took the samovar, a pot, a copper container, and relish and onions. They sat next to each other on a carpet. Her mother started the conversation, saying that Abbas, a servant in the same house where Marokh worked, had proposed to her. This morning when the house was empty Abbas's mother had come to ask for her hand. They wanted to sign the marriage contract next week. They would give twenty-five tomans as a gift for the bride's mother, thirty tomans to the bride in case there was a divorce, as well as a mirror, candlesticks, a Koran, a pair of shoes, sweets, a bag of henna, a taffeta scarf, brocaded chintz trousers... Her father, fanning himself with a fan hemmed around the edges, sucking a piece of sugar in the corner of his mouth and drinking tea, nodded and said offhandedly, "Good enough. Congratulations. There's no objection." He didn't show any surprise or happiness and didn't express any opinion. It was as if he was afraid of his wife. But Abji Khanom was furious as soon as she heard this news. She couldn't listen to the rest of the agreements and on the pretext of prayers she got up without intending to and went downstairs to the main room which had five entrances. She stared at herself in a small mirror she had. In her own eyes she appeared old and broken down, as if these few minutes had aged her several years. She examined the wrinkle between her eyebrows. She found one white hair. With two fingers she pulled it out. She stared at it for a while under the light. Where she pulled it from she felt nothing.

Several days passed. There was quite a commotion at home. They went back and forth to the bazaar and bought two silk outfits, a water pitcher, glasses, embroidery, a rose water sprinkler, a drinking container, a night cap, a box of cosmetics, eyebrow paint, a bronze samovar, painted curtains, everything imaginable. Since the mother wanted a great deal for her daughter, whatever trinkets from the home came into her hands she would put aside for Marokh's trousseau. Even the hand-woven prayer carpets that Abji Khanom had asked her mother for several times and which she hadn't given to her she put aside for Marokh. During these several days Abji Khanom silently and apprehensively watched these things, pretending not to notice. For two days she pretended to have a headache and rested. Her mother repeatedly scorned her, saying, "When is sisterhood valuable, if not now? I know it's from jealousy, and no one reaches his goal from that. Besides, ugliness and beauty aren't in my hands, it's God's work. You saw that I wanted to give you to Kalb Hosein, but they didn't like you. Now you're pretending to be sick so you won't have to do anything. From morning till night you pretend to be pious, while I must strain my weak eyes sewing."

Furious with the jealousy which had overflowed her heart, Abji Khanom answered from under the quilt, "Enough, enough. She tries to put a brand in a heart of ice. Such a bridegroom you found her! Whenever you hit a dog someone like Abbas will appear in this town. What kind of taunt are you giving me? It's clear that everyone knows what kind of a man Abbas is. Now don't make me spell out that Marokh is two months pregnant. I saw that her stomach has swollen, but I didn't show that I noticed it. I no longer consider her my sister."

Her mother became very angry. "May God strike you dumb. Go and die. I hope you die, shameless girl. Go and get lost. Do you want to stain my daughter's reputation? I know this is just jealousy. You are dying because nobody will marry you with that face and figure. Now out of grief you slander your own sister. Didn't you say that God in his own Koran has written that a liar is a big sinner, eh? God had mercy on others that he did not make you pretty... Every other hour you leave the house on the pretext of going to a sermon. You're the one who makes people gossip... Go, go. All this praying and fasting isn't worth the curse of Satan for people who have been deceitful. You're just fooling people."

This kind of talk passed between them for the next several days. Marokh stared at these scuffles astonished and said nothing, until the night of the ceremony arrived. All the neighbours and the local unladylike women had gathered together, their eyes and eyebrows painted black, their faces white and their cheeks red. The women wore print *chadors*, had straight fringes and sported baggy cotton trousers. Among them Naneh Hasan was in the limelight. Simpering and smiling, she had tilted her head and was playing the drum. She sang whatever came to her mind:

> Oh friends, congratulations. With the blessing of God, congratulations.
> We came, we came again, we came from the bridegroom's home –
> Everybody's pretty as the moon, everybody's a king, everybody's got almond eyes.
> Oh friends, congratulations. With the blessing of God, congratulations.
> We came, we came again, we came from the bride's home.
> Everybody's blind, everybody's lethargic, everybody's with sick eyes.
> Oh friends, congratulations. We have come to take the angel and the fairy.
> With the blessing of God, congratulations.

She would repeat this same thing over and over. They came and went, cleaning trays by the fountain, rubbing them with ashes. The smell of vegetable stew permeated the air. Someone shooed a cat out of the kitchen. Someone wanted eggs for an omelette. Several small children had taken each other's hands and were sitting down and getting up saying, "The small bath has ants; sit down and get up." They lit bronze fires in rented samovars. Unexpectedly they had news that the lady of the house where Marokh was a maid was coming to the ceremony with her daughters. On two tables sweets and fruit were arranged and they put two chairs at each table. Marokh's father was pacing pensively, thinking that his expenditure had been great. But Marokh's mother was insisting that for the approaching night they should have a puppet show. In all this tumult there was no sign of Abji Khanom. She had been gone since two in the afternoon. No one knew where she was. Probably she had gone to listen to a sermon.

When the candles were lit and the ceremony was over, everyone had gone except for Naneh Hasan. They had joined the hands of the bride and groom who were sitting beside each other in the main room. The doors were closed. Abji Khanom entered the house. She went directly to the room next to the main room to take off her *chador*. As soon as she entered she noticed that they had pulled down the curtain in the main room. Out of curiosity she lifted a corner of the curtain from behind the glass. Under the light of the lamp, she saw her sister Marokh, looking prettier than ever with make-up and painted eyebrows, beside the bridegroom, who seemed to be about twenty. They were sitting in front of a table filled with sweets. The bridegroom put his hand around Marokh's waist and said something in her ear. It looked as if they had noticed Abji Khanom or maybe her sister had recognized her. To spite Abji Khanom, they laughed and then kissed. From the end of the courtyard came the sound of Naneh Hasan's drum. She was singing, "Oh friends, congratulations..." A feeling of hatred mixed with jealousy overcame Abji Khanom. She dropped the curtain and went and sat on the pile of bedding which they had put near the wall. Without opening her black *chador* she rested her chin in her hands and stared at the ground at the flower patterns of the carpet. She counted them and they seemed to her to be something new; she noticed the pattern of their colours. She either didn't notice anyone coming and going, or she wouldn't lift her head to see who it was. Her mother came to the door of her room and said to her, "Why don't you eat supper? Why do you make yourself suffer? Why are you sitting here? Take off your black *chador*. Why have you left it on like a bad omen? Come and kiss your sister. Come and watch them from behind the glass. The bride and groom look like the full moon. Aren't you happy for them? Come on, say something, finally. Everyone was asking where her sister was. I didn't know what to say."

Abji Khanom only raised her head and said, "I've eaten supper."

* * *

It was midnight. Everyone was asleep with the memory of his own wedding night and dreaming happy dreams. Suddenly, as if somebody were thrashing in water, the sound of splashing woke everybody abruptly. At first they thought a cat or a child had fallen into the fountain. With bare heads and feet they lit the lights. They searched everywhere but found nothing extraordinary. When they came back to go to sleep Naneh Hasan saw that Abji Khanom's slippers had fallen near the cover of the water reservoir. They brought the light forwards and saw Abji Khanom's body floating on the water surface. Her braided black hair had wrapped around her throat like a snake. Her rust-coloured clothes clung to her body. Her face shone with splendour and luminosity. It was as if she had gone to a place where there existed neither ugliness nor beauty, neither marriage nor funerals, neither laughter nor crying, neither happiness nor sorrow. She had gone to heaven.

The Stray Dog

(from *The Stray Dog*)

(translated by Deborah Miller Mostaghel)

V ARAMIN SQUARE WAS MADE UP of several small shops – a bakery, a butcher's shop, a chemist, two cafés and a hairdresser's, all of which served to fulfil the most basic needs of life. Beneath the powerful sun the square and its residents were half burnt, half broiled. They longed for the first evening breeze and the shade of the night. The people, the shops, the train and the animals had ceased their activity. The warm weather weighed heavily on them and a fine mist of dust, continually increased by the coming and going of cars, shimmered under the azure sky.

On one side of the square was an old sycamore tree whose trunk was hollow and rotten but whose crooked, rheumatic branches had spread out with a desperate stubbornness. In the shade of its dusty leaves a large, wide bench had been placed from which two little boys with loud voices were selling rice pudding and pumpkin seeds. Thick muddy water pushed itself with difficulty through the ditch in front of the café.

The only building which attracted attention was the well-known tower of Varamin, half of whose cracked, cylindrical body and cone-shaped top was visible. Even the sparrows that had built nests in the crevice where bricks had fallen from the tower were quiet from the force of the heat and were having a nap. The moaning of a dog was the only sound to break the stillness at intervals.

The dog was from Scotland and had a smoky grey snout and black spots on his legs, looking as if he had run through a marsh and been splashed with slime. He had drooping ears, a bristling tail, and matt, dirty fur. Two human eyes shone in his woolly face. A human spirit could be seen in the depths of his eyes. Even in the darkness which had overtaken his life, there was in his eyes something eternal and shining, something which held a message that couldn't be understood. It was neither brightness nor colour: it was something indefinable. Not only did there exist a similarity between his eyes and human eyes, but also a kind of equality could be seen. Two hazel eyes full of pain, torment and hope, eyes that can only be seen in the face of a wandering dog. But it seemed as if no one saw or understood his pained, pleading looks. In front of the bakery the errand boy would hit him. In front of the butcher's the apprentice would throw stones at him. If he took shelter in the shade of a car, a heavy kick from the driver's shoe would greet him. And when everyone else grew tired of tormenting him, the boy who sold rice pudding took special pleasure in torturing him. For every groan the dog gave, he would be hit in the side with a stone. The sound of the boy's loud laughter would rise above the moans of the dog, and he would say, "God damn." It was as if all the others were on the boy's side, craftily and slyly encouraging him and then doubling up with laughter. They all hit the dog for God's sake, since in their opinion it was quite natural that they should hurt the unclean dog which their religion had cursed and which they believed had seventy lives.

Eventually, the rice pudding boy's torment forced the animal to flee down the alley which led towards the tower. He didn't really flee, he dragged himself with difficulty, on an empty stomach, and took shelter in a water channel. He laid his head on his paws, let his tongue hang out and, half asleep, half awake, looked at the green field which waved before him. His body was exhausted and his nerves were overwrought.

In the moist air of the water channel a special tranquillity enveloped him from head to foot. In his nostrils the different odours of half-dead weeds, an old damp shoe, the smell of live and dead animals brought to life half-suppressed memories.

Whenever he looked carefully at the green field, his instinctive desires would awaken, and memories of the past would be brought to his mind afresh, but this time the sensation was so powerful that it felt as if a voice he could hear next to his ear was compelling him to move about, jump and leap. He felt an inordinate desire to run and frolic in the green fields.

This was his inherited feeling: all his ancestors had been bred among the green open fields of Scotland. But his body was so exhausted that it didn't allow him to make the slightest movement. A painful feeling mixed with weakness overcame him. A handful of forgotten feelings, lost feelings had reawakened. Once, he had had various duties and responsibilities. He knew himself bound to answer his master's call, to drive out strange people and dogs from his master's home, to play with his master's child, to act one way with acquaintances and another with strangers, to eat on time, to expect being fondled at a certain time. But now all these ties had been removed.

All of his attention had narrowed down to finding a bit of food, fearfully and tremblingly, in the rubbish heap, while taking blows and howling all day – this had become his only means of defence. Formerly he had been courageous, fearless, clean, and full of life, but now he had become timid, the butt of people's vengeance. Whatever noise he heard or whatever moved near him caused him to tremble. He was even frightened of his own voice. He had become accustomed to rubbish. His body itched, but he didn't have the heart to search for fleas or to lick himself clean. He felt he had become part of the garbage, and something in him had died, had gone out.

Two winters had passed since he had found himself in this hell. During this time he hadn't eaten a full meal, or taken a peaceful nap. His lustre and passions had been stifled. Not a single person had laid a caressing hand on his head. Not one resembled his master in appearance – it seemed that in feelings, disposition and behaviour, his owner was a world away from these people. It was as if the people he had formerly been with were closer to his world, understood his pain and his feelings better, and protected him.

From among the smells which assailed his nostrils, the one that dizzied him the most was the smell of that boy's rice pudding: that white liquid which was so similar to his mother's milk and which brought to mind the memories of his childhood. Suddenly a numbness took hold of him. He remembered as a puppy sucking that warm, nutritious liquid from his mother's breast while her warm, firm tongue licked his body clean. The strong odour he had breathed in his mother's embrace, next to his brother, the strong, heavy smell of his mother and her milk, revived in his nostrils.

When he had sucked his fill, his body grew warm and comfortable. A liquid warmth flowed through his veins, his head separated heavily from his mother's breast, his body quivered with pleasure from head to tail, and a deep sleep followed. What pleasure greater than this was possible? To instinctively press his paws against his mother's breast, and with no special effort the milk would come out. The fluffy body of his brother, his mother's voice, all of this was full of pleasure. He remembered his old wooden doghouse, the games he used to play in that green garden with his brother.

He would bite his floppy ears, they would fall on the ground, get up, run; and later he found another playmate, too, his owner's son. He would run after him at the end of the garden, bark, take his clothes in his teeth. In particular, he could never forget the caresses his owner had given him, the lumps of sugar he had eaten from his hand. Still, he liked his owner's son better, because they had been playmates and the boy would never hit him. Later, he suddenly lost his mother and brother. Only his owner and his owner's wife and son and an old servant were left. How well he distinguished their smells and recognized from afar the sound of their footsteps. At lunch and supper he would circle the table and smell the food, and sometimes against her husband's will his owner's wife would kindly give him a titbit. Then the old servant would come, calling, "Pat... Pat..." and would pour his food in a special dish which was beside his doghouse.

Natural needs caused Pat's misfortune, because his owner wouldn't let him out of the house to go after female dogs. As luck would have it, one autumn day his owner and two other people who often came to their house and whom Pat knew got in the car. Pat had travelled with his owner in the car several times, but today he was agitated. After several hours of driving, they got out in Varamin Square. His owner and the two others passed through the alley beside the tower, but suddenly there

187

was the unexpected stench of a bitch, that special smell that Pat was searching for, and all at once he was driven crazy. He sniffed in different places and finally entered a garden through a water channel.

Twice near dusk the sound of his owner's voice calling "Pat! Pat!" reached his ears. Was it really his voice, or was the echo of his voice sounding in Pat's ears?

Although his owner's voice had a strong hold on Pat, because it reminded him of all the obligations and duties that he owed him, still a power superior to that of the outside world compelled him to stay with the bitch. He felt that his ears had grown too heavy and dull to hear sounds outside himself. Strong feelings had awakened in him, and the smell of the bitch was so powerful that he felt giddy.

All his muscles, all his body and his senses, were beyond his control, so that they were no longer obedient to him. But it wasn't long until people came with sticks and shovel handles and shouts and drove him out through the water channel.

Dizzy, giddy and tired, but light and relieved, as soon as Pat came to himself he went to look for his master. In several side alleys a faint odour of him had remained. He looked everywhere, leaving traces of himself at intervals. He went as far as the ruins outside the town. Then Pat returned because he realized that his owner had gone back to the square, but from there his faint scent got lost among others. Had his owner gone and left him behind? He felt agitated and fearful. How could Pat live without his master, his God? For his owner was like a god to him. But at the same time he was certain that his owner would come to look for him. Frightened, he began running up and down the roads; his efforts were wasted.

When night fell he returned to the square, tired and exhausted. There was no trace of his master. He circled the village a few more times, finally going to the water channel that led to the bitch, but the entrance had been blocked with rocks. With peculiar enthusiasm, Pat dug at the ground with his paws in the hope of being able to enter the garden, but it was impossible. Disappointed, he napped there.

In the middle of the night Pat jumped awake at the sound of his own moans. Frightened, he got up. He prowled about in the alleys helpless and perplexed. At length he felt very hungry. When he returned to the square, the odour of different foods reached his nostrils. The smells of leftover meat, fresh bread and yoghurt were all mingled together, but at the same time he felt guilty for trespassing. He must beg from these people who resembled his owner, and if another rival shouldn't turn up to drive him out, little by little he could obtain the right to this territory. Perhaps one of these beings who had food would take care of him.

Trembling with fear, he went cautiously towards the bakery, which had just opened and from which the strong smell of baked bread diffused in the air. Somebody with a loaf of bread under his arm said to him, "Come... Come!" How strange his voice sounded in Pat's ears! The man threw a piece of warm bread in front of him. After hesitating a moment, Pat ate the bread and wagged his tail. The man put the bread down on the shop bench. Fearfully and cautiously, he laid his hand on Pat's head. Then, with both hands, he undid Pat's collar. How comfortable Pat felt: it was as if all the responsibilities, obligations, and duties were lifted from his shoulders. But when he wagged his tail again and went towards the shop owner, he met a heavy kick in the side and retreated, moaning. The owner of the shop went and carefully dipped his hands in the water of the ditch. Pat still recognized his collar hanging in front of the shop.

From that day on, aside from kicks, rocks, and beatings from the club, Pat had earned nothing from these people. It was as if they were his sworn enemies and took pleasure in torturing him.

Pat felt that he had entered a new world which didn't belong to him and in which no one understood his feelings. He passed the first few days with difficulty, but he adjusted by and by. On the right-hand side of the alley, where it turned, he discovered a place where rubbish was thrown. In the refuse many delicious titbits could be found, such as bones, fat, skin, fish heads, and many other things which he couldn't identify. After scavenging he would spend the rest of the day in front of the butcher's shop and the bakery. His eyes were glued to the butcher's hands, but he received more blows than delicious morsels. Eventually he came to terms with his new way of life. Of his past life only a handful of hazy, vague memories and some scents remained, and whenever things were particularly hard for him, he would find a measure of consolation and escape in this lost heaven of his, while involuntarily the memories of that time would take shape before his eyes.

But the thing that tortured Pat more than anything else was his need to be fondled. He was like a child who had always been cursed and made a scapegoat, but whose finer feelings had not yet been extinguished. Especially in this new life full of pain and torment, he needed to be caressed more than before. His eyes begged for this fondling, and he was ready to lay down his life for the person who would be kind to him or stroke him on the head. He needed to display his kindness to someone, to sacrifice himself for someone, to show someone his feelings of worship and loyalty, but it seemed that no one would take his part. In every eye he looked at he saw nothing but hatred and mischief. Whatever movement he made to attract the attention of these people, it seemed to rouse their indignation and wrath still more.

While Pat was napping in the water channel, he moaned and woke up several times, as if he were having nightmares. Presently he felt very hungry. He smelt grilled meat. A treacherous hunger tortured his insides so much that he forgot his helplessness and his other pains. He arose with difficulty and went cautiously towards the square.

* * *

At this time, amid noise and dust, a car entered Varamin Square. A man got out of the car, walked towards Pat and patted his head. This man was not his owner. Pat wasn't fooled, because he knew his owner's scent very well. But why had somebody come to caress him? Pat wagged his tail and looked doubtfully at the man. Hadn't he been tricked? But there was no longer a collar around his neck to pat him for. The man turned and patted him once more. Pat followed him, his surprise increasing, because the man went inside a shop that Pat knew well, from which the smell of food came. The man sat on a bench by the wall. He was served warm bread, yoghurt, eggs and other things. He dipped pieces of bread in the yoghurt and threw them in front of Pat. At first hurriedly, then more slowly, Pat ate the bread, his good-natured hazel eyes full of unhappiness riveted to the man's face in thanks, his tail wagging. Was he awake, or was he dreaming? Pat ate a full meal without being interrupted by blows. Could it be possible that he had found a new owner? In spite of the heat, the man got up. He went down the same alley to the tower, paused there a bit, then passed through winding alleys. Pat followed him, until he went out of the village. The man went to the same ruin, which had several walls, to which his owner had gone. Perhaps these people, too, followed the scent of their females? Pat waited for him in the shade of the wall. Then they returned to the square by a different route.

The man laid his hand on Pat's head again and after a brief walk around the square, he went and got into one of those cars that Pat knew. Pat didn't have the courage to jump up. He sat next to the car and looked at the man.

All at once the car started in a cloud of dust. Without hesitation, Pat ran after the car. No, this time he didn't want to let the man get away from him. He panted and in spite of the pain he felt in his body, he leapt up and ran after the car with all his strength. The car left the village behind and passed through fields. Pat reached the car two or three times but then fell back. He had gathered all his strength, and his despair forced him to run as fast as he could. But the car went faster than he did. He had made a mistake. Not only was he unable to reach the car, but he had become weak and broken and suddenly he felt that his muscles were no longer in his control. He was not able to make the slightest move. All his effort had been in vain. He actually didn't know why he had run or where he was going. He had come to a dead end. He stood and panted, his tongue hanging out. It had grown dark before his eyes. His head hanging, he pulled himself laboriously away from the road and went into a ditch beside the field. He lay on the hot moist sand, and with his instinct, which was never deceptive, he felt that he could not move any more from this spot. His head was dizzy. His thoughts and feelings had become vague and dark. He felt a severe pain in his stomach, and his eyes looked glazed over with sickness. In the midst of writhing and spasms, he lost control of his legs little by little. A cold sweat covered his body. It was a mild, intoxicating coolness...

* * *

Near dusk three hungry crows flew over Pat's head. They had smelled him from afar. One of them cautiously landed near him and looked carefully. When it was certain that Pat was not yet completely dead, it flew up again. The three crows had come to tear out his hazel eyes.

The Broken Mirror

(from *Three Drops of Blood*)

(translated by Deborah Miller Mostaghel)

O DETTE WAS AS FRESH as the flowers that blossom at the beginning of spring, with a pair of alluring eyes the colour of the sky and blonde hair which always hung in wisps by her cheeks. With a pale, delicate profile she would sit for hours in front of her window. She would cross her legs, read a novel, mend her stockings or do embroidery. But it was when she played the Garizari Waltz on her violin that she pulled at my heartstrings.

The window of my room was opposite the window of Odette's room. How many minutes, hours, and maybe even whole Sundays I would watch her from my window: especially at night when she took off her stockings and got into bed.

In this way a mysterious relationship had developed between us. If I didn't see her for one day, it was as if I had lost something. Some days I would look at her so long that she would get up and close her window. We had been watching each other for two weeks, but Odette's glance was cold and indifferent. She did not smile or make any move to reveal her feelings towards me. Basically her expression was serious and self-contained.

The first time that I came face to face with her was one morning when I had gone to the café at the end of our alley to have breakfast. When I came out, I saw Odette. Her violin case was in her hand and she was going towards the metro. I said

197

hello and she smiled. Then I asked if I could carry her violin case. She nodded her head in answer and said "Thanks". Our acquaintance started with this one word.

From that day on, when we opened our windows, we talked to each other from afar with hand motions and gestures. But it always resulted in our going down to the Luxembourg Gardens and meeting each other. Afterwards we would go to a film or to the theatre, or spend several hours together in some other way. Odette was alone at home. Her stepfather and her mother had gone on a trip, and she remained in Paris because of her job.

She spoke very little. But she had the temperament of a child: she was wilful and stubborn, and sometimes she infuriated me. We had been friends for two months. One day we decided to go that evening to the Friday market at Neuilly. That night Odette wore her new blue dress and seemed happier than usual. When we came out of the restaurant, she spoke of her life all the way on the metro, until we came out opposite Luna Park.

A large crowd was coming and going. All kinds of amusements were spread along the street. Entertainers were performing. There were shooting games, lottery games, sweet-sellers, a circus, small electric cars that went around a track, balloons which revolved around themselves, rides, and various exhibits. The sounds of girls' screams, conversation, laughter, murmuring, and the noise of motors and different sorts of music were mingled together.

We decided to go on a car ride. It was a train of cars which went around in a circle and when it was moving, a cloth would cover it, making it look like a green worm. When we wanted to get on, Odette gave her gloves and purse to me so they wouldn't fall during the ride. We sat close beside each other. The ride started and the green cover slowly rose and hid us from the eyes of the onlookers for five minutes.

When the cover fell back, our lips were still pressed together. I was kissing Odette and she was not holding back. Then we got out, and while walking, she told me that this was only the third time she had come to the Friday market, because her mother had forbidden her. We went to look at several other places. It was midnight when, tired and worn out, we finally started to return. But Odette didn't want to leave. She stopped at each show, and I was obliged to wait. Two or three times I dragged her by the arm, and she was forced to come with me, until she stopped in front of the stand of somebody who was selling Gillette razor blades. He was delivering a speech and demonstrating how good they were and inviting people to buy. This time I became really infuriated. I pulled her arm hard and said, "This has nothing to do with women." But she pulled her arm away and said, "I know. I still want to watch."

I went towards the metro without answering her. When I got home, the alley was deserted and Odette's window was dark. I went into my room and turned on the light. I opened the window, and since I wasn't sleepy, I read for a while. It was one in the morning. I went to close the window and go to sleep. I saw that Odette had come and was standing in the alley by the street light beneath her window. I was surprised by her behaviour. I slammed the window shut. As I started to undress, I realized that Odette's beaded purse and her gloves were in my pocket and I knew that her money and door key were in the purse. I tied them together and dropped them out the window.

Three weeks passed and during all that time I paid no attention to her. When her window opened, I closed mine. In the meantime it happened that I had to make a trip to London. The day before I left for England, I ran into Odette at the end of the alley, going towards the metro with her violin case in her hand. After saying hello and exchanging a few pleasantries, I told her about my trip and apologized for my behaviour that night. Odette coldly opened her beaded purse and handed me a small mirror which was broken in the middle. She said, "This happened that night you threw my purse out of the window. You know this will bring bad luck."

I laughed in answer and called her superstitious, and promised her that I would see her again before I left, but unfortunately I couldn't make it.

After I had been in London about a month I received this letter from Odette:

Paris, 21st September 1930

Dearest Jamshid,
You don't know how lonely I am. This loneliness hurts me. I want to say a few words to you tonight, because when I write to you it's as if I am speaking with you. If I address you familiarly please excuse me. If you only knew how much I am suffering!

How long the days are – the hands of the clock move so slowly that I don't know what to do. Does time seem so slow to you too? Perhaps you've met a girl there, although I'm sure that your head is always in a book, just the way you were in Paris, in that tiny room that is always before my eyes. Now a Chinese student has moved in, but I've hung a heavy curtain across my window so that I won't be able to see out, because the person that I loved isn't there. It's just like the refrain in the ballad says: "A bird that's gone to another land won't come back."

Yesterday Helen and I went walking in the Luxembourg Gardens. When we got to that stone bench, I remembered the day we sat on the same bench and you spoke of your country, and how you made me all those promises and I believed them. And now I've become an object of ridicule to my friends, and people talk about me. I always play the Garizari Waltz to remember you. The picture we took in the Bois de Vincennes is on my table. When I look at your picture it reassures me. I say to myself, "No, this picture doesn't fool me!" But alas, I don't know if you share my feelings or not. But ever since that night my mirror broke, the very mirror that you gave me yourself, my heart has been warning me of some unfortunate event. The last day that we saw each other, when you said that you were going to England, my heart told me that you were going very far and we would never see each other again. And the thing that I worried about has happened. Madame Burle asked, "Why are you so sad?" and she wanted to take me to Brittany, but I didn't go with her, because I knew that I would get worse.

Never mind – what's over is over. If I'm sounding cross, it's because I'm feeling depressed. Please forgive me, and if I've harassed you I hope you will forget me. You'll tear up my letters, won't you, Jimmy?

If only you knew how much pain and sorrow I'm in at this moment. I'm tired of everything. I'm disillusioned with my daily work, although it wasn't like this before. You know, I can't bear to be left hanging any longer, even if it becomes a cause of grief to others. All of their sorrow can't equal mine. I have decided to leave Paris on Sunday. I'll take the six-thirty train and go to Calais, the last city that you passed through. Then I'll see the blue water of the ocean. That water washes all misfortunes away. Every moment its colour changes, and it laps the sandy shore with its sad, enchanting murmur. It foams. The sand nibbles the foam and swallows it and then those very same waves will take my last thoughts with them, because when death smiles at someone, it draws him to it with this smile. Perhaps you will say that she couldn't do such a thing, but you will see that I don't tell lies.

Accept my distant kisses,

Odette Lasour

I sent two letters in answer to Odette, but one of them remained unanswered and the second was stamped "Return to Sender" and came back to me.

The next year, when I returned to Paris, I went as quickly as possible to Rue Saint Jacques, where my old house was. From my room a Chinese student was whistling the Garizari Waltz. But the window of Odette's room was shut, and a paper had been stuck on the front door which said "To Let".

Davoud the Hunchback

(from *Buried Alive*)

(translated by Deborah Miller Mostaghel)

"NO, NO. I WILL NEVER FOLLOW THIS PATH. I must completely close my eyes to it. It brings happiness to others, while for me it's full of pain and torture. Never, never…" Davoud was talking to himself, striking the ground with the short yellow-coloured stick which he had in his hand, and with which he struggled along, as if he kept his balance with difficulty. His big head was sunken between his thin shoulders onto his protruding chest. From the front he appeared hollow, terrible, and repulsive: thin withered lips, thin curved eyebrows, drooping eyelashes, sallow colour, prominent bony cheeks. But when someone looked at him from a distance with his coat covering his hump-back, his long disproportionate hands, his big hat pulled down on his head, and especially the serious attitude he assumed, hitting his stick with force on the ground, he seemed rather more laughable.

From the intersection of Pahlavi Avenue he had turned into a street out of the city and was going towards the Government Gate. It was near dusk and the weather was slightly warm. On the left, in the vague light of the sunset, the mud-covered walls and brick columns thrust their heads towards the sky in silence. On the right was a gully that had just been filled and next to that at intervals, half-built brick houses were visible. Here it was fairly empty, and sometimes a car or a droshky would pass which raised a little dust into the air even though water had been sprinkled on the road. Saplings had been planted on both sides of the street, by the gutter.

He was thinking that from the beginning of his childhood up to the present he had always been the object of other people's ridicule or pity. He remembered that the first time the teacher in the history class said the inhabitants of Sparta used to kill deformed children all the students turned around and looked at him, and it had made him feel strange. But now he wished that this law had been enforced everywhere in the world, or at least that, as in most places, they would have banned syphilitic people from marrying, since he knew that all this was his father's fault. The scene of his father's death, the pale face, bony cheeks, sunken blue eyes, half-open mouth, passed before his eyes just as he had seen it: his old syphilitic father, who had taken a young wife and all of whose children had been born blind or lame. One of his brothers who had survived was dumb and an idiot and had died two years ago. He would say to himself, "Maybe they were the lucky ones!"

But he remained alive, weary of himself and others, and everyone avoided him. He had grown somewhat accustomed to living for ever a life apart. From childhood in school he was left out of sports, jokes, races, ball games, leapfrog, tag and all the things which brought about the happiness of his classmates. During playtime he would crouch in the corner of the school playground holding a book in front of his face and watching the children stealthily from behind it. But there was a time when he truly worked, and he wanted to find superiority over the others at least through study. Day and night he worked, and because of this one or two of the lazy students became friendly with him, because they wanted to copy his exercises and his solutions to maths problems. But he knew that their friendship was insincere and was to their advantage, since he saw that the students tried hard to be friends with Hasan Khan, who was handsome, well-built, and wore nice clothes. Only one or two people among the teachers showed Davoud any consideration and attention, and this wasn't for his work but because they pitied him, since even with all his labour and hardship he couldn't complete his work.

Now he remained empty handed. Everyone avoided him. His acquaintances would be embarrassed to walk with him, women would say "See the hunchback!" This made him more angry than anything else.

Twice, several years before, he had asked for a girl's hand. Both times the women had ridiculed him. By coincidence one of them, Zibandeh, lived near here in Fisherabad. They had seen each other several times, and they had even talked to each other. In the afternoons when he came home from school he used to come here to see her. The only thing he could remember was that she had a mole by her lip. Later when he sent his aunt to ask for her hand that same girl had ridiculed him and said, "But is there a dearth of men, that I should become the wife of a hunchback?" No matter how much her father and mother had beaten her, she hadn't accepted. She kept saying, "But is there a dearth of men?" But Davoud still loved her, and this counted as the best memory of his youth. Even now, wittingly or unwittingly, he mostly wandered here, and the past memories would become fresh again before his eyes. He was disappointed in everything. Mostly he went for walks alone and kept aloof from crowds because he suspected that everyone who laughed or talked quietly to his friend was talking about him, was making fun of him. With his brown staring eyes and fierce attitude he would laboriously move his neck and the upper half of his body and would pass on looking down contemptuously. When he went out all his senses were attuned to others, all the muscles of his face were tense. He wanted to know other people's opinion about him.

He was passing slowly by the side of a gutter and sometimes he stirred the water with the end of his stick. His thoughts were frenzied and distressed. He saw a white dog with long hair who lifted its head because of the sound of his stick hitting against a rock, and it looked at him as if it was sick or on the verge of death. It couldn't move from its place and once again its head dropped to the ground. He stooped down with difficulty. In the light of the moon their eyes met. A strange thought occurred to him: he felt that this was the first time that he had seen a simple and sincere look and that both of them were unfortunate and unwanted, rejected and useless, driven out from human society. He wanted to sit by this dog, who had dragged its misery out of the city and had hidden it from men's eyes, and take it in his embrace, press its head to his protruding chest. But he thought that if someone passed by here and saw, he would make fun of him even more. It was dusk. He passed by the Yusef Abad Gate. He looked at the circle of the incandescent moon, which in the calm of this sorrowful and tender evening had come up from the shore of the sky. He looked at the half-built houses, the piles of bricks which they had heaped on each other, the sleepy background of the city, the tin roofs of the houses, the blue-coloured mountain. Grey blurred curtains were passing before his eyes. No one could be seen, near or far. The distant muffled sound of singing was coming from the other side of the gully.

He lifted his head with difficulty. He was tired, extremely sad and unhappy, and his eyes burned. It was as if his head was too heavy for his body. Davoud left his walking stick by the side of the ditch and went over to the other side. Without intending to, he walked towards the rocks and sat down beside the road. Suddenly he became aware of a woman in a *chador* who was sitting near him beside the ditch. His heartbeat speeded up. Suddenly the woman turned her head and said with a smile, "Hushang! Where were you until now?" Davoud was surprised by the women's easy tone, surprised that she had seen him and hadn't been startled. It was as if he had been given the world. From her question it was evident that she wanted to talk with him, but what was she doing here at this time of night? Was she decent? Maybe she was in love. He took a chance, saying to himself, come what may, at least I've found someone to talk to, maybe she'll give me comfort. As if he had no control over his own tongue he said, "Miss, are you alone? I'm alone too. I'm always alone. I've been alone all my life."

His words weren't yet finished when the woman, wearing sunglasses, turned her head again and said, "Then who are you? I thought it was Hushang. Whenever he meets me, he tries to be funny."

Davoud didn't follow much of this last sentence, and he didn't understand what the women meant. But he didn't expect to, either. It had been a long time since any woman had talked to him. He saw this woman was pretty. Cold sweat streamed down his body. With difficulty he said, "No, miss, I'm not Hushang. My name is Davoud."

The woman answered with a smile, "I can't see you – my eyes hurt. Aha, Davoud!... Davoud the Hunch..." she bit her lip. "I'm Zibandeh. Don't you know me?" The curled hair which had covered her cheek moved, and Davoud saw the black mole at the corner of her lip. He throbbed from chest to throat. Drops of sweat rolled down his forehead. He looked around. No one was there. The sound of the singing had come near. His heart beat. It beat so fast that he couldn't breathe. Without saying anything, trembling from head to foot, he got up. Sobs choked his throat. He picked up his cane. With heavy steps rising and falling he went back the same way he had come and with a scratchy voice he whispered to himself, "That was Zibandeh! She didn't see me... Maybe Hushang was her fiancé or husband... Who knows? No... Never... I must close my eyes completely!... No, no I can't any more..."

He pulled himself along to the side of the same dog that he had seen, sat and pressed its head to his protruding chest. But the dog was dead.

Madeleine

(from *Buried Alive*)

(translated by Deborah Miller Mostaghel)

THE NIGHT BEFORE LAST I WAS THERE, in that small living room. Her mother and her sister were there too. The mother wore a grey dress and the daughters wore red dresses. The furniture, too, was of red velvet. I was resting my elbow on the piano and looking at them. There was silence except for the record player, from which was coming the stirring, sorrowful song of 'The Volga Boatman'. The wind roared; drops of rain beat against the window. The rain trickled, and with a constant sound blended with the melody of the record. Madeleine sat in front of me, thoughtful and gloomy, with her head leaning on her hand, listening. I looked stealthily at her brown, curly hair, bare arms, lively, childish neck and profile. This mood she was in struck me as being artificial. I thought she should always run, play and joke. I couldn't imagine that thoughts came to her or that it was possible for her also to be sad. I liked her childish and unrestrained attitude.

This was the third time that I had met her. I was introduced to her first at the seaside, but she had changed a lot since then. She and her sister had been wearing bathing suits. They had been carefree, with cheerful faces. She was childlike, mischievous, with shining eyes. It was near dusk. The waves of the sea, the music from the casino – I remembered everything. Now they wore the reddish purple dresses that were stylish this year, whose long skirts covered them to the ankles. They looked aged, apprehensive and seemed preoccupied with life's problems.

The record stopped, cutting off the distant, choked tune which was not unlike the waves of the sea. To liven things up, their mother spoke of school and the activities of her daughters. She said that Madeleine was a top student in art. Her sister winked at me. I smiled outwardly and gave short, perfunctory answers to their questions. But my thoughts were elsewhere. I was reviewing from the beginning my acquaintance with them. About two months ago, during the summer vacation just gone by, I had gone to the seaside with one of my friends. It was warm and crowded. We went to Trouville. In front of the railway station we took a bus. Through the forest beside the sea, our bus slipped among hundreds of cars, amid the sound of horns and the smell of oil and gasoline diffused in the air. The bus shook. Sometimes a view of sea appeared beyond the trees.

Finally we got off at one of the stations, Ville Royale. We passed through several alleys lined on each side with walls of stone and mud. We arrived at a small bun-shaped beach which had been built up on a rise by the sea. In the small square opposite the sea, a small casino could be seen. Around it, on the hills, houses and small villas had been built. Lower down, near the water, there was sand, and beyond that there were the waves. There, small children, alone or with their mothers, were busy playing ball or digging in the sand. A handful of men and women in bathing suits were swimming or were running into the water a little way and coming back. Others, on the sand, were sitting or lying in the sun. Old men lounged under striped umbrellas, reading newspapers and furtively watching the women. We, too, went in front of the casino, with our backs to the water, and sat on the long, wide edge of the sea wall. The sun was about to set. The tide was coming in, and the waves pounded on the shore. The sun sparkled on the waves in triangles of light. A big black ship could be seen going through the mist to the port of Le Havre. The air became slightly cool. The people near the water were coming up by and by. At this point my friend got up and shook hands with two girls who had come near us. He introduced me. They came and sat beside us on the high edge of the sea wall. Madeleine, with a large ball in her hand, sat beside me and started to talk as if she had known me for years. Sometimes she would get up and play with the ball in her hands and then she would come and sit beside me again. I'd tease her, grab the ball from her and then give it back to her and our hands would touch. Slowly we pressed each other's hands. Her hand had a delicate warmth. I glanced furtively at her breasts, her bare legs, her head and neck. I thought to myself how nice it would be to lay my head on her breast and sleep right there by the sea. The sun set and a pale moonlight gave this small, remote beach an intimate, family atmosphere. Suddenly a dance tune sounded from the casino. Madeleine, her hand in mine, started to sing an American dance tune, 'Mississippi'. I pressed her hand. From a distance the brightness of the lighthouse cast a half-circle of light on the water. The roar of the water hitting the shore could be heard. People's shadows were passing in front of us.

At this point, while these images were passing before my eyes, her mother came and sat at the piano. I moved aside. All at once I saw Madeleine get up like a sleepwalker. She went and searched through the sheet music scattered on the table, separated one piece, took it and put it in front of her mother, and came with a smile to stand near me. Her mother started to play the piano. Madeleine sang softly. It was the same dance tune that I had heard in the Ville Royale – the same 'Mississippi'.

Dash Akol

(from *Three Drops of Blood*)

(translated by Deborah Miller Mostaghel)

E VERYONE IN SHIRAZ KNEW that Dash Akol and Kaka Rostam hated each other. One day Dash Akol was squatting on a bench at the Domil Teahouse, his old hangout. Beside him was a quail cage with a red cover over it. With his fingertip he twirled a piece of ice around in a bowl of water. Suddenly Kaka Rostam came in. He threw Dash Akol a contemptuous look and with his hand in his sash went and sat on the opposite bench. Then he turned to the teahouse boy and said "S-s-son, bri-bring some tea."

Dash threw a look full of meaning at the boy, so that he became apprehensive and ignored Kaka's order. The boy took the dirty teacups out of a bronze bowl and dipped them into a bucket of water. Then one by one he dried them very slowly. A scratchy sound arose from the rubbing of the towel against the cups.

This snub made Kaka Rostam furious. Once again he yelled, "A-a-are you deaf? I-I-I'm talking to you!"

The boy looked at Dash Akol with an uncertain smile, and Kaka Rostam snarled, "D-d-devil take them. P-p-people who th-th-think they're so great will c-c-come tonight and p-prove it, if they're any g-g-good."

Dash Akol was whirling the ice around in the bowl, noticing the situation slyly. He laughed impudently, showing a row of strong white teeth shining beneath his henna-dyed moustache, and said, "Cowards brag, but pretty soon it will be evident who's the better man."

Everyone laughed. They didn't laugh at Kaka Rostam's stuttering, because they knew he stuttered, but because Dash Akol was very well known in the town. No "tough guys" could be found who hadn't tasted his blows. Whenever he would drink a bottle of double-distilled vodka in Nolla Ashaq's house and then take on all comers at the corner of Sare Dozak, he would be more than a match for Kaka Rostam. Even fellows much stronger than Kaka Rostam wouldn't dare to fight him. Kaka himself knew that he was not a match for Dash Akol, because he had been wounded twice at his hands, and three or four times Dash Akol had overpowered him and sat on his chest. Unluckily, several nights before, Kaka Rostam had seen the corner empty and had started boasting. Dash Akol arrived unexpectedly, like an avenging angel, and heaped insults on his head. Dash had said to him, "Kaka, you sissy, it seems you've been smoking too much opium... It's made you pretty high. You know what, you'd better stop this vile, dastardly behaviour. You're acting like a hoodlum, and you aren't a bit ashamed. This certainly is some kind of beggary that you've picked up as a business, I swear if you get really drunk like this again I'll smoke your moustache off. I'll split you in half."

Then Kaka Rostam had set off with his tail between his legs. But he developed a grudge against Dash Akol, and he was always looking for an excuse to take revenge.

Everybody in Shiraz liked Dash Akol, because, although he challenged any man at the corner of Sare Dozak, he didn't bother women and children. On the contrary, he was kind to people, and if some miserable fellow bothered a woman or

threatened someone, he wouldn't be able to get away from
Dash Akol in one piece. Dash Akol was usually seen to help
people. He was benevolent, and if he was in the mood he would
even carry people's loads home for them. But he couldn't stand
to be second to anyone, especially not to Kaka Rostam, that
opium-smoking, phoney busybody.

Kaka Rostam sat infuriated by this contempt which had been
shown him. He chewed his moustache, and he was so angry
that if someone had stabbed him, he wouldn't have bled. After
a few minutes, when the volley of laughter died down, everyone
was still except the teahouse boy. Wearing a collarless shirt,
nightcap, and black twill trousers, the boy held his hand over
his stomach, and writhed with laughter, nearly worn out. Most
of the others were laughing at his laughter. Kaka Rostam lost
his temper. He reached out and picked up the crystal sugar bowl
and threw it at the boy. But the sugar bowl hit the samovar,
which rolled off the bench to the floor together with the teapot
and broke several cups. Then Kaka Rostam got up, his face
flushed with anger, and went out of the teahouse.

The teahouse keeper examined the samovar with a distressed
air and said, "Rostam, the legendary hero, had only one suit
of armour. All I had was this dilapidated samovar." He uttered
this in a sad tone, but because of the allusion to Rostam,
people laughed even harder. The teahouse keeper attacked the
boy in frustration, but Dash Akol with a smile reached into his
pocket, pulled out a bag of money, and threw it to him.

The teahouse keeper picked up the bag, hefted it, and smiled.

At this point a man with a velvet vest, loose trousers, and a felt
hat rushed headlong into the teahouse. He glanced around, went
up to Dash Akol, greeted him, and said, "Hajji Samad is dead."

Dash Akol raised his head and said, "God bless him!"

"But don't you know he's left a will?"

"I don't live off the dead. Go and tell somebody who does."

"But he's made you the executor of his will."

As if these words awakened Dash Akol from his indifference, once again he looked the man up and down, rubbing his hand on his forehead. His egg-shaped hat was pushed back, showing his two-toned forehead, half of which was burnt brown by the sun and half of which had remained white from being under the hat. Then he shook his head, took out his inlaid pipe, slowly filled it with tobacco, tapped it with his thumb, lit it, and said, "God bless Hajji now that it's over, but that wasn't a good thing he did. He's thrown me into a sea of trouble. Well, you go, I'll come after."

The person who had entered was Hajji Samad's foreman. Taking long steps, he went out of the door. Dash Akol frowned in thought. He puffed on his pipe reflectively. Somehow it was as if dark clouds had suddenly stifled the cheerful, happy atmosphere of the teahouse. After Dash Akol emptied the ashes from his pipe he got up, gave the quail cage to the boy, and went out of the teahouse.

When Dash Akol entered Hajji Samad's courtyard, the reading of the Koran was over. There were only a few readers left and some men to carry the Koran who were grumbling over their fee. After waiting a few minutes by the fountain, he was taken into a big room whose sash windows opened onto the courtyard. Hajji's wife came and stood behind a curtain, and after the usual greetings and pleasantries Dash Akol sat on a mattress and said, "Ma'am, may God keep you in good health. May God bless your children." The woman said in a choked voice, "On the night that Hajji fell ill, they brought His Eminence the Imam* Jomeh to pray at his bedside, and in the presence of all Hajji announced you as the executor of his will. Probably you knew Hajji from before?"

"We met five years ago on a trip to Kazeroon."

"Hajji, God bless him, always said that if there was only one real man, it was Dash Akol."

"Ma'am, I like my freedom more than anything else, but now that I've been obliged by the dead, I swear by this ray of light that if I don't die first, I'll show those cabbage heads."

Then as he lifted his head, he saw from between two curtains a girl with a glowing face and alluring black eyes. They had looked at each other for not even a moment when the girl, as if she felt embarrassed, dropped the curtain and stepped back. Was she pretty? Perhaps. In any case her alluring eyes did their work and Dash Akol was ravished. He blushed and dropped his head.

It was Marjan, the daughter of Hajji Samad. She had come out of curiosity to see the famous Dash Akol, who was now her guardian.

The next day Dash Akol began to work on Hajji's affairs. With an expert in second-hand goods, two men from the neighbourhood, and a secretary, he carefully registered and inventoried everything. Whatever was extra he put in the storeroom, locking and sealing the door. Whatever would bring anything he sold. He had the deeds of Hajji's lands read to him. He collected what was owed to Hajji and paid his debts. All of these things were accomplished in two days and two nights. On the third night, tired and worn out, Dash Akol was passing near Sayyed Haj Qarib Square on his way home. On the way he ran into Imam Qoli Chalengar, who said, "Now it's been two nights that Kaka Rostam has been expecting you. Last night he was saying that you left him up in the air. He says that you've got a taste of high life and you've forgotten your promise."

Dash Akol remembered well that three days before in the Domile Teahouse Kaka Rostam had challenged him, but since he knew what kind of man Kaka was and knew that Kaka had plotted with Imam Qoli to shame him, he didn't pay any attention and continued on his way. On the way all his senses were concentrated on Marjan. No matter how much he wanted to drive her face away from before his eyes, it would take shape more firmly in his imagination.

Dash Akol was a big man of thirty-five, but he wasn't good looking. Seeing him for the first time would dampen anyone's spirits, but if someone sat and talked to him or heard the stories about his life which people were always telling, he would become fascinated. When one didn't consider the sword scars going from left to right, Dash Akol had a noble and arresting face: hazel eyes, thick black eyebrows, broad cheeks, narrow nose, black beard and moustache. But his scars spoilt everything. On his cheeks and forehead were the marks of sword wounds which had healed badly, leaving raw-looking furrows on his face. Worst of all, one of them had drawn down the corner of his left eye.

His father was one of the great landowners of Fars Province. When he died all his property went to his only son. But Dash Akol took life easy and spent money recklessly. He didn't consider wealth and property important. He passed his life freely and generously. He had no ties in life, and he generously gave all his possessions to the poor and empty-handed. Either he would drink vodka and raise hell in the streets or he would spend his time getting together with a handful of friends who had become his parasites. All his faults and virtues were confined to these activities, but the thing which seemed surprising was that the subject of love had never come up for him. Although several times his friends had talked him into coming to bull sessions, he never took part in the conversation. But from the day he became Hajji Samad's executor and saw Marjan, his life changed completely. On the one hand he considered himself obliged to the dead and under a burden of responsibility; on the other hand, he had lost his heart to Marjan. But the responsibility weighed on him more than anything. He had wasted his own wealth and had also squandered part of his own inheritance through carelessness. Now every day from early morning when he awoke he thought only of how to increase the income of Hajji's estate. He moved Hajji's wife and children into a smaller house. He rented out their private house. He brought in a tutor for the children. He invested their money, and from morning until night he was busy chasing after Hajji's affairs.

From this time on Dash Akol completely gave up prowling around at night and daring others to fight. He lost interest in his friends, and he lost his old enthusiasm. But all the men who had been his rivals, incited by the mullahs who felt themselves cheated of Hajji's wealth, found a little legroom for themselves, and they made sarcastic remarks about Dash Akol. Talk of him filled the teahouses and other gathering places. At the Pachenar Teahouse people often discussed Dash Akol, saying things like, "Speaking of Dash Akol – he doesn't dare any more, his tongue's frozen. That dirty dog. They really got rid of him.

Now he sniffs around Hajji's door. Seems like he is scrounging something. Now when he comes around Sare Dozak he drops his tail between his legs and slinks by."

Kaka Rostam, carrying a grudge in his heart, stuttered, "Th-th-there's no f-f-f-fool like an old fool. The guy has f-f-fallen in love with Ha-Ha-Hajji Samad's daughter! He's sh-sh-sh-sheathed his butter knife! He's thrown d-d-dirt in people's eyes. He m-m-made a false r-r-r-reputation for himself and got to be Hajji's e-e-e-executor. He'll steal them all b-b-b-blind. Lucky d-d-dog."

People no longer put stock in Dash Akol and no longer held him in awe. In every place he entered, people were whispering in each other's ears and making fun of him. Dash Akol heard this talk here and there, but he didn't show it and didn't pay any attention, because his love of Marjan had grown so strong within him and had so upset him that he had no thought except for her.

At night he would drink alcohol in his distress, and he had a parrot to amuse himself with. He sat in front of the cage and told his grievances to the parrot. If Dash Akol asked for Marjan's hand, her mother would gladly give Marjan to him. But on the other hand, he didn't want to become tied to a wife and child, he wanted to be free, just as he had been raised. Besides, he suspected that if he married the girl who had been put into his keeping, he would be doing something wrong. What was worse than everything else was that every night he would look at his drooping eye, and in a rough tone he would say aloud, "Maybe she doesn't like me; maybe she'll find a handsome young husband. No, it's not a manly thing to do... She's fourteen years old and I'm forty... But what shall I do?

This love is killing me. Marjan... You've killed me... Who shall I tell... Marjan... Leaving you has destroyed me!"

Tears welled up in his eyes and he drank glass after glass of vodka. Then, with a headache, he fell asleep in his chair.

But at midnight, when the city of Shiraz, with its twisting alleys, exhilarating gardens, and purple wines, went to sleep; when the quiet, mysterious stars were winking at each other in the pitch black sky; when Marjan with her rosy cheeks was breathing softly in her bed and the day's events were passing before her eyes, it was at that time that the real Dash Akol, the natural Dash Akol, with all his feelings, fancies, and desires, with no embarrassment, would come out of the shell which the etiquette and customs of society had built around him. It was then that he would come out of the thoughts which had been inculcated in him since childhood; and freely he hugged Marjan tight and felt her slow heartbeat, her fiery lips and her soft body, and he covered her cheeks with kisses. But when he leapt awake he would curse himself, and curse life, and like a madman he paced up and down his room. He muttered to himself, and in order to kill the thought of love in him, he would busy himself for the rest of the day with running after and taking care of Hajji's affairs.

But an important event, one which should not have happened, took place: a husband appeared for Marjan, and what a husband, who was both older and less attractive than Dash Akol. At this event Dash Akol didn't turn a hair. On the contrary, with extreme contentment he busied himself preparing the trousseau, and he organized a fitting celebration for the wedding night. He took Hajji's wife and children to their own home again and designated the large room with sash windows for entertaining the male guests. All the important people, the merchants and dignitaries of Shiraz, were invited to the festivities.

That day at five in the afternoon, when the guests were sitting around the room cheek by jowl on the priceless carpets and rugs and the big wooden trays of sweets and fruit had been placed in front of them, Dash Akol entered, with his old rough appearance and manner, but with his unruly hair combed and wearing new clothes, a striped robe, a sword belt, a sash, black trousers, cloth shoes, and a hat. Three other people entered behind him with notebooks and pads. All the guests looked him up and down. With long steps Dash Akol went up to His Eminence the Imam Jomeh, and said, "Sir, Hajji, God bless him, made his will and threw me into a sea of trouble for seven years. His youngest son, who was five years old, is now twelve. These are the accounts of Hajji's property." He pointed to the three people standing beside him. "Until today, whatever has been spent, including the expenses of this evening, I have paid from my own pocket. From now on I will go my way, and they will go theirs!"

When he reached this point he stifled a sob. Then without adding anything or waiting for an answer, he dropped his head and with his eyes full of tears went out of the door. In the alley he breathed a sigh of relief. He felt that he had become free and that the burden of responsibility had been lifted from his shoulders, but his heart was broken. He took long, careless steps. As he walked, he recognized the house of the Jewish vodka maker, Mullah Ashaq. Without hesitation he went down the damp steps and entered an old, sooty courtyard which was surrounded by small dirty rooms with windows full of holes like beehives and whose fountain was covered with moss. The smells of fermentation, of feathers, and of old cellars diffused in the air. Mullah Ashaq, skinny, with a dirty nightcap, a goatee beard and covetous eyes, came forwards, laughing artificially.

Dash Akol said gloomily, "By your moustache, give me a bottle of the best to refresh my throat." Mullah Ashaq nodded his head, went down the cellar steps, and after a few minutes came up with a bottle. Dash Akol took the bottle from his hand. He hit the neck against a pillar. The top broke off, and he drained half the bottle. Tears gathered in his eyes, he stifled a cough, and wiped his mouth on the back of his hand. Mullah Ashaq's son, who was a sallow, scrawny, dirty child, with a swollen stomach, an open mouth, and snot hanging on his upper lip, was looking at Dash Akol. Dash Akol put his finger under the lid of a salt cellar which was on a shelf in the courtyard and laid salt on his tongue.

Mullah Ashaq came forwards, clapped Dash Akol on the shoulder and said, "That's the way, fellow." Then he fingered the material of Dash Akol's clothes and said, "What's this you're wearing? This robe is out of style. Whenever you don't want it, I'll pay a good price."

Dash Akol laughed dejectedly. He took some money from his pocket, put it in the palm of Mullah Ashaq's hand, and left the house. It was near dusk. His body was warm, his thoughts were distressed, and his head ached. The alleys were still damp from the afternoon rain and the smell of mud walls and orange blossoms mingled in the air. Marjan's face, her rosy cheeks, black eyes and long lashes, the curly hair on her forehead appeared vaguely and mysteriously before Dash Akol's eyes. He remembered his past life; memories passed before him one by one. He remembered the outing he had made with his friends to the tombs of Saadi and Baba Kouhi. Sometimes he smiled, sometimes he frowned. The one thing he was certain of was that he was afraid of his house – that the state of affairs had become intolerable for him. It was as if his heart had been torn out. He wanted to go far away. He thought that again tonight he would drink and tell his troubles to the parrot! All of life for him had become small, futile, and meaningless. Meanwhile he remembered a poem. Out of boredom he murmured it: "I envy the parties of prisoners / Whose refreshments are chain links." He remembered another poem and recited it a little louder.

> My heart has gone crazy, oh wise ones.
> The crazed man is bound with a chain.
> Bind my heart with a chain of prudence,
> Or its madness will break out again.

He recited this poem in a sad hopeless tone, but as if he had lost interest, or was thinking of something else, he fell silent.

It had grown dark when Dash Akol reached Sare Dozak. This was the same square where in the old days Dash Akol would take on all comers, and no one had dared tangle with him. Without intending it, he went and sat on a stone bench in front of a house. He took out his pipe, filled it, and drew on it slowly. It occurred to him that this place was more run down than it had been; the people looked different to him, just as he himself had changed and broken down. He saw things hazily. His head ached. Suddenly a dark shadow appeared coming towards him, saying, as it approached, "Even the d-d-dark night knows who's the b-b-better man."

Dash Akol recognized Kaka Rostam. He stood up, put his hands on his hips, spat on the ground, and said sarcastically, "God damn your coward father. You think you're the better man? You haven't even learnt where to pee."

Kaka Rostam laughed mockingly, came close, and said, "I-i-i-it's a long t-t-time we haven't seen you around here. Tonight there's a w-w-w-wedding at Hajji's house. Didn't they let y-y-you—"

Dash Akol interrupted, "God knew what he was doing when he gave you only half a tongue. I'm going to take the other half tonight." He pulled out his sword. Kaka Rostam reached for his sword also. Dash Akol drove his sword into the ground, folded his arms across his chest and said, "Now I dare you to pull that sword out of the ground."

Kaka Rostam suddenly attacked him, but Dash Akol hit the back of his hand so hard that the sword flew out of his grasp. At the sound, a handful of passers-by stopped to watch, but no one dared to come forwards or try to separate them.

Dash Akol said with a smile, "Go on, pick it up, but hold it tighter this time, because tonight I want to settle our accounts!"

Kaka Rostam came forwards with clenched fists and they grappled with each other. They rolled on the ground for half an hour, sweat dripping from their faces, but neither one gained the upper hand. In the middle of the struggle Dash Akol's head hit hard against the cobblestones. He nearly lost consciousness. Kaka Rostam, too, despite the murder in his heart, felt that his power of resistance was exhausted, but suddenly his glance fell on Dash Akol's sword, which was within his reach. With all his strength he pulled it out of the ground and drove it into Dash Akol's side. He pushed it so hard that neither could move any more.

The onlookers ran forwards and lifted up Dash Akol with difficulty. Drops of blood splattered on the ground. He clutched his wound, dragged himself next to the wall a few steps, and fell to the ground again. Then they raised him and carried him to his house.

The next morning, as soon as the news of Dash Akol's wounding reached Hajji Samad's house, Vali Khan, Hajji's oldest son, went to see how he was. When he reached Dash Akol's bedside, he saw him stretched out deathly pale in bed. Bloody froth had bubbled from his lips, and his eyes had darkened. He breathed with difficulty. In a state of torpor, Dash Akol recognized Vali Khan. In a half-choked, trembling voice he said, "In the whole world... that parrot... was all I had... please... please... give it to..."

He fell silent again. Vali Khan took out his handkerchief and wiped the tears from his eyes. Dash Akol lost consciousness, and an hour later he died.

Everybody in Shiraz cried for him.

That afternoon, Marjan placed the parrot's cage in front of her and sat looking at the parrot's colourful wings, its hooked beak, and its round, lustreless eyes. Suddenly the parrot, in a rough, scratchy tone, said, "Marjan... Marjan... You killed me... Whom shall I tell... Marjan... Loving you... has destroyed me."

Tears streamed from Marjan's eyes.

The Man Who Killed His Passions

(from *Three Drops of Blood*)

(translated by Deborah Miller Mostaghel)

The passions are dragons,
Perhaps sleeping, but never slain,
In the proper circumstances,
They'll rise up again.

Mowlavi*

REGULARLY EVERY MORNING, Mirza Hoseinali, wearing a black buttoned-up frock, pressed trousers and shiny black shoes, came walking steadily out of one of the alleys near Sar Cheshme.* He passed in front of the Sepas-Selar Mosque, went through Safi Ali Shah Alley, and went to school.

He didn't look around as he walked. It was as if his thoughts were directed towards something special. He had a pure, dignified face, with small eyes, prominent lips and a brown moustache. His beard was always trimmed. He was very humble and quiet.

Occasionally around sunset, the thin figure of Mirza Hoseinali could be discerned from afar outside the city gate, walking very slowly, hands linked behind his back, head down, back bent. Sometimes he would stand and whisper to himself for a while, as if he were searching for something.

The principal of the school where he taught and the rest of the teachers neither liked nor disliked him. Perhaps he made a mysterious impression on them. In contrast to the teachers, the students were satisfied with him, because he had never been seen to be angry or to beat anybody. He was very calm and reserved, and he behaved in a pleasant manner towards the students. Because of this he was known for lacking authority, but in spite of that reputation, the students were polite in his class and were apprehensive of him. The only person with whom Mirza Hoseinali had a warm relationship and with whom he sometimes had discussions was Sheikh Abelfazl, the teacher of Arabic, who was very pretentious. Sheikh Abelfazl was always talking about the degree to which he had mortified his flesh and the wondrous things he had done. For a long time he had been in a state of religious rapture, and he hadn't spoken for several years. He saw himself as a philosopher, heir to Avicenna, Mowlavi, and Galen. But in reality he was one of those selfish phoney mullahs who liked to show off his knowledge. In any conversation that arose he would immediately insert a proverb or an esoteric Arabic sentence, or he would cite a poem as evidence, and then with a victorious smile he would look for the effect of his words in the faces of those present. And it was strange that Mirza Hoseinali, the teacher of Persian and history, apparently modern and without pretension, should choose Sheikh Abelfazl of all people to be his friend. Sometimes he would take the Sheikh to his home, and sometimes he went to the Sheikh's house.

Mirza Hoseinali was from an old family, and was a knowledgeable, well-rounded man. People were impressed that he had graduated from the Darolfonoun. For two or three years he had travelled with his father on duty, but when he returned from the last trip he stayed in Tehran and chose the teaching profession, so that, even though he knew it was a difficult responsibility, he would have time to turn his attention to his own interest.

From childhood, from the time a mullah started to come to their house to tutor him and his brother, Mirza Hoseinali showed a special talent for learning the literature, poetry, and philosophy of the Sufis. He even wrote poetry in the Sufi style. Their teacher, Sheikh Abdollah, who considered himself a Sufi, paid special attention to his pupil. He indoctrinated him with mystic thoughts and described the mystic state for him. He had especially told him about the distinguished position of Mansour Hallaj, who by the mortification of his passions had elevated himself to such a position that even on the gallows he refused to stop saying "I am God". This story seemed very poetic to young Mirza Hoseinali. And finally one day Sheikh Abdollah declared to him, "With the nature that I see in you, if you follow the Way of Truth, you will attain excellence." Mirza Hoseinali always remembered this thought. It took root and grew in his brain, and he always wished for a suitable time to begin devoting himself to asceticism. Later he and his brother entered the Darolfonoun School. There also, Mirza Hoseinali did very well in Arabic and literature. Mirza's younger brother was not of the same mind. He would mock him and say, "These fancies will only make you fall behind in life and give up your youth for nothing." But in his heart Mirza Hoseinali laughed at his brother's words; he considered his brother's thoughts materialistic and small, and he became even more stubborn in his determination. On account of this difference of opinion they separated after their father's death.

Something which reinforced Mirza's resolution was that on a recent trip to Kerjan he met a dervish* who, in the course of conversation, confirmed the words of his teacher, Sheikh Abdollah, and promised that if he should take up mysticism and discipline himself, he would reach a position of eminence. Thus it was that for five years Mirza Hoseinali had chosen seclusion and had closed the door to family and friends. He lived alone, and after his teaching, he would begin his main occupation at home.

His house was small and neat as a pin. He had an old housekeeper and an errand boy. As soon as he entered the door, he took his clothes off with care, hung them up, put on a long grey robe, and went into his library. He had allocated the largest room in the house for his library. At one corner beside the window a white mattress was spread. On it were two pillows. In front of it was a low table on which were several volumes, a pile of paper, a pen and an inkpot. The covers of the books on the table were worn. Many other books were stacked on shelves built into the wall.

The subject matter of these books was Gnosticism, mysticism, and ancient philosophy. His only recreation and pleasure was reading these books, and until midnight, behind the table under the oil lamp, he would pore over them and read. He would interpret them to himself and whatever seemed to him difficult or doubtful he would make a note of and later discuss with Sheikh Abelfazl. Not because Mirza Hoseinali was unable to understand their meaning: on the contrary, he had passed many of the spiritual stages and could penetrate hair-splitting ideas and the fine points of some Sufi poems better than Sheikh Abelfazl. He let these things inside, and he had created within himself a world beyond the material world. This had become a cause of egotism, because he considered himself to be superior to others, and he had complete faith in this superiority.

Mirza Hoseinali knew that there existed a secret in the world which the great Sufi had discovered, and it was evident to him that to begin the search he would need a preceptor, someone who would guide him. Sheikh Abdollah had told him, and he would read, that "because the initiate's thoughts are scattered at the beginning, he should concentrate on the teacher in order to collect his thoughts."

Thus it was that after searching a great deal he found Sheikh Abelfazl, even though he was not to Mirza's taste and knew nothing except for how to pass judgement. Whenever the Sheikh encountered something difficult, he would say that it was too soon and he would explain it later, as if he were working with a child. In the end the only thing that Sheikh Abelfazl recommended to Mirza was to kill his passions. The Sheikh considered this the beginning of everything. In other words, by means of asceticism one could prevail over the senses, and the Sheikh delivered detailed lectures full of *hadith** which he had prepared about killing the passions. Among the things he said was: "Your worst enemy is inside you". Another was: "Your fight is with your passions". He quoted Chadi, who said: "Whoever kills his passions is a crusader". He also quoted the poem:

> If the self can't be contained
> It must somehow be restrained;
> The fatal sword of ignorance
> Should be sheathed in continence.

Another one he liked was:

> To kill the passions should be our delight,
> Man's highest honour is winning that fight.

Among other things which Sheikh Abolfazl preached there was this: "The seeker of the Truth should hold in contempt wealth, position, splendour, power and pomp, because the greatest wealth and pleasure is the subduing of the passions." He quoted Maktabi, who said:

> Win the battle over self,
> And attain eternal wealth.

And he said, "Know, oh friend of the Way, that if you are seduced once by the bodily senses, you have walked in the valley of death, just as Sanai says:

> Keep your passions under control
> If you would have them your slave.
> Give them control and they will send
> A thousand like you to the grave.

"And as Sheikh Saadi says:

> If you help a man attain his ends
> He'll help you achieve your desire.
> The passions are different: foes, not friends.
> Instead of helping, they'll rule you entire.

"And learned men of the Way have considered the passions as a vicious dog which must be bound by the chain of self-discipline and which one must avoid letting free. But the disciple must not become proud and reveal hidden secrets to the uninitiated. He should consult the preceptor at every difficulty. As Khawje Hāfiz, God bless him, says:

> 'This gallows was erected,' someone said,
> 'For giving secrets. Now the giver's dead.'"

Mirza Hoseinali had always had a special interest in asceticism and Indian philosophy, and he wished to go to India to pursue his studies. He wanted to meet members of Indian religious sects and learn their secrets. Thus he was not surprised by the suggestion that he should control his passions. On the contrary, he greeted it wholeheartedly, and the same day, when he returned home, he opened his handwritten copy of the *Masnvai** to find an omen. As luck would have it, these lines came up:

> The passions do not keep their promises
> For breaking faith they should be doomed to die.
> The passions and their purpose both are base
> And do their best themselves to justify.
>
> In this society the passions fit
> As aptly as the corpse fits in the grave.
> The passions may be shrewd and full of wit
> But to the temporal world they are as slaves.
>
> Since in no afterlife do they have a part,
> Leave them for dead. But God, who can't despise,
> Can make his inspiration touch their heart –
> From lifeless dust a being will arise.

This augury became the reason that Mirza Hoseinali decided definitely to spend all his effort in overcoming his natural instincts and devoting himself to asceticism. At first, the more profoundly he studied Sufi books, the more emphasis he put on this struggle. In the *Treatise of the True Light* it was written:

> Oh master! Discipline yourself for some time
> and occupy your passions in this endeavour,
> until your false ideas leave and in their
> place comes the truth.

In the *Conzelor Romus* of Mir Hoseini he read:

> Destroy the passions, and their power break,
> As you would destroy a vile snake.

In the book of Marsad ol'Bad it was written:

> Know that when the initiate starts the struggle on the path of
> asceticism and the purification of the heart, the way to the Kingdom
> of Heaven appears to him; and at every stage secrets will unfold
> themselves to him befitting his state.

And in the poetry of Naser Khosro he read:

> There stands a dragon over your treasure,
> Slay it, and find sorrow turns to pleasure.
> To appease it, as the coward tries,
> Forfeits claim to that endless prize.

All of these threatening verses full of fear and hope, the writing
of which had worn out countless pens, left little doubt in Mirza
Hoseinali that the first step towards the goal was the killing
of the devilish and animal passions, passions which prevented
mankind from reaching the truth. Mirza Hoseinali wanted
to purify his passion both through thought and reason and
through rigour and struggle. Approximately a week of this
passed, but then he began to be discouraged. The reason for
this loss of hope was doubt and suspicion, especially after
becoming involved with such poems as these by Hāfiz:

> Seek not the mystery of the universe,
> Rather tell tales of musicians and wine.
> For solving the riddle of our existence
> Requires a wisdom which no one can find.
> Enjoy each pleasant note that comes along,
> For no one knows the ending of life's song.

Although Mirza Hoseinali knew that words such as "wine", "cupbearer", "tavern", "wine seller", and so on are mystical terminologies, still, in spite of this explanation, some of Khayyam's quatrains were very difficult for him and left him confused. For example:

No one has seen Heaven and Hell, oh heart.
From there none has returned, news to impart.
Our hopes and fears are idle, for we have
Nothing except the names from which to start.

Or this quatrain:

Khayyam, if you are drunk with wine, rejoice,
Happy with the beloved of your choice.
Because the end of life is nothingness,
Be glad that end has not yet stilled your voice.

These masters invited one to pleasure, whereas he had forbidden himself all pleasures. This thought produced a bitter regret in him for his past life – that life in which he had given up so much and which he had made so difficult for himself. Even now his days were painfully spent seeking imaginary ideas! For twelve years he had been giving himself sorrow and affliction. Of pleasure, of the happiness of youth, he had no share, and now, too, he was empty-handed. This doubt and hesitation had turned all his thoughts into frightening shadows which followed him everywhere. Especially at night, when he turned and twisted in the cold bed. Alone, no matter how much he wanted to think about spiritual worlds, as soon as he fell asleep and his thoughts grew dim, a hundred demons would tempt him. How many times did he leap awake in fright and pour cold water on his head and face? The next day he would eat less, and at night he would sleep on straw, because Sheikh Abelfazl was always reciting this poem for him:

> The passions are like furies, hard to restrain,
> The more they get, the louder they complain.

Mirza Hoseinali knew that if he slipped, all his efforts would be wasted. Because of this, he intensified the torturing and mortification of his body. But the more he disciplined himself, the more the demon of lust tortured him, until he decided to go to his only friend and teacher, Sheikh Abelfazl, relate his problems, and get complete instructions from him.

It was near dusk when this thought occurred to him. He changed his clothes, buttoned his frock, and with measured steps set out for the home of the teacher. When he arrived he saw a man standing angrily in front of the house. He was shouting and tearing his hair and saying aloud, "Tell the Sheikh tomorrow I'll take him to court, he'll have to answer me there. He took my daughter to be a maid and ruined her and took all her money. Either he has to marry her, or I'll tear him apart. I've been dishonoured…"

Mirza Hoseinali couldn't bear it any more. He went forwards and said softly, "My good man, you've made a mistake. This is the house of Sheikh Abelfazl."

"That's the same villain I'm talking to, that same godless sheikh. I know he's home, but he's hiding. If he had nerve enough to come out I'd tear him limb from limb. For sure I'll see him tomorrow."

When Mirza Hoseinali realized that the case was serious, he moved off and went away slowly, but these words were enough to awaken him. Could it be true? Hadn't he made a mistake? Sheikh Abelfazl, who had been recommending to him before anything else to kill the passions, hadn't he himself been able to succeed in this endeavour? Had he slipped, or had he been fooling Mirza? It was very important that he should know this. If it were true, then had all the Sufis been like this, saying things which they didn't believe themselves? Or was this typical only of his teacher, and had he found a phoney among the prophets? If this were the case, could he go and tell all his spiritual tortures and his misfortunes and then have the Sheikh recite several Arabic sentences, give him harder instructions, and laugh at him in his heart? No, he had to clear things up this very night. For a while he paced crazily about the empty streets. Then he found himself in a crowd. Without thinking of anything in particular, he walked slowly among the same people he had considered inferior and materialistic. Inside himself he felt their materialistic, ordinary life, and he desired to walk among them for a long while, but he turned once more towards Sheikh Abelfazl's house, as if he had made a sudden decision. This time no one else was there. He knocked on the door and told his name to the woman who answered it. It was a little while before she opened the door for him. When he entered the room he saw Sheikh Abelfazl, with his squinting eyes, pockmarked face, and beard dyed the colour of plum jam, sitting on a carpet. He was telling his beads and several volumes of books were open beside him. As he saw Mirza he sprang to his feet, said "Ya Allah" and cleared his throat. In front of him was an open handkerchief on which was some stale bread and an onion. The sheikh looked at Mirza and said, "Come in. Partake of a humble supper with a poor man for the evening."

"We thank you very much… Excuse me if I'm causing trouble. I was just passing by. I only came—"

"Not at all, nonsense. My house is yours."

Mirza Hoseinali wanted to say something, but suddenly there arose the sound of shouts and uproar, and a cat leapt into the room with a cooked partridge in its mouth and a yelling woman on its tail. While Mirza Hoseinali watched, Sheikh Abelfazl suddenly threw his cloak at it, and wearing only a shirt and underpants, reached out and grabbed a club from the corner of the room and ran after the cat like a madman. Mirza Hoseinali forgot what he wanted to say and stood transfixed. After a quarter of an hour, panting and with a burning face, Sheikh Abelfazl entered the room and said, "You know, according to religious law, if a cat causes more than seven hundred dinars worth of damage it is a holy duty to kill it."

Mirza Hoseinali had no longer any doubt that this was a very ordinary man and that what the old man had charged was completely true. He got up and said, "Excuse me for bothering you… With your permission I'll leave."

Sheikh Abelfazl accompanied him to the door. When Mirza reached the alley he breathed a sigh of relief. Now it was proved for him. He recognized what kind of a man the Sheikh was and understood that this show and intrigue and trickery had been for his sake. He would eat a partridge, then, in order to fool people, he would set the table with dry bread and mouldy cheese or a withered onion to make himself seem pious. He instructed Mirza to eat nothing but an almond a day, while he himself got the maid pregnant and recited with relish this poem of Attar's:

Don't shed blood, like the wild beast, oh son,
That unbefitting food try hard to shun.
Be happy with a morsel or a grain,
Through fasting keep your passions bound in chains.
In fasting strive for excellence, and find
You'll achieve distinction from your kind.
Don't merely keep food from the passions hidden,
But refuse all thoughts on things forbidden.

It was dark. Once more Mirza Hoseinali entered the crowd of people. Like a lost child he walked aimlessly in the dusty, crowded streets. In the light of the streetlamps he looked at faces. All of them were dull and sad. His head felt empty, and there was a pressure in his heart which had grown unbearable. These people whom he had considered base, bound to their stomachs and lusts, gathering money, he now knew to be wiser and better than he, and he wished to be one of them. But he said to himself, "Who knows?" Maybe there was someone among them even worse off than he. Could he judge from appearances? Wouldn't a beggar on the street become happier with just one coin than the richest person? Meanwhile all the money in the world couldn't do anything to alleviate Mirza Hoseinali's pain. This time all the frightening nightmares which usually came to him were stronger and quicker in their attack. It occurred to him that his life had passed uselessly. Frenzied, confused memories of thirty years passed before him. He felt himself to be the most unfortunate and useless of creatures. Periods of his life appeared to him from behind dark clouds. Some episodes would shine out suddenly, then they would disappear. All of it was monotonous, tiring, and heart-rending. Sometimes a brief, vain happiness appeared like lightning flashing from a cloud. Everything seemed mean and useless to him: what a worthless struggle! What an absurd chase! He muttered to himself and bit his lips. His youth had been wasted in seclusion and darkness, without pleasure, without happiness, without love, weary of himself and others. How many people sometimes feel themselves more lost, more homeless than a bird which cries in the darkness of the night? He could no longer believe anything. This meeting of his with Sheikh Abelfazl had cost him dearly, because it had turned all his thoughts inside out. He was tired and thirsty, and a devil or a dragon had awakened in him which continually wounded and poisoned him. Now a car passed him, and in its lights his angry face, trembling lips and open, expressionless eyes were frighteningly illuminated. He was gazing into space, with a half-open mouth, as if he were laughing at something out of reach. He felt a pressure at the base of his skull which extended to his forehead and temples and caused wrinkles to appear between his eyebrows.

Mirza Hoseinali had felt pain beyond human endurance. He was acquainted with hopeless hours, with distress and misfortune, and he knew a kind of philosophical pain which doesn't exist for the mass of people. But now he felt himself immeasurably lost and alone. Life for him had become nothing but a mockery and a lie. He recited to himself, "What do I have to show for life? Nothing!"

This line from a poem drove him mad. Pale moonlight shone from behind the clouds, but he passed in the shadows. This moon, which previously had been so enchanting and mysterious for him and with whom he had communed during long hours outside the city gate, now seemed a cold, heartless and meaningless brightness. It angered him. He remembered the warm days, the long hours of study. He remembered his youth.

While other boys his age were busy with pleasure, he would spend the summer days dripping with sweat, studying Arabic grammar with other students. Then they would go to take part in discussions with their theology teacher, Sheikh Mohammad Taqi. Squatting in full gathered trousers, a bowl of ice water in front of him, he fanned himself, and if they made a mistake in one vowel sign of an Arabic word, he shouted and the veins of his neck stood out, as if the world were ending.

Now the streets were empty and the shops were closed. When he entered Allah-o-Duleh Street the sound of music aroused him. Over a blue door in the glow of an electric light he read the name "Maxim". Without hesitating he pushed back the curtain in the doorway, entered, and sat down at a table.

Since Mirza Hoseinali wasn't used to bars, having never set foot inside such places, he looked around in amazement. Cigarette smoke mingled with the smell of fried meat and cabbage. A short man with a heavy moustache and rolled-up sleeves stood behind the bar working out sums on an abacus. A row of bottles was arranged next to him. A bit further away, a fat woman was playing the piano, while a thin man beside her played the violin. Drunken customers with strange faces, some from Russia and the Caucasus, sat at the tables. Meanwhile, a rather pretty woman with a foreign accent came up to his table and said with a smile, "Won't you buy me a glass of wine, darling?"

"Certainly."

Without hesitation the woman called a waiter and ordered an alcoholic drink he had never heard of. The waiter placed a bottle of wine and two glasses in front of them. The woman poured the wine and offered it to him. Mirza Hoseinali reluctantly drank the first glass. His body grew warm, his thoughts mixed up. The woman plied him with glass after glass of alcohol. A mournful wailing came from the violin. Mirza Hoseinali felt free and peculiarly happy inside. He remembered all the praise and glorification of wine he had read in Sufi poetry. In the pitiless brightness of the light he saw crow's feet around the eyes of the woman seated next to him. After all his self-restraint, now his lot had become a yellow, sour-tasting wine and a heavily made-up, used, rough-haired woman. But he liked it that way. He felt he wanted to lower himself so that he could better destroy and ruin the being he had become through so much pain. He wanted to plunge from the purest, brightest thoughts into the darkest pleasure. He wanted to become a laughing stock, have people jeer at him. He wanted to find a route of escape for himself through madness. In this hour he knew himself capable of every kind of insanity. He murmured to himself:

> During this time of poverty
> Have pleasure, feast, and revelry.
> The philosopher's stone of existence
> Can turn a beggar to a Croesus.

Opposite him, the Russian woman laughed. Everything Mirza Hoseinali had read in Sufi poetry in praise of wine appeared before his eyes. He felt it all; he could read all the mysteries and secrets in the face of the woman who was sitting opposite him. At this time he was happy, because he had attained what he had wished for. Through the delicate mist of the wine he saw what he could never have imagined, what Sheikh Abelfazl couldn't even dream, what other people couldn't even conceive. Another world, full of secrets, became apparent to him. He understood that those who had forbidden this world had taken all their words and comparisons and allusions from it.

When Mirza Hoseinali got up to pay the bill he couldn't stand on his feet. He took out his wallet, gave it to the woman, and with his arm around her they went out of Maxim's. In the droshky, Mirza Hoseinali laid his head on the woman's breast. He breathed the smell of her powder. The world was whirling before his eyes. The lights were dancing. The woman sang a mournful song in her Russian accent.

The droshky stopped at Mirza Hoseinali's house. He entered the house with the woman, but he didn't go to the bed of straw where he usually slept. He took her to the white mattress which was spread in his library.

Two days passed, and Mirza Hoseinali didn't go to his work at school. On the third day was written in the newspaper: "Mister Mirza Hoseinali, a young, hardworking teacher, has committed suicide for unknown reasons."

Buried Alive

(from *Buried Alive*)

(translated by Deborah Miller Mostaghel)

I'M SHORT OF BREATH, tears pour from my eyes, my mouth tastes sour. I'm dizzy, my heartbeat is laboured, I'm exhausted, beaten, my body is loosened up. I have fallen without volition on the bed. My arms are punctured from injections. My bed smells of sweat and fever. I look at the clock on the small table beside the bed. It's Sunday, ten o'clock. I look at the ceiling of the room, from the middle of which hangs a light bulb. I look around the room. The wallpaper has a pink and red flower design. At intervals two blackbirds sit opposite each other on a branch. One of them has opened his beak as if he is talking to the other. This picture infuriates me, I don't know why, but whichever direction I turn, it's before my eyes. The table is covered with bottles, wicks, and boxes of medicine. The smell of burnt alcohol, the smell of a sickroom, has pervaded the air. I want to get up and open the window, but an overwhelming laziness has nailed me to the bed. I want to smoke a cigarette, but I have no desire for it. It hasn't been ten minutes since I shaved my beard, which had grown long. I came and fell in bed. When I looked in the mirror I saw that I'd become very wasted and thin. I walked with difficulty. The room is a mess. I'm alone.

A thousand kinds of astonishing thoughts whirl and circle in my brain. I see all of them. But to write the smallest feeling or the least passing idea I must describe my whole life, and that isn't possible. These reflections, these feelings, are the result of my whole life, the result of my way of life, of my inherited thoughts, of what I've seen, heard, read, felt, or pondered over. All these things have made up my irrational and ridiculous existence.

I twist in the bed. I jumble my memories together. Distressed and mad reflections press my brain. My head hurts, throbs. My temples are hot. I twist and turn. I pull the quilt over my eyes. I think – I'm tired. It would be good if I could open my head and take out all the soft, grey, twisted mass of my brain and throw it all away, throw it to a dog.

Nobody can understand. Nobody will believe. To somebody who fails at everything they say, "Go and lay your head down and die." But when even death doesn't want you, when even death turns its back on you, death which won't come and which doesn't want to come!…"

Everyone is afraid of death but I'm afraid of my persistent life. How frightening it is when death doesn't want one and rejects one! Only one thing consoles me. It was two weeks ago, I read in the paper that in Austria a person tried thirteen times to kill himself in different ways and each time he almost succeeded: he hanged himself and the rope broke, he threw himself in the river and they pulled him out, and so on… Finally, for the last time, when the house was empty he slashed his wrists with a kitchen knife, and this thirteenth time he died!

This gives me consolation!

No, no one decides to commit suicide. Suicide is with some people. It is in their very nature, they can't escape it. It is fate which rules, but at the same time it is I who have created my own fate. Now I can no longer escape it, but I cannot escape from myself.

Anyhow, what can be done? Fate is stronger than I am. What fancies I get! As I was lying in bed I wished to be a child. The same old nursemaid who used to tell me stories, pausing to swallow, would be sitting here at my head. I would be lying just like this, tired out in bed, and she would elaborately tell me stories and my eyes would slowly close. Now that I think about it, some of the events of my childhood come easily to mind. It is as if it were yesterday. I see that I'm not very far from my childhood. Now I see the whole of my dark, base, and useless life. Was I happy then? No, what a big mistake! Everyone supposes children are lucky. No, how well I remember. I was even more sensitive then. Then I was a phoney and a sly fellow. On the surface I may have laughed or played, but inside, the least biting remark or the smallest unpleasant, worthless occurrence would occupy my mind for long hours, and I would eat my heart out. By no means should a character like mine survive. The truth is with those who say that heaven and hell are inside a person. Some are born lucky and some unlucky.

I look at the red pencil stub with which I am making these notes in bed. It was with the same pencil that I wrote out the meeting place and the note to the girl whom I had just got to know. We went to the pictures together two or three times. The last time it was a talking film rather that a silent one. As part of the programme, a well-known Chicago singer sang 'Where is My Sylvia?' I enjoyed it so much that I closed my eyes to listen. I can still hear his powerful and captivating voice. The theatre rang with the sound. It seemed to me that he should never die. I couldn't believe that some day this voice might become silent. His mournful tone made me sad, even while I was enjoying it. Music played high and low. The quivering and wailing which came from the strings of the violin made it seem as if the bow were being drawn across my veins. The entire fabric of my body was impregnated with the music; it made me tremble and carried me down the path of imagination. In the darkness I fondled her breasts. Her eyes grew heavy. I felt strange. I remember it was a sad and poignant state which can't be expressed. I kissed her moist, fresh lips. She was blushing. We hugged each other. I didn't follow the film. I was playing with her hands, and she was pressing herself against me. Now it's as if it was a dream. Nine days have passed since we last parted. We had arranged that the next day I would bring her to my room. Her house was near the Montparnasse cemetery. That day I went to get her. I got off the metro at the corner. A cold wind was blowing and the weather was cloudy and overcast. I didn't know what happened, but I changed my mind. Not that she wasn't attractive, or that I didn't like her, but some power held me back. No, I didn't want to see her any more. I wanted to cut all ties with life. Without thinking I went into the cemetery. At the entrance the watchman had wrapped himself in a dark blue cape. An immense silence ruled there. I strolled slowly, staring at the gravestones, the crosses above them, the artificial flowers and grass next to or on top of the graves. I read the names of some of the dead. I regretted not being in their place. I thought to myself how fortunate all these people were!... I was envious of the dead whose bodies had disintegrated under the ground. Such a strong feeling of jealousy had never arisen in me before. It seemed to me that death is happiness and a blessing which one is not given lightly. I don't know exactly how much time passed. I stared, stunned. I had entirely forgotten the girl. I didn't feel the cold. It was as if the dead were closer to me than the living. I understood them better. I turned back. No, I didn't want to see that girl any more. I wanted to put everything aside. I wanted to give up and die. What ridiculous thoughts come to me! Maybe I'm babbling.

For several days I had been telling my fortune with cards. I don't know how it happened that I had come to believe in superstition, but I took my fortune-telling seriously. In other words I had nothing else to do; I couldn't do anything else. I wanted to gamble with my future. I made a wish to do away with myself. My wish would come true, the cards told me. One day I realized that I had been telling my fortune with cards for three and a half hours without stopping. First I shuffled, then I arranged one card face up on the table and five other cards face down in a row, then on the second card, which was face down, I put one card down, and so on. I had learnt this game in childhood and I was passing my time with it.

A week or so ago I was sitting in a café. Two people in front of me were playing backgammon. One of them, red-faced, bald-headed, a cigarette sticking out from under his hanging moustache, was listening with a dim-witted expression. The other said, "I've never won at gambling. I lose nine times out of ten." I stared at them dully. What did I want to say? I don't know. Anyway, I went out in the streets, walking mechanically. Several times it occurred to me to close my eyes and walk in front of a car, let its wheels pass over me, but it was a hard way to die. Even then, how could I be sure? Perhaps I might remain alive. This is the thought that drives me crazy. Thinking like this, I passed intersections and crowded places. In the middle of this hustle and bustle, this ringing of car horses' hooves, these wagons and automobile horns, this noise and commotion, I was alone. In the midst of millions of people it was as if I was sitting in a broken boat lost in the middle of the ocean. I felt as if I had been driven out in disgrace from the society of men. I saw that I wasn't made for life. I was reasoning with myself, walking monotonously. I would stop and look at the paintings in store windows. I would stare for a while. I regretted not having become a painter. It was the only job that I liked and that pleased me. I thought to myself that only in painting could I find a small consolation for myself. A postman was passing me and from behind a pair of glasses he was looking at the address on a letter. What did it make me think of? I don't know. Perhaps I remembered the postmen of Iran, the mailman who came to our house.

It was last night. I pressed my eyes together, but I couldn't fall asleep. Disjointed thoughts, exciting images appeared before my eyes. They weren't dreams because I hadn't yet fallen asleep. They were nightmares. I was neither asleep nor awake, but I saw them. My body was enervated, beaten, sick and heavy. My head hurt. These frightening nightmares kept passing before my eyes. Sweat dripped from my body. I saw a package of paper opening in the air. It dropped sheet by sheet. A group of soldiers passed, their faces invisible. The dark, terrifying night was filled with frightening and angry figures. When I wanted to close my eyes and give myself up to death, these startling images would appear. A volcanic circle whirling about itself, a corpse floating on a river, eyes looking at me from every direction. Now I remember well the crazy, angry figures swarming towards me. An old man with a bloody face had been tied to a column. He was looking at me, laughing; his teeth glittered. A bat was hitting my face with its cold wings. I was walking on a tightrope. Below it was a whirlpool. I was slipping. I wanted to scream. A hand was laid on my shoulder. An icy hand was pressing my throat. It seemed that my heart would stop. The groans, the sinister groans which came from the night's darkness, the faces cleaned of shadows – these things appeared and disappeared of their own accord. What could I do in the face of them? They were at once very near and very far. I wasn't dreaming them because I hadn't yet fallen asleep.

* * *

I don't know if I have fooled everyone or if I have been fooled, but there is one thought which is driving me crazy. I can't stop myself from laughing. Sometimes I choke with laughter. So far nobody has understood what's wrong with me. They've all been fooled! It's been a week that I've been pretending to be sick, or else I've caught a strange ailment. Willy-nilly I picked up a cigarette and lit it. Why do I smoke? I don't know myself. I hold the cigarette between two fingers of my left hand. I lift it to my lips. I blow the smoke into the air. This is also an ailment!

Now when I think about it my body trembles. It's no joke – for a week I tortured myself in various ways. I wanted to become ill. The weather had been cold for several days. First I went and turned the cold water on myself. I left the bathroom windows open. Now when I think of it, I get the creeps. I was gasping, my back and chest hurt, I told myself that now everything was over. The next day my chest would hurt badly, and I would be confined to bed. I would make it worse and then put an end to myself. The next morning when I woke up I didn't find the smallest sign of a cold. Again I took off my clothes. When it got dark I locked the door, turned off the light, opened the window and sat in the stinging cold. A sharp wind was blowing. I trembled violently. I could hear my teeth chattering. I looked outside. The people who were coming and going, their black shadows, the cars which were passing, all appeared small from the sixth floor of the building. I had surrendered my naked body to the cold, and I was writhing. At this point it occurred to me that I was crazy. I laughed at myself. I laughed at life. I knew that in this big playhouse of the world everybody plays in a certain way until his death arrives. I had taken up this role because I thought I would be carried off the stage sooner. My lips were dry. The cold burned my body. I warmed myself until I dripped with sweat, then all at once I stripped. All night I lay on the bed and trembled. I didn't sleep at all. I got a mild cold, but as soon as I took a nap the illness completely went away. I saw this didn't help either. For three days I didn't eat anything, and every night I stripped and sat in front of the window. I would make myself tired. One night until morning I ran on an empty stomach through the streets of Paris. I got tired and went and sat on the cold damp steps in a narrow alley. It was past midnight. A drunken worker reeled by. In the vague mysterious gaslight I saw a man and a woman passing and talking together. Then I got up and started to walk. Homeless wretches were sleeping on the street benches.

Finally I took to bed from weakness, but I wasn't sick. My friends came to see me. I made myself tremble in front of them, and I acted sick so well that they were sorry for me. They thought I would die the next day. I said my heartbeat was laboured. When they left the room I mocked them. I said to myself that there seemed to be only one thing in the world I could do well. I should have become an actor!...

How did I pull off the same trick on the doctors that I did on my friends? Everyone believed that I was truly sick. Whatever they asked, I said, "My heartbeat is laboured", because sudden death can only be attributed to a heart attack; otherwise, a simple chest pain could hardly be fatal.

This was a miracle. When I think of it, a strange feeling comes over me. I had been torturing myself for seven days. If, at the insistence of my friends, I had a cup of tea, I'd get better. It was frightening. The illness would completely go away. How badly I wanted to eat the bread alongside the tea, but I didn't do it. Every night I would say to myself that finally I had become bedridden. Tomorrow I wouldn't be able to get up. I went and brought the capsules that I had filled with opium. I put them in the drawer of the small table beside my bed so that when the illness had really thrown me and I couldn't move, I could bring them out and swallow them. Unfortunately the illness wouldn't come and didn't want to come. Once when I was obliged to eat a piece of bread with tea in front of one of my friends, I felt that I was well, all well. I became scared of myself, my own endurance frightened me. It's terrifying. It's unbelievable. I am in my right mind as I write this. I'm not speaking nonsense. I remember well.

What was this strength that had appeared in me? I saw that none of my plans had worked. I really had to become ill. Yes, the fatal poison is there in my bag, a swift poison. I remembered the rainy day that I bought it with lies and pretexts and a thousand difficulties, pretending to be a photographer. I gave a false name and address. Potassium cyanide, which I had read about in a medical book and whose signs I knew: convulsion, difficulty in breathing, agony when taken on an empty stomach. Twenty grams of it kills immediately or within two minutes. So that it wouldn't spoil in the air I had wrapped it in a chocolate wrapper, covered this with a layer of wax, and put it in a crystal bottle with a stopper. It was a hundred grams, and I kept it with me like a precious jewel. But fortunately I found something better than that – smuggled opium, and that in Paris! The opium which I had been after for such a long time, I found by accident. I had read that dying by taking opium is better and more wholesome than doing so by cyanide. Now I wanted to make myself really sick and then take the opium.

I unwrapped the potassium cyanide. I shaved off about two grams from the egg shaped ball and put it in an empty capsule: I sealed it with glue and swallowed it. Half an hour passed. I felt nothing. The surface of the capsule, which had touched the poison, tasted salty. I took out the cyanide again. This time I shaved off about five grams and swallowed the capsule. I went and lay down on the bed. I lay down as if I would never get up again!

This thought could drive anyone mad. No, I didn't feel anything. The killer poison didn't work on me! I'm still alive, and the poison is lying there in my bag. In the bed my breath comes with difficulty, but that's not the result of the drug. I have become invincible, invincible like those in legends. It's unbelievable, but I must go. It's futile. I feel rejected, useless, good for nothing. I should end things as soon as possible and go. This time it's not a joke. The more I think the more I see that nothing holds me to life, nothing and no one…

I remember it was the day before yesterday. I was pacing my room like a madman, going from one side to the other. The clothes hanging from the wall, the sink, the mirror in the cupboard, the picture on the wall, the bed, the table in the middle of the room, the books scattered on it, the chairs, the shoes placed under the cupboard, the suitcases in a corner of the room, passed continually before my eyes. But I wasn't seeing them, or else I wasn't concentrating. What was I thinking of? I don't know – I was pacing around to no purpose. Suddenly I came to myself. I had seen this frenzied pacing somewhere else and it had attracted my attention. I didn't know where, then I remembered. It was in the Berlin zoo that I had seen wild animals for the first time. Those that were awake in their cages walked in this same way, just like this. I too had become like those animals. Perhaps I even thought as they did. Inside I felt that I was like them. This mechanical walking around in a circle. When I bumped into the wall I naturally felt that it was a barrier, and turned around. Those animals do the same thing...

I don't know what I'm writing. The clock goes tick-tock right in my ear. I want to pick it up and throw it out of the window. This frightening sound that beats the passing of time into my head with a hammer!

For a week I had been making myself ready for death. I destroyed all the papers and things I had written. I threw away my dirty clothes so that when my things were being investigated nothing dirty would be found. I put on the new underwear I had bought, so that when they pulled me out of bed and the doctor came to examine me I would look presentable. I picked up a bottle of eau de cologne and sprinkled in the bed so it would smell good. But since none of my actions was like those of other people, I wasn't sure this time either. I was afraid of my diehard self. It was as if this distinction and superiority aren't given to one easily. I knew that nobody dies for free...

I took out the pictures of my relatives and looked at them. Each one of them appeared before me reflecting my own observations of them. I liked them and I didn't like them. I wanted to see them and I didn't want to. No, those memories were too bright before my eyes. I tore up the pictures; I was not attached to anything. I judged myself and saw I had not been a kind person. I had been created hard, rough, and weary. Maybe I wasn't always like this, but life and the passage of time have made me so. I have no fear of death. On the contrary, an illness, a special madness had appeared in me so that I was drawn by the magnetism of death. This isn't recent, either. I remembered a story from five or six years ago. In Tehran one early morning I went to Shah Abad Avenue to buy opium from a druggist. I put three tomans in front of him and said, "Two rials of opium."

Wearing a henna-dyed beard and a skullcap on his head and uttering holy words, he looked at me shrewdly, as if he were a physiognomist or could read my thoughts and said, "We don't have change."

I took out a two-rial coin to give him. He said, "No, we don't sell it at all." I asked why and he said, "You're young and ignorant. You might suddenly decide to eat the opium, God forbid." I didn't insist.

No, no one decides to commit suicide. Suicide is with some people. It's in their very nature. Yes, everyone's fate is written on his forehead; some people are born with suicide. I always mocked life, the world and its peoples all seemed like a game, a humiliation, something empty and meaningless. I wanted to sleep a dreamless sleep and not wake up again. But since people see suicide as a strange thing, I wanted to make myself ill, to become worn out and weak, and when everyone thought I was really sick, to eat the opium, so that people would say, "He fell ill and died."

* * *

I am writing in bed. It's three in the afternoon. Two people came to see me. They just left. I'm alone. My head is spinning, my body is comfortable and calm. There's a cup of milk and tea in my stomach. My body is loose, feeble, and feverish. I remembered a pretty tune I heard once on a record. I want to whistle it but I can't. I wished I could hear that record again. Right now I neither like life nor dislike it. I am alive but without will or desire; a superior power is holding me. I have been bound in the prison of life with steel chains. If I were dead they would take me to the Paris mosque. I would fall into the hands of those damn Arabs and I would die again. I am sick and tired of them. In any case it wouldn't make any difference to me. If they threw me into a sewer after I died it would be the same for me, I would rest easy. Only my family would cry and weep. They would bring my picture, praise me, all of the usual rot. All of this seems foolish and futile to me. Probably a few people would praise me, a few would criticize, but finally I would be forgotten. I am basically selfish and without charm.

The more I think about it the more I see that continuing this life is futile. I am a germ in the body of society, a harmful being, a burden on others. Sometimes my madness breaks out again. I want to go away, far away, to a place where I could forget myself, to go very far, for example go to Siberia, in wooden houses, under pine trees, with grey skies, snow, lots of snow, among the Mujiks, go and start my life over again. Or, for example, go to India, under the shining sun, in the dense forests, among strange people; go somewhere where no one knows me, nobody knows my language. I want to feel everything within myself. But I see I wasn't made for this. No, I'm lazy and good for nothing. I was born by mistake. I'm untouchable, driven from pillar to post. I have closed my eyes to all my plans, to love, to delight. I put everything aside. From now on I may be considered among the dead.

Sometimes I make big plans, I see myself worthy of every job and every thing. I say to myself, "Yes, only people who have washed their hands of life and have been disappointed in everything can accomplish great things." Then I say to myself, "What's the use? What purpose would it serve? Madness, everything is madness. No, do away with yourself, and leave your corpse to rot. Get lost, you weren't made for life. Leave off being philosophical, your existence has no value, you can't do anything." But I don't know why death was coy. Why didn't it come? Why couldn't I succeed with my plan and become comfortable? I had tortured myself for a week and this was the return I got! Poison didn't affect me. It's unbelievable; I can't believe it. I didn't eat, I tried to get pneumonia, I drank vinegar. Every night I thought I had come down with a severe case of tuberculosis, but in the morning when I got up my health was better than the day before. Who can I tell this to? I didn't even get a fever. But I haven't dreamt, nor have I taken narcotics. I remember everything well. No, it's unbelievable.

Now that I've written this down I am feeling a little better. It consoles me. It's as if a heavy burden has been lifted from my shoulders. How good it would be if everything could be written. If I could have made others understand my thoughts I would. No, there are feelings, there are things, which can't be conveyed to others, which can't be told, people would mock you. Everybody judges other people on the basis of his own values. Language, like man himself, is imperfect and incapable.

I'm invincible. Poison didn't affect me. I ate opium to no effect. Yes, I've become invincible. No other poison will affect me. Finally I realized that all my life was wasted. It was the night before last – I decided that before this mockery started to arouse suspicion, I would end it. I went and took out the capsules of opium from the drawer of the small table. There were three, approximately the size of an ordinary stick of opium all together. I picked them up. It was seven o'clock. I asked for tea from downstairs. They brought it and I drank it down. By eight, no one had come to see me. I closed the door from inside. I went and stood in front of the picture that was on the wall. I looked at it. I don't know what occurred to me, but in my eyes he was a stranger. I said to myself, "What relationship does this person have with me?" But I know that face. I had seen it a lot. Then I came back. I felt neither frenzy, nor fear, nor happiness. All the things I had done and the things I wanted to do and everything seemed to me to be useless and empty. Life seemed completely ridiculous. I looked around the room. Everything was in its place. I went in front of the cupboard mirror and looked at my flushed face. I half closed my eyes, opened my mouth a little bit and held my head bent like a dead man's. I said to myself, "Tomorrow morning I'll look like this. First, no matter how much they knock, no one will answer. Till noon they'll think I'm sleeping. Then they'll break the lock, enter the room, and see me like this." All of these thoughts passed like lightning through my mind. I picked up a glass of water. Coolly I told myself it was an aspirin, and swallowed the first capsule. The second and third also I swallowed hastily one after another. I felt a slight trembling inside me. My mouth smelled like opium. My heart beat a little faster. I threw the half-smoked cigarette in the ashtray. I took a scented wafer from my pocket and sucked it. I looked at myself once more in the mirror. I looked around the room – everything was in its place. I told myself that now everything was over. Tomorrow even Plato couldn't bring me back to life. I straightened the clothes on the chair by the bed. I pulled the quilt over myself. It had absorbed the smell of eau de cologne. I switched off the light and the room darkened. Part of the wall and the foot of the bed were slightly lit by the weak glow that came from the window. I had nothing else to do. Good or bad, I had brought things to this point. I lay down. I turned. I was fearful that someone might come to see how I was and be insistent. However, I had told everyone that I hadn't been able to sleep for several nights, so that they would leave me alone. I was very curious at that time, as if an important event had taken place or I was going to go on an exciting trip. I wanted to feel death well. I had concentrated my senses, yet I was listening for sounds outside. As soon as a footstep came, my heart would cave in. I pressed my eyelids together. Ten minutes or so went by. Nothing happened. I had occupied myself with different thoughts till I felt the pills begin to work, but I didn't regret this decision of mine, nor was I afraid. First I became heavy. I felt tired. This feeling was more in the pit of my stomach, like when food isn't well digested. Then this feeling travelled to my chest and then to my head. I moved my hands. I became thirsty. My mouth had turned dry.

I swallowed with difficulty. My heartbeat slowed. A short time passed. I felt that warm, pleasant air was being given off from my body, more from the extremities like the fingertips, the tip of the nose, and so on... At the same time I knew that I wanted to kill myself. I realized that this news would be unpleasant for some people. Everything seemed amazing. All of this seemed childish, absurd, and laughable to me. I thought to myself that now I was comfortable and I would die easily. What did it matter whether others would be sad or not, would cry or not? I greatly desired that this should happen and I feared lest I should move or think in such a way that I would prevent the opium from working. My only fear was that after all this trouble I might remain alive. I feared that dying might be difficult and that in despair I might cry out or want someone to help me. But I said that no matter how hard it was, opium puts one to sleep and he feels nothing. Sleep – I would sleep and I wouldn't be able to move from my place or say anything, and the door was locked from inside!...

Yes, I remember well. These thoughts came to me. I heard the monotonous sound of the clock. I heard the footsteps of people who were walking in the guesthouse. It seemed as if my sense of hearing had become sharper. I felt that my body was flying. My mouth had become dry. I had a slight headache. I had almost fallen into a faint. My eyes were half open. My breathing was sometimes fast, sometimes slow. From all the pores of my skin this pleasant heat flowed out of my body. It was as if I too were going out after it. I really wanted its intensity to increase. I had plunged into an unspeakable ecstasy. I thought whatever I wanted to. If I moved I felt that it would be a hindrance to the flowing out of this warmth. The more comfortably I lay the better it was. I pulled my right hand out from under me. I rolled over and lay on my back. It was somewhat unpleasant. I returned to the first position, and the effect of the opium became stronger. I wanted to feel death fully. My feelings had grown strong and magnified. I was amazed that I didn't fall asleep. It was as if all of my existence was leaving my body happily and wholesomely. My heart beat slowly. I breathed slowly. I think two or three hours passed. At this point someone knocked on the door. I realized it was my neighbour, but I didn't answer him and I didn't want to move from my place. I opened my eyes and closed them again. I heard the sound of his door opening. He washed his hands and whistled to himself. I heard everything. I tried to think happy, pleasant thoughts. I was thinking of the past year. The day when I was sitting in the boat and they were playing instruments. The waves of the sea, the rocking of the boat, the pretty girl sitting opposite me: I had plunged into my thoughts. I was running after them, as if I had wings and was soaring through space. I had grown so light and nimble that it can't be explained. The difference of being under the pleasurable influence of opium is as great as the difference between light seen ordinarily or seen through a chandelier or a crystal prism which separates it into different colours. In this state any simple, empty thoughts which come to people become enchanting and dazzling of themselves. Any passing and empty thought appears entrancing and splendid. If a scene or a vista passes through one's mind, it becomes limitlessly large, space swells, the passing of time is imperceptible.

At this time I felt very happy. My senses undulated above me. But I felt that I wasn't asleep. The last feeling that I remember of the pleasure and ecstasy of the opium is that my legs had become cold and senseless, my body motionless. I felt that I was going, drifting far away. But as soon as its influence waned, an infinite sorrow gripped me. I felt that my senses were returning. It was very difficult and unpleasant. I was cold. For more than half an hour I trembled violently. I could hear my teeth chattering. Then came fever, burning fever, and sweat poured from my body. My heart laboured, my breathing had become difficult. The first thought that occurred to me was that all my work was undone, and things hadn't turned out as they should have. I was surprised at my useless endurance. I realized that a dark power and an unspeakable misfortune were fighting me.

With difficulty I sat up partly in the bed. I pressed the light switch. It became light. I don't know why my hand went towards the small mirror that was on the bedside table. I saw that my face had swollen and had a sallow colouring. Tears fell from my eyes. My heart struggled hard. I told myself that at least my heart was ruined. I turned off the light and fell back in the bed.

No, my heart wasn't ruined. Today it's better. A bad product has no buyers. The doctor came to see me. He listened to my heart, took my pulse, looked at my tongue, took my temperature, the same things that doctors do everywhere, as soon as they see a patient. He gave me a mixture of baking powder and quinine. He didn't understand at all what my pain was! No one can understand my pain! These medicines are laughable. There in rows on the table are seven or eight kinds of medicine. I was laughing to myself. What a theatre this is.

The clock ticks incessantly by my ear. From outside come the sounds of car and bicycle horns, the clang of trains. I look at the wallpaper, the deep purple leaves and white flowers. At intervals on the branches two blackbirds are seated facing one another. My head is empty, my stomach twisting, my body broken. The newspapers which I have thrown on top of the cabinet lie there in odd positions. When I look it suddenly seems as if everything is strange to me. I even seem a stranger to myself. I wonder why I'm still alive. Why do I breathe? Why do I get hungry? Why do I eat? Why do I walk? Why am I here? Who are these people that I see, and what do they want from me?...

Now I know myself well, just the way I am, no more, no less. I can't do anything. I have fallen on the bed tired and exhausted. My thoughts revolve, whirl, hour by hour. I have become bored in their hopeless circle. My own existence astonishes me. How bitter and frightening it is when someone feels his own existence! When I look in the mirror I laugh at myself. To me my face seems so unknown and strange and laughable...

This thought has occurred to me many times: I've become invulnerable. The invincibility that has been described in legends is my tale. It was a miracle. Now I believe all kinds of superstitions and rubbish. Amazing thoughts pass before my eyes. It was a miracle. Now I know that in his endless cruelty, God or some other snake in the grass created two kinds of beings: the fortunate and the unfortunate. He supports the first group, while making the second group increase their torture and oppression by their own hands. Now I believe that a mean, brutal force, an angel of misfortune, is with some people.

* * *

Finally I've been left alone. The doctor left just now. I've picked up paper and pencil. I want to write. I don't know what. Either I have nothing to write or I can't write because there's so much. This itself is a misfortune. I don't know. I can't cry. Maybe if I could it would soothe me a little bit! I can't. I look like a lunatic. I saw in the mirror that my hair is a mess. My eyes are open and empty. I think my face shouldn't have looked like this at all. Many people's faces don't go with their thoughts. This really irritates me. All I know is that I hate myself. I eat and hate myself, walk and hate myself, think and hate myself. How obstinate. How frightening! No, this was a supernatural power, a loathsome disease. Now I believe these kind of things. Nothing will affect me any more. I took cyanide and it had no effect on me, I ate opium and I'm still alive! If a dragon bites me, the dragon will die! No, no one would believe it. Had these poisons spoilt? Wasn't the amount sufficient? Was it more than the normal dose? Had I mistaken the amount when I looked in the medical book? Or does my hand turn the poison into antidote? I don't know. These thoughts have come to me hundreds of times. There's nothing new in them. I remember I have heard that when a scorpion is surrounded by a ring of fire it stings itself – isn't there a ring of fire around me?

Outside my window on the black edge of the tin roof, where rainwater has collected, two sparrows are sitting. One of them puts its beak into the water, then lifts its head. The other one, crouching next to it, is pecking at itself. I just moved. Both of them chirped and flew off together. The weather is cloudy. Sometimes the pale sun appears behind a bit of cloud. The tall buildings opposite are all covered with soot, black and sad under the pressure of this heavy, rainy weather. The distant, suffocated sound of the city can be heard.

There in the drawer of my table are the malicious cards with which I told my fortune, those lying cards which fooled me. The funniest thing is that I still tell my fortune with them!

What can be done? Fate is stronger than I am.

It would be good if, with the experience of life that a person has, he could be born again and start his life anew. But which life? Is it in my hands? What's the use? A blind and frightening force rules us. There are people whose fate is directed by a sinister star. They break under this burden, and they want to be broken...

I have neither wishes nor grudges left. I have lost whatever in me was human. I let it be lost. In life one must become either an angel, a human being, or an animal. I became none of these. My life was lost forever. I was born selfish, clumsy, and miserable. Now, it is impossible for me to go back and adopt another way. I can't follow these useless shadows any more, grappling with life, what firm reason and logic do you have? I no longer want to pardon or to be pardoned, to go to the left or to the right. I want to close my eyes to the future and forget the past.

No, I can't flee from my fate. Aren't they the truth, these crazy thoughts, these feelings, these passing fancies which come to me? In any case they seem more natural and less artificial than my logical thoughts. I suppose I am free, yet I can't resist my fate. My reins are in the hands of my fate, fate is what pulls me from one side to another. The meanness, the baseness of life, which can't be fought against. Stupid life.

Now I am neither living nor sleeping. Nothing pleases me and nothing bothers me. I have become acquainted with death, used to it. It is my only friend. It is the only thing which heartens me. I remember the Montparnasse Cemetery. I don't envy the dead anymore. I am now counted in their world. I, too, am with them. I am buried alive...

I'm tired. What trash have I written? I say to myself, "Go, lunatic, throw away the paper and the pencil, throw them away. That's enough rambling. Shut up. Tear it up, lest this rubbish fall into somebody's hands. How would they judge me? But I wouldn't be embarrassed, nothing is important to me. I laugh at the world and whatever is in it. However harsh their judgement of me might be, they don't know that I have already judged myself even harder. They'll laugh at me; they don't know that I laugh at them more. I am sick of myself and of everyone who reads this trash.

These notes and a pack of cards were in his drawer. He himself was lying in bed. He had forgotten to breathe.

Paris, Esfand 11, 1308
(3rd March 1928)

Notes

p. 7, *Nouruz*: The national festival of Iran. It begins on 21st March and lasts for thirteen days. It is the custom to spend the last day of Nouruz picnicking in the country.

p. 24, *Shah Abdolazim*: A mosque and cemetery situated among the ruins of Rey, a few miles south of Tehran. Rey (the Rhages of the Greeks) was an important centre from at least the eighth century BC and continued to be one of the great cities of Iran down to its destruction by Genghis Khan in the thirteenth century AD.

p. 27, *krans… abbasi*: Coins worth respectively five pence and one pence.

p. 37, *bed unrolled*: In old Persia bedsteads were not used. The bed roll (mattress, sheet, pillows and quilt) was stowed away in the daytime and unrolled on the floor at night.

p. 39, *Karbala*: The burial place of the Shia martyr Hosein, the Iraq city of Karbala is one of the Muslim holy cities to which pilgrimages are made. Water in which a little earth from Karbala had been steeped was employed as medicine.

p. 40, *Nishapur… Balkh*: A reminiscence of a quatrain of Omar Khayyam:

> Since life passes, whether sweet or bitter,
> Since the soul must pass the lips, whether in Nishapur or in Balkh,
> Drink wine, for after you and I are gone many a moon
> Will pass from old to new, from new to old.

p. 57, *Ezrail*: The Angel of Death.

p. 60, *huzvaresh*: A convention of Pahlavi writing by which the scribe substituted an Aramaic word for a Persian one.

p. 68, *korsi*: A stool under which is placed a lit brazier and over which blankets are spread. People recline with the lower part of their bodies under the blankets.

p. 72, *begged… get better*: It is the custom on the last Wednesday before Nouruz for people to disguise themselves and go begging. The alms received on this occasion are believed to bring good luck.

p. 80, *La elaha ell' Allah*: "There is no god but God", part of the Muslim profession of faith.

p. 89, *dirhems… peshiz*: Medieval coins, corresponding roughly to the modern *kran* and *abbasi* respectively.

p. 96, *besmellah*: "In the name of God". The formula pronounced by Muslims at the beginning of any important undertaking.

p. 97, *sneeze… pause*: A Persian superstition requires that, if anyone present should sneeze, any action which one may have been about to undertake be postponed.

p. 98, *got pregnant at the baths*: It was popularly believed that women could become pregnant through using the public baths, which were frequented (at different hours) by men also. The belief could be exploited to provide an explanation of otherwise inexplicable pregnancies.

p. 99, *first leap… old man's face*: Another popular belief was that a baby would resemble the person at whom the mother happened to be looking when it stirred for the first time in the womb.

p. 109, *Karbala*: See note to p. 39.

p. 123, *Darolfonoun*: The name of a school in Tehran.

p. 133, *Pass Qale*: A village north of Tehran.

p. 135, *Aide Qorban*: A day of sacrifice in the Muslim religion.

p. 141, *I divorced my wife three times*: According to Islamic law a divorce comes into effect when the husband tells the wife, "I divorce you". At this point the couple can remarry if they wish. However, if the husband tells the wife "I divorce you, I divorce you, I divorce you", then they cannot remarry unless the wife marries someone else first and is divorced from him. This person is called a legalizer.

p. 147, *the Shah Abdolazim cemetery*: A cemetery in southern Tehran containing the tomb of Shah Abdolazim, a holy figure.

p. 151, *Pah Chenar*: A village outside of Tehran.

p. 152, *thirteenth day of Mehr 1311*: The date given refers to the Muslim solar calendar. 1311 A.H. corresponds to 1932 AD.

p. 153, *Bandargaz*: An Iranian port on the Caspian Sea.

p. 165, *Flandon*: Hedayat says "E. Flandon and P. Coste were two well-known Iranologists, who ninety years ago did important research about ancient Iran. This section has been taken from Flandon's notes." They published *Voyage on Perse* in 1851.

p. 172, *Muharri and Safar*: Months of mourning for the deaths of holy figures in the Shi'a branch of the Muslim religion.

p. 172, *the passion plays*: Plays re-enacting the martyrdoms of Muslim religious figures.

p. 223, *Imam*: A title given to certain religious leaders in the Muslim religion.

p. 235, *Mowlavi*: Persian poet and philosopher of the thirteenth century.

p. 235, *Sar Cheshme*: A square in Tehran.

p. 237, *dervish*: A wandering preacher or holy man.

p. 239, *hadith*: The body of transmitted actions and sayings of the Prophet Mohammad and his companions.

p. 241, *Masnvai*: A famous book of poetry by Mowlavi.

Acknowledgements

The Publisher wishes to thank Nushin Arbabzadah for her extensive editorial work and Homa Katouzian for writing the introduction.

ALMA CLASSICS

ALMA CLASSICS aims to publish mainstream and lesser-known European classics in an innovative and striking way, while employing the highest editorial and production standards. By way of a unique approach the range offers much more, both visually and textually, than readers have come to expect from contemporary classics publishing.

LATEST TITLES PUBLISHED BY ALMA CLASSICS

www.almaclassics.com